Sing
Sorrow
Sorrow

for Simon

Sing
Sorrow
Sorrow

Dark and Chilling Tales

Editor: Gwen Davies

SEREN

seren is the book imprint of
Poetry Wales Press Ltd
57 Nolton Street, Bridgend, Wales, CF31 3AE
www.seren-books.com

ISBN 978-1-85411-530-0

Cover photograph: Stacey Lee as Elizabeth Báthory by Gordon Crabb,
www.gordoncrabb.co.uk

Cover design: Charlotte Petty

Inner design and typesetting by www.eifionjenkins.co.uk

Printed by Short Run Press, Exeter

The publisher works with the financial assistance of
the Welsh Books Council.

Mixed Sources

Product group from well-managed
forests and other controlled sources
www.fsc.org Cert no. SA-COC-002112
© 1996 Forest Stewardship Council

FSC

My father lost me to The Beast at cards.

Angela Carter
'The Tiger's Bride'
from *The Bloody Chamber*

And if Fiammarosa was sometimes lonely in her glass palace, and sometimes wished both that Sasan would come more often, and that she could roam amongst fjords and ice-fells, this was not unusual, for no one has everything they can desire.

AS Byatt
'Cold'
Elementals: Stories of Fire and Ice

And of all the hounds he had seen in the world, he had never seen dogs of this colour – they were a gleaming shining white, and their ears were red.

The Mabinogion
(First Branch)
translated by Sioned Davies

Contents

Puck's Tale

Niall Griffiths

I received the telegram at my lodgings in Arles; Puckeridge had been released from prison unexpectedly early, due to some sort of Home Secretarial interference and investigation into his case and a decision made in the House that the sentence that had been imposed on him – for tax evasion or fraud, I don't quite remember the details – was unduly harsh. I smiled – or perhaps 'smirked' is the *mot juste* – to read it, recalling Puckeridge's Harrow connections and his tales of fagging for seniors who would go on to become prominent back-benchers and the like. Reciprocal back scratching, it seems, occasionally reaches across the decades. The telegram was sent by Boothby, the only one of our group to know my whereabouts, and went on to implore me to cut short my tour of Napoleonic battlefields, or at least break it, and attend the 'welcome home' dinner to be given in Puckeridge's honour at our Soho club two evenings hence. Well, I mused to myself, I'd been in France for more than a month and was growing rather tired of ambling around grassy earthworks, and my imaginative powers of picturing them denuded of vegetation and crouched behind by cowering uniformed men under fiery skies were on the wane. Plus, my lodging house was presided over by a wearyingly fat and clucking Gallic matriarch whose squashed egg of a nose would, every night when I returned, dart sniffing around my face to test for the smell of *pastis*. Plus the coffers were running dry. And plus – yes, I admit it – I'd missed Puckeridge. So I made, with dispatch, to Le Havre and caught the next available packet to Dover, where I lodged for a night to refresh myself and to telephone Boothby to warn him of my impending arrival.

'My chap!' he boomed out of the earpiece. 'Hope you've brought oceans of claret for us to sink!'

Never a man for metaphorical cohesion or clarity, our Boothby.

I slept well and breakfasted late the next morning. I hadn't read an English newspaper in several weeks and was intrigued by the lead item, which concerned the disappearance of several children in central London, most of them in the Bloomsbury area. Nine or ten of them, a mixture of boys and girls, gone – simply vanished. Police, as is customary in these cases, were 'baffled'. The latest had been reported as missing only the night before last, when I was futilely attempting to snatch some slumber on the ragged Sleeve, as I'd become habituated to calling that stretch of perpetually angry sea that mercifully separates the civilised from the Gaul. Pictures of this child adorned the railway station at Dover: HAVE YOU SEEN THIS BOY? they asked, above a badly reproduced image of a smiling and ringletted cherub. There was mention of a reward. I silently wondered if such fuss would've been granted a child whose only available image would show him dirt-streaked and sullen and tyke-ish. Undoubtedly not: no. The vanished children were all, it seemed, issue of the professional classes; hence the media agitation. Some things will never change.

London, when I arrived there around dusk that evening, was much as I had left it some weeks earlier; loud and cramped and violent and voracious, its air both saturated and inspissated in equal measure by the hanging greasy fog. Disembarking at Marylebone, unsure whether the thick and cloying mist that enveloped me was steam from the trains or the choking exhalations of the city itself, I felt immediately, and happily, at home, so much so that I delayed my cab journey to Soho for the time it took to enjoy a relaxed cigarette and a languid appreciation of the London traffic on the pavement outside the station concourse. The solidity of an English thoroughfare under my shoes. The welcome fixity of myself under that delightful, dirtied and darkening sky. This is wonderful, I thought. This is what I miss with a real and authentic, if low-level, pain, when I'm away.

The same poster that I'd seen in Dover was affixed, many times over, to the oily bricks of the wall that flanked the cab-rank; the same question manifold above the same shy smile, the same fair curls. And the matter was on everybody's lips – the city's collective mind seemed preoccupied with it. I caught snatches of several conversations, all 'ooh' and 'aah' and 'isn't it shocking' and 'poor little mites' and 'the parents must be *distraught*', and my cab-man, as I suspected he would, launched himself into a monologue about it the second I'd settled into my seat behind his brilliantined cannonball of a head.

'It's them bladdy Jews. Them Zionists, innit? Human sacrifice, it's in their religion. Burnt offering they call it. To appease their god. Not like us, see. My bravver, he lives in Tottenham, and I'm tellin ya, you do *not* let your nippers go aht alone in that area. Not safe, see. Bladdy full of them it is, all wiv them hats and them coats and them bits of hair comin dahn. See, if you read the Torah, their holy book as they call it, it tells them that…'

Ah yes, some things never change. I settled back in my seat and let the fellow drone on, let the flat timbre of his voice lull me and soothe me, provide a calming soundtrack to the flickering screen of my window. The omnibuses, the hawkers, the crushed and rushing crowds. My London. The dirty urchins crowding the window when we were forced to halt temporarily at the junction at the lower end of Tottenham Court Road, their large eyes and scabbed lips, their filthy little palms held out beseeching and empty. I lowered my window and dispensed pennies and farthings. On he droned, my driver, and I was hovering on the verge of sleep when he pulled up in Soho, the jerk of the brakes jolting me back alert.

'...pull the bladdy lever myself, I would. Here we go, squire, Greek Street.'

I paid and tipped the chap and stood on the pavement a moment to let Soho soak into my skin. My Soho, my London. It was wondrous to be back. How I miss it when I'm away. I went into my club, checked in my overcoat, and was ushered into the dining room to hails and halloos from my group; Boothby, whose plump cheeks had already assumed the maroon hue of the bucket of claret he'd evidently imbibed; Shaftoe, whose cicatriced skin shone in the firelight and who gripped his gold-topped cane with a withered claw as he rose beaming to greet me; and Puckeridge, poor Puck, newly released Puckeridge, thinner, much thinner, than he was when I last saw him, dark rings around his eyes and tightly set lips, the demeanour, indeed, of a man who did not wish to be where he was. If I'd expected his new liberation to have enervated and energised him in any way at all, then I was in error. The man looked profoundly unhappy.

'Sit, Hackett, sit,' said Shaftoe, gesturing at an empty chair. 'You've missed the soup but the beef will shortly be making an appearance.'

'Vile bilge anyway,' said Boothby, apropos the soup, I imagined. 'Stilton and watercress. Ugh. Sooner suck a sock. Red?'

He filled my glass. I looked at Puckeridge.

'Welcome back,' I said.

He responded with a small smile, nothing else. It's the strain of his incarceration, I thought; Wandsworth gaol would flatten the fizz of life in the stoutest of men. Wine and beef will help him effervesce, I reasoned, but was, again, wrong. Oh, he ate heartily and quaffed strongly, as had always been his wont, yet he said very little and not even our many toasts to his reappearance into society could raise anything more than a weak and slight smile on his bloodless lips. Boothby, on several occasions, saw fit to prod Puckeridge in the ribs and exhort him to 'cheer up, man!' but all he elicited was a wince. Shaftoe, for his part, rolled up his sleeve to reveal his defleshed stick of an arm and regale the gathering, once again, with the oft-heard tale of the tiger attack he endured in India; such a story would usually have Puckeridge in thrall, but all he did was nod. The man was not with us. He was elsewhere.

After dinner – excellent beef and passable claret, a great deal of each – we were shown into the smoking room with cigars and a decanter of brandy. We sat in a loose semicircle around the built-up fire, in swallowing armchairs which gave off a deep, rich, leathery and evocative smell. The wine, and now the brandy, had empinkened faces and loosened tongues and Shaftoe, the nearness of the flames making the scar tissue on his face and forehead more than usually reflective, drained his glass, re-filled it, and asked: 'So, Puckeridge, tell us, if you will. Wandsworth gaol. The regime inside its walls. Does it deserve the fearsomeness of its reputation? Had you to endure a *dreadful* level of buggery?'

Again that barely perceptible smile, if 'smile' can be suitably applied to a mere wrinkling of the lip.

'Not an absolutely *unbearable* amount, Shaftoe, no. Sorry to disappoint.'

'A toast!' yelled Boothby, not for the first time that evening. 'No doubt this one will provoke the same level of disinterestedness and indifference as have its several predecessors, but dash it if I don't try again anyway. Welcome back, Puckeridge. We'll drink to your reappearance.'

We did. Puckeridge didn't. This wasn't the Puckeridge I knew. I refilled my glass and asked him outright: 'Damn it, Puckeridge, what's wrong, man? You're a shell of the man I knew. You have a markedly haunted countenance. You're amongst friends here, man. If we can help, we assuredly will, but we need at least some notion of the type of assistance required.'

Puckeridge glanced at Shaftoe, sipped at his brandy, rubbed some ash off his trouser leg. Sipped more brandy. Scratched his ear. Coughed.

'For God's sake, man!' Shaftoe thumped the floor with his cane. 'Out with it. You're like a fellow with fleas. All evening we've had to endure your face bearing the sour expression of a chap who's fallen into a vat of dollymops and re-emerged sucking but his thumb. Speak to us, for God's sake. This gathering's in *your* honour.'

Puckeridge nodded. 'You're right, of course. I will speak, yes. It's the very least you fellows deserve. But at some point this evening I fear that I must affect an abrupt departure. I'm hoping that it will occur *following* what I'm about to tell you, but if, well, if you should look up and find this chair that I'm sitting in now unexpectedly empty, well, I'll hopefully pre-empt your forgiveness. And hope still further that, should that moment arise, I'll have been granted time enough to furnish you with sufficient information to allow you all to formulate some sort of reason as to why.'

Ah, prolix Puckeridge. More like his old self. Shaftoe's cane, however, thumped with impatience on the polished parquet floor.

'Get on with it, Puckeridge,' he rumbled out of his furrowed neck. Not for the first time I marvelled at the power of the cat that had put such deep maroon grooves into that throat, and stripped that arm almost entirely of flesh and muscle. 'We haven't got all night, man.'

Puckeridge made a sound that might've been a chuckle.

'No', he said, 'you haven't.' He re-lit his cigar and exhaled, nodding at Boothby through a cloud of rising smoke that, for an instant, assumed the shape of a human skull.

'Our friend Boothby here has, this evening, used the word "reappearance". You have no idea how apt that is. You're all aware, no doubt, of the recent abductions of children in this area.'

'"Abductions", Puckeridge? Strong word.'

'Yet an accurate one, Hackett. As accurate, in this context, as the word *dread*.'

'Dread?'

'As in crippling fear, yes. I knew this moment would come again. Would reappear, as it were. And I've been dreading it. That is, anticipating its reappearance with a terror that fills my soul.'

Mine was not an especially happy childhood. I wasn't deprived, in the sense that today's sociologists, so-called, use that word; no, I wanted for very little, in the harsh embrace of my parents' shrill and public love. But I was an only child, and congenitally shy, and unnaturally tall for my age, and so, of course, I became a brunt for the mischief and mild malice of the local children. I won't bore you with a tabulation of my torments. Suffice to say that my best friends were all imaginary, long past the age when it was acceptable for them to be so.

So it was entirely foreseeable that I should fall under Merryweather's influence. Merryweather was everything I wasn't, and embodied in his stout person everything I desired to be: alive with energy, animated by an adventurous spirit, ready to burst with confidence. He seemed to move in an attractive and sunlit haze generated by his own personality. He took me under his wing. Had I developed more certain tools of objective self-analysis and perspicacity, I would've realised that I was being treated and used in the same way that I treated and used the guinea pigs that my parents would buy me as, largely, educational equipment through which I could develop a sense of personal responsibility, empathy, what have you.

In truth, however, I don't suppose that I really cared about Merryweather's motives; I was simpy happy to have his companionship and protection. Is it so wrong to bask in reflected glory? One still accepts the comforts of the cast warm rays. Ask any sunbather or naturist.

Merryweather's family was impressively well off, even by the standards of Bloomsbury at that prosperous time. They kept a pile in Suffolk, where they'd summer, and would, for a fortnight or so in late June, invite some of Merryweather's London friends up for relaxation and activity; orienteering in the woods, raft-building, the rudiments of agricultural knowledge to be gleaned in the kitchen garden and on the smallholding. That kind of thing. This was intended, I suspect, mainly to keep Merryweather content; familial felicity was the aim, I fear, rather than philanthropy. Merryweather could tantrum like a dervish if he was bored or frustrated or otherwise dissatisfied. But, again, I cared not a fig for the motives. Why should I? I was in the countryside; I was washed by the sun, I was catching trout in the streams, shooting pigeons and rabbits in the meadows, lying in the long grass, swimming in the plunge-pool with MacReady, the groundsman. I was enjoying myself as I never had before. Life was a constant joy of discovery. I was living purely in the moment. I was deliriously happy.

And then came the Open Day. This, I was to discover to my initial chagrin, was when the hall and its grounds became public property for a day, and the children from the local village were invited in for games and food. I hadn't been told about this, and so was unprepared; indeed, no sooner had I been informed of what was about to happen by Merryweather's brusque mother than the lawn was swarmed over by brawny and mud-crusted children, snot-nosed whelps in torn breeches and malodorous headgear, boots nailed through at the toe and heel, if they were shod in anything other than layers of accumulated filth at all. In actuality, there were only four children – two of either gender – but to me, looking out through the mullioned windows of the games room, it seemed that MacReady had broken open an ants' nest of them and released the things in their scurrying thousands across the lawn. I'm not ashamed to say that I recoiled from the sight; a physical, bodily adverse reaction, as if instinctively away from some vile and slimy, excrementitious thing come upon unexpectedly. Pure envy, of course. Those ugly pups would make demands on the attentions of my friends. And yes, there they were, on the lawn already; Merryweather excitedly making preparations for a game of croquet, MacReady piggybacking one of the girls – the one with the *particularly* bad dentition – down to the pond. Someone was calling my name: Puck. Come and play, Puck. But I stayed in the games room and sulked. Was only tempted out onto the lawn when Merryweather's mother appeared with the enticement of orange squash. I wordlessly knocked a ball around the lawn with a wooden mallet for an hour or so. I went for a silent and desultory group walk along the riverbank. With a protruding lower lip I ate more than my fair share of currant cake in the gazebo by the lake and barely managed to restrain myself from administering a slap when one of the boys complained as I helped myself to a fourth slice. I'd never known such outrage as that which flamed in my breast that day. I felt like I'd been given a much-valued and yearned-for gift, only to have it smithereened in front of my eyes. I was filled with shock for what I felt was betrayal on the part of Merryweather and MacReady, and with hate for the ugly bucktoothed brood from the dung-encrusted huts of the nearby village. Forgive my shrug; I do not mean to suggest facile dismissal. But that's the kind of boy I was, and what's done is done.

At sundown we returned to the house for the day's closing and, I was informed, customary activity: a game of hide-and-seek. I welcomed the notion; I thought to secrete myself in some impossible-to-find cubby-hole or trunk, of which there were many in that rambling mansion, thence to sleep and awaken with the intruders gone and paradise thereby regained, but the Fates that day were bent on blighting my life and I was chosen, with Merryweather, to be 'It'. He led me into the games room to count to one hundred whilst the village children vanished like flies into the bowels of the house and there something unexpected happened: at the call of 'coming-ready-or-not', Merryweather nudged me and told me in a whisper to follow him and we crept out of the house and ran across the lawn and down to the lake where, in the gazebo, I found food and blankets and drink. This, said Merryweather, was where we would spend the night. He'd made surreptitious preparations for a comfortable sleep-out. The children will shortly get bored and tired and wander home, he explained, else they'll fall asleep in their hiding-places and appear rubbing their eyes at the breakfast table whereupon we'd congratulate them on winning the game and send them home to their hovels with a pat on the lousy head. That night, explained Merryweather, we were to seek nobody but ourselves. The incisive maturity of that comment startles me even now. At some point that night MacReady joined us in the gazebo, and told us, with a chuckle, that none of the children had reappeared as yet. They must've all fallen asleep in their chosen secret spots. Like satiated mice in a loaf of bread, he said. Or happy cats scattered across an old sofa.

In the morning, and much to my initial dismay, the dining room was full of adults, big and bearded adults, rag-clad, twisting their caps at their chests, their faces soiled and creased and concerned and weathered. The ostentatious deference they evinced towards Merryweather's parents masked, even a boy of my age could see, a profound worry: none of the children had returned home. They'd been out all night. *We be terrible werrited, sor, we be.* That's what they said. I found such bumpkins more amusing than perturbing, after a few minutes in their company. They were nothing to be afraid of, with their servility and cowering carriage. Their accents were ludicrous and laughable to my ears. The stereotype of their attire – trousers held up with string, the several layers of frayed shirts and waistcoats – prompted in me a kind of pitying disdain. They even postponed a search for their children so they could eat the breakfast that the Merryweathers generously offered them, an act either gluttonous or slavish, either of which was beneath my contempt. These adults were defeated and weary and bleached of all personality. They were attenuated and scared and they walked through mud without leaving a footprint. They were everything their childen were not.

At this point, Puckeridge broke his tale to re-light his cigar and re-fill his glass with brandy. The firelight had put his eyes into pits of ink and made the seams in his face appear like canyons. His exhaled smoke was a hand this time, a skeletal hand, grey fingers of smoky bone reaching for the ceiling beams and breaking apart before they could touch.

Shaftoe thumped his cane. 'Well?'

'Well, what?'

'The children, man. Where were the children?'

Were I following tradition I should say here that, despite the big and brisk fire, the room had taken on a chill, but life does not obey literary convention. Indeed the opposite had occurred, and the flames had warmed the room appreciably, as fires are supposed and intended to do; so much so, in fact, that despite Puckeridge's story I could feel sleep beginning to whisper on my skin. The others, also, seemed to be feeling the heat's soporific effects; the only proof that Boothby was awake was the constant lifting of his glass to his mouth, and Shaftoe's usual growl had become a mumble, a murmur, as if he spoke through a duck-down pillow pressed to his face. Only Puckeridge seemed alert.

'We found… traces,' he said. 'Of what sort I shall tell you. But before that, and forgive the Conradian structure of my narrative, I must tell you something of the history of the Merryweather house. A tale within a tale, if you will. Not so much a diversion or tangential distraction, more an essential ingredient. You'll see why.'

A silver cylinder of ash tumbled down Puckeridge's waistcoat. The scars on Shaftoe's skin shone. Boothby gulped his brandy, as did I.

'This is what I was told after the Open Day. After we'd found what we found in that house. All houses have their secret histories, of course, some stranger than others. Before the Merryweathers bought that mansion in Suffolk, it had been for centuries in the hands of the Sinclairs, a Maud

Sinclair, to be precise, at the time that concerns us. A widow, she'd lost her husband on the veldt and was raising her daughter alone. Can't have been easy. Not in a house that size; the outlay for maintenance must've been colossal, I imagine. And with no constant breadwinner...'

'Get on with it, Puckeridge,' grumbled Shaftoe.

'Of course, yes.' Puckeridge smiled and held a placatory palm outwards. 'Forgive me. My trend is not toward the terse. Maud re-married, rather too quickly it was thought, but who could blame the woman? Think of her footsteps echoing through the draughty corridors of that mansion. Her sobbing bouncing back to her off the damp and crumbling walls. Her beau was a yeoman from the village: a common labourer. The courtship was whirlwind. He was marrying for money, *that* was the general consensus and flavour of village gossip. He had no love for Maud, or for her daughter, but at twenty years Maud's junior his eye gave a twinkle when he contemplated the material comforts of his life after her passing. This is what people were saying but Maud, of course, refused to hear it; she had companionship again. She was no longer lonely. The child it was who caught the man in congress with the maid in the scullery one morning. And it was the child who ran to inform her mother, and who was caught by the man and summarily killed on the lawn, in broad daylight, strangled to death. Maud, brought running from her gardening by the cries of her daughter, discovered her husband with his gnarled hands around her child's blue and lifeless throat and, acting purely on instinct, one imagines, plunged her shears into her husband's back. Killed him outright. Consider: Maud awoke that morning with a beloved child and husband. Not two hours after taking her toast and tea she had neither.'

'Good Lord,' said Shaftoe. 'All very unpleasant and sad, I'm sure. But what in God's name has this to do with the children?'

'Did you find the children?' someone asked. Was this me speaking? I think it was, after a fashion. But I didn't recognise my own voice. 'You said you found "traces". What did you discover, Puckeridge?'

Boothby raised his glass to his lips. The room was very warm.

'On the inside of a wardrobe in the east wing's master bedroom we found the garments terribly torn, shredded and bloodstained, as if in a great rage. As if your tiger, Shaftoe, had been shut up in there. In a bathroom, we found the word HELP scratched into a mirror, written backwards. The inside of a wooden trunk in one of the corridors was splintered and hacked at, evidence of a terrible panic; seeing it, and young as I was, I thought of how a coffin lid must look if one had been buried alive. And under the bed in one of the guest rooms, sunk into the wooden frame, were a child's fingernails. They'd been ripped out at the roots. Imagine the horror of that child. Now imagine the determination and force of whatever it was that dragged that child out from under the bed.

'No bodies were ever found. MacReady was arrested and arraigned, but the case collapsed for lack of evidence, and besides, MacReady had an alibi; he'd been with myself and Merryweather in the gazebo much of the night. He it was, however, who told me the tale of Maud Sinclair. He it was who reckoned that Maud's second husband still lived, in a way and in some unknowable form, driven to revenge himself – or itself, perhaps – on the children, on *all* children, whom he blamed for shortening his physical life and robbing him of its future comforts. What MacReady *didn't* say, but what I myself began to feel might be closer to accuracy, was that though the body dies, some urges can never die and will, like fleas, jump from man to man; the urge itself becomes the pilot, we the mere vessels. That's what I've come to believe. I have to believe it. Conjecture, you may think, but what is indisputable is that the Merryweather house has lain empty for some years, because every family who has moved in there has left shortly afterwards, minus their children. Abducted, the papers all said. Playing on the lawn and never seen again. Check the records. The house has been empty for years. I've been keeping my eye on it. I heard recently that its present owners are applying for planning permission to turn it into an orphanage.'

Something spat and exploded in the fire: a sap pocket in a log, perhaps. When we looked away from the flames, Puckeridge had gone; his chair was empty. Then I think the heat and the alcohol exacted their inevitable price and I fell asleep because all of a sudden I was alone in the room by the smouldering ashes and I returned to my lodgings to retrieve my things and made straight for Dover. HAVE YOU SEEN THIS GIRL? asked the posters on the train. It may have been the same poster as yesterday or maybe another child had vanished overnight, I don't know. I'm afraid I didn't give the thing sufficient attention to ascertain.

The House Demon

Maria Donovan

When the old woman was a young bride she had left a cup of tea on the hearth and begged the house demon to go with her to their new home. He yawned, tired out from tidying the mess she and her new husband had made, first with their hasty wedding and now with their packing; it was winter, too cold for travelling; and he didn't like the manners of the new husband, who was eyeing the household treasures she'd refused to pack until the day of leaving – the family samovar, the silver biscuit tin.

The house demon drank his tea, and was just settling more comfortably when he heard the husband say, 'Where you're going there'll be no place for these old superstitions. The Minister won't stand for it, see!'

She didn't argue, but that night she left her husband's high-topped boots before the fire, and whispered, 'Please come with us. We hope you will be happy there.' The demon lay all night on the coals thinking it over. She had always been kind, showing him the proper respect, and she was the last of her line. Without him how would she speak to the ancestors? Who would tell the old stories? Tales of Uncle Yasha and his wooden teeth, the winter the family had to burn them to keep warm.

When morning came the house demon said goodbye to his friends the mice, popped a hot coal into the breast pocket of his coat, pulled one of the husband's boots into the fire and climbed inside.

At once he fell into a half-slumber so that he only heard voices as if from behind a thick curtain – the new husband shouting at his wife because he had only one boot to wear and it was snowing.

Through the grinding hours by train, the demon was only half awake. A boat rolled them over the salt water; another train jerked them through the press of a great city. Then once more the slamming of doors, and a giant owl hooting through the night. The last part of the journey they made by moonlit road, climbing to a lonely house a few miles inland and a thousand feet above the sea.

The demon woke up to blow on the coal he'd brought from home and help the new wife light their first fire in the kitchen stove. When it was blazing, he hopped up onto a shelf, and sat looking down at the poor woman searching for the trunk that held the samovar. The husband was shifty and silent. Only when she burst into tears did he admit to having sold her treasures before the journey started.

'We'll need every penny,' he warned. 'And here you'll have to get used to the kettle and the pot and not sit about all day drinking tea.'

It was a thick-walled house that would be cool in summer. The kitchen door had a cat flap through which the house demon stuck his head to breathe the air. From behind the garden shed peeped one of the outdoor demons of that country, a shy creature with untrimmed nails, who managed the woodpile. Across two fields the house demon thought he saw, halfway up a tree in the coppice marking the boundary of their land, another demon with a mossy beard, the sort of wild thing that can only bark and squeal.

The husband brought home a kitten but his wife sneezed once and refused to keep it (mice are mice, after all, even in a new country). The grateful demon worked hard in the house and she set out milk and biscuits for him every night, which he shared with his new friends. 'More crumbs!' the husband would say, and set mousetraps. Whenever they snapped, he rushed to look – but the demon sprang them all with the tip of the poker.

Children meant more work. They seemed to think the house kept order by itself, and stole the treats their mother gave the demon. Just once a year they liked to set out on the hearth in the parlour a strange meal of raw carrot, a small pie filled with sticky fruit and spices, and a thimbleful of sherry. Still, the house demon had to be quick before the husband crept down in the night.

The voices of the ancestors seemed far away and very faint.

One morning, while the family were at breakfast, the demon was sitting above the stove, swinging his legs, sniffing the bacon and watching the youngest daughter crawling on the hearthrug, when she sat back on her padded bottom and reached out her arms to him. He was so surprised he nearly fell off his shelf, but her father leapt up, shouting, 'No! Hot, hot!' smacking her hands and making her cry.

Not long after the youngest daughter started school, she heard her playmates talking about the tooth fairy and the money she brought in the night. Eagerly, the little girl told them all about the house demon, who polished her shoes ready for morning. That afternoon the Minister, then still a young man, with fervent eyes gleaming under a wide-brimmed hat, came knocking at the house.

'You have a demon here,' he said. 'We'll have to do something about it!' He went from room to room, book in hand, darting looks into corners and flicking sudden drops of water as if to catch him by surprise. At first the demon was amused: he sat on the stairs picking his teeth and listening.

'It's only the hobgoblin,' said his mistress. 'He came with me from the old country, a good spirit. Nothing to fear!'

'Fear?' said the Minister, sniffily. '*I* am not afraid of demons; I only fear for your immortal soul.'

The house demon leapt onto the Minister's shoulder, peered under his hat and thought about tweaking his nose, but the mistress shook her head. They let him go on calling out the names of all the demons he knew and commanding them, 'Be gone!'

He knows a lot of names I've never heard of, thought the house demon, but he doesn't know mine. On went the Minister, letting his voice ring out and liking the sound of it so much he did not notice the broken cry as the demon of the woodpile's name was called. This poor shy creature disappeared as if the sky had closed over him. The house demon banged a door with his fist. Now there would be no one to stack the logs when the wind pushed them over; they would tumble on the wet ground and soak up the rain, sputter in the fire, tarring up the chimney.

Spots of rust soon appeared on the saws and hatchets, giving the husband more cause to grumble. The demon of the coppice drew closer and lurked in the hedge. When the children ran past they felt something grab at their hair.

Relentless winters, dark and damp. The husband promised his wife he'd build her a conservatory where she could sit and sew in good light, for here it snowed only once every three years and then it lay bright for no more than a week. The children threw snowballs and made snowmen and the youngest daughter cried when their stone eyes fell out in the warmth of midday. The demon risked the back garden at twilight to press them back into their icy sockets.

When at last the husband built the glass room for his wife, the first thing she sewed there was for the house demon: a green jacket, snug against the wind. The husband asked why she bothered with that 'stiff old stuff', when the grandchildren had so many soft supermarket clothes to wear. She just reached for the scissors and clipped a thread as if he hadn't spoken.

Years on, in the time of the old woman's dying, the demon crouched on the bedpost watching her breathe, hoping she would open her eyes and see him, hair and beard neatly combed, buttons polished on his green jacket. He was listening for the voices of the ancestors, anxious to know when they would gather her in.

The youngest daughter, grey in her hair, had come back to help out, but in the evenings she went downstairs to phone her brothers and sisters. Sometimes she cried or said things like 'At least she'll see Dad again'. But the house demon could not say where he had gone.

When the others came on weekend visits, bringing their own children, always thinking *this* might be the last time, he stalked out, disgusted with them all. Every neglected job in the house was waiting for him, and he threw himself into a haphazard frenzy of cleaning, snarling the spiders out of their corners, snatching at the dead heads of geraniums over-wintering in the conservatory. When he brushed up the scarlet petals they smeared the blue-tiled floor.

The grown-ups came out of the bedroom and went round the house looking at all the things that would soon belong to them: the demon spat at their feet and flew upstairs to take his place on the bedpost again. The grandchildren, all sizes, were still there, looking scared and saying, 'What shall we do?' One by one they tiptoed up to kiss poor old Granny on the cheek. But their routine sobbing only made her frown.

Once, she opened her eyes, pushed herself up in bed, and cursed them all – the dead husband who'd brought her to this place, her children, the whole tribe, in a tongue she'd not used to anyone but the demon for over fifty years – because she would die here, and not where the bones of her ancestors could be found.

The demon sat on the coffin while they nailed it down. When the body of his mistress had been taken away, he crawled inside the stove and lay there for a long time, not moving. The ancestors had not come. He heard voices, muffled, but it was only the adult children, arguing. Should they sell or let the house? Put in central heating? They cried a bit and clinked glasses and laughed about the old Minister, feeble in body but insisting he must be the one to see Mother safely into the next world. 'He'll be there himself soon enough.' 'Do you remember when he came to cast out her demon?' '*You* always thought it was real.' And the youngest daughter, defensively, 'Well, Mum did!'

Later, he woke to the sound of someone alone in the house, weeping. There was the youngest daughter eating biscuits at the kitchen table and crying into a cup of tea. Choking, she wet the tip of her finger and picked up every crumb.

The stove was cold, the house empty. Even the mice had gone. Biscuits the youngest daughter had left in the cupboard were nibbled and damp. He ate them anyway, shivering through the rooms. Everything of value had been taken, down to the quilt from the old woman's bed. He found an old pair of her shoes, sat in one, then the other. Nothing – only the agony of everything that is past.

Other people moved in. The old stove went and instead came a boiler that fed on oil and roared when it liked; the radiators were too narrow to sit on.

Then once more the people left and only the postman came near. The house demon snapped at his hand, startled by the letters forced in. They piled up. Sometimes he waited all day, sitting on the heap, sliding down at last to the cold tiled floor to lie on his back in the darkening hallway.

The oil ran out. The lights went off. A man whistled in through the door, wearing overalls, carrying a box of tools and a coil of tape. He went round turning off the water and wrapping toilet, bath, shower and sinks with black-and-yellow lines that said 'Do not...!' – until the house looked like a crime scene.

The house demon went to sleep in the ashes. Through the long winter, when rain pattered down the chimney and the wind stirred, he dreamed of flying, looking for his lost mistress, Uncle Yasha, anyone who could tell him where to go. Once round the village he flew, and down to the Minister's house where the old man, tucked up by the fire, dozed with the Bible slipping from his lap.

In springtime the house demon roused himself to his own chilly hearth. Down the chimney came birdsong and a cloud of voices murmuring, 'Home, home, home'. He called up to them, 'Yes! Here I am!'

A comet of bees dived down the chimney, following their queen, erupting out of the mouth of the fireplace, zooming around the dark parlour and away up the stairs towards the light, the first window. The buzzing comet threw itself against the glass, shrinking, until the windowsill was layered with the quivering and the dead. They smelt of nectar and pollen, the wealth of the outdoors. Guiltily, with his long fingernails, the demon tore out their stings and poison sacs, tossed them in a pile and sucked their honey baskets clean.

His hair and beard grew long – in fits of rage and weeping he tore out great handfuls. The buttons hung loose from his mildewed jacket; his leather boots were dirty, cracked and stiff. In one of the bedrooms damp brought down the ceiling, leaving powder and debris on the carpet and a hole into the attic that let in cluster flies. Dark spots appeared on the white plastic frame inside the conservatory; without ventilation it stank in the heat of summer. Black mould bloomed in the corners of the unheated rooms.

People came to view the place. If they complained about the state of it, he stuck bee stings into their legs and squeezed in the poison.

More often than not he slept and in his dreams roared through the house, tearing out the doors and eating them like biscuits.

On a bright day, after a fall of snow, came new people, who said the place had Potential: they talked of fixing it up, cosifying the kitchen, putting in a brand new wood-burning stove. The wife wore a dress of velvet sewn with mirrors and stars. 'We could love this house,' she said.

But the demon didn't hear. They had left the door open to freshen the air and he had drifted out with the smell of mould and damp. He wandered the garden, not thinking of where he was going until from the tangled hedge there came a growl and a laugh, enough to make him hurry back. But the estate agent was already locking the door: the couple were going away to 'think it over'.

The demon went all around, looking in the windows, peering in through the letterbox, climbing on the roof and sniffing down the chimney, but the house was closed against him. The only shelter left open was the shed. Inside, a dusky light fell through dirty windows on a family of old wellingtons, big and small, waiting in a row. He thought of getting inside them, but they were already taken by slugs and spiders.

Propped with his back against the shed door, he dreamed the smell of a leather boot and the warmth of a coal in his pocket. Then he was soaring away from the house over snowy fields towards the village bell tower, cut out black against a deep-blue starry sky. The only window open was at the Minister's house, where a woman in a blue tabard stood blowing out smoke.

The Minister was calling; the woman pinched out her unfinished cigarette and snapped it away in a tin. When she went back to the bedroom, the demon rode on her shoulder. The Minister's eyes were shut. As the demon leapt on the bed, the Minister opened his eyes sharply, but saw only the woman standing over him with a spoonful of pink liquid. He opened his mouth wide, showing a coated tongue, and sucked down his medicine.

'Ugh!' he said. 'You've been smoking!' Then he leaned forward. 'Too many pillows.'

'The doctor said you were better to sleep sitting up.'

Undaunted, the Minister struggled to pull a pillow out from behind him, but the demon had hold of it and wouldn't let go. The old man gave up, leaned back and closed his eyes again. The woman looked at her watch and said, 'I'll be downstairs if you need me.'

After a while, the Minister opened his eyes. He heard the sound of TV laughter from below and called out, 'Nurse! Nurse!' But she didn't come back.

He reached behind him to tug at one of the pillows and was jerked forwards. All the pillows flew out and thumped to the floor. Something pushed him back, and settled on his chest, cold and heavy as treasure.

The demon, warmed a little by the Minister's body, leaned over and whispered in the old man's ear. The Minister wanted to cry out: he could feel the cold flame on his cheek, sharp claws around his heart, the air snapping in his ears. But no words came.

The demon pinched the Minister's nose until the end turned white; he slapped the old man's cheeks.

'Say my name,' he hissed. He tore two buttons from his green jacket and placed them on the Minister's eyelids. 'Show me where you sent her!' he screamed, pressing down hard with vengeful thumbs.

An hour passed before the TV was turned off and the woman climbed the stairs. She saw the pillows on the floor and the grey old man flat on his back. His eyes were almost closed, his mouth fallen open.

She hurried over and touched his cold lips, but her fingers came away slippery with powder; bending to look inside his mouth, she found it full of ashes.

Box

Deborah Kay Davies

I don't have many things. Things hold you back, weigh you down, trip you up. That's bad. There may come a time, unexpected as a visit from the vicar, when you need to vamoose; leg it, pronto. Then all those fab things, those cute, thingy things you hoard and gloat over, will be the death of you. Or maybe not. Who knows? Possessions are like rusty, open cans lobbed in a quivering, crystalline rock pool. My advice: keep it simple, keep it small; think transportable, for blessed saint Frig's sake. Then again, advice can be tricky. Broadly speaking, never trust it. Advice is the bucket of petrol thrown at a fire.

I live by what I say. I have a strongbox. Exactly the right size and weight to expedite a hasty exit. No one knows where the key is. Secrets are like chocolate truffles with open safety pins inside; handle with care. Don't squander secrets. Don't drool them out when you're a-snooze. Don't you know people are as voracious as seagulls for your secrets? They'll snatch them up with precision, fly high and bang! drop them onto the rocks, expose them, pink and boneless, beadily watch them wincing in the bright light. Too late to blub then.

So my box is mucho importanto. In it I keep items that are in danger of slipping away. It's weird; things can get in, and things can get out. Both are undesirable. It's all crap, this in, out, in, out malarkey. Holding on, shall we say, is a bit of a challenge. And God, how I've always shunned those in my past. Some nights, when the hours are like conjoined twins who share a heart and one is dying, I extricate my key and check out my stuff. Oh my beautiful, schmootiful box! And of course, its lovely, bulky key. The key you would never find without some kind of hi-tech, sophisticated machine. Or surgically skilled, latex-clad fingers. Sufficient to say it is about my person. My key gives me pleasure in its own knobbly, unique way. Hey, life is tray diffiseelay, mon ami. Take what you can, when you freaking can. Don't judge.

My box is covered in hammered metal. It looks like pewter – that lovely, gloomy colour: sort of Monday-morning rainy. Everybody surely knows that shade. My box is hard and cold. Impregnable. The screws are impossible to shift; the power of my mind holds everything together. It's a gift I have, and no shiny-shoed, slimey, smooth-haired sod will soft-talk the truth of it from me. No-siree-bob, not even torture would be effective. I say that torture is like a sandwich you might offer to some starving, orphaned child, made with fragrant crusty bread, filled with shavings from the end-of-day butcher's block. But then, I say a lot of things. Blah blah blah.

Crikey Moses. The things in my box. Who'd have thought it? Not me, missus. Not when I started. Now, who knows where things might end? It's exhilarating. Wow, with a lovely big knob on. Here's a thing; I don't have to open my box to see what's inside; I *know*. But it's fun, somehow, getting it all out. First, there is my little folding knife. I've always thought; who knows when you might need a tiny knife like this? I ensure the blade is sharp and bright. Ready for action, so to speak. Be prepared, as the good old Guides say. Or is it the weird old Scouts? And then again, who gives a shit? So anyway, I was saying; be prepared: life is a stinking, blood-soaked bran-tub. And you never know when you may need to slice or dice something. Something that gets on your tits, clouds your vision, gives you boils. Caution! Knife-ist at work! If you've got a little blade, you've got the answer: the promise of peace, a hint of calm, a way to change. A chance maybe, to sleep, zone out, leave it all behind.

Box. Contents thereof: a lovely length of slippery ribbon, the knot still clogged with a nest of hairs, the ends spoiled by a spatter of tears. And then, weighting it down, a disk of scalp as crisp as a cracker. No one knows how I came by my ribbon, but certain things are true; there was a spooky winter wood, a pink hooded coat, a nylon rope between two trees, a blood-blossomed ankle, a chance to run, a chase, some tripping and rolling in the undergrowth, quite funny, and a clean cut. Oh, and a few surprisingly deep grunts down amongst the holly. Don't ask me. I can't remember much. Memory. It's like that photo an ex-lover took when you were wasted and pleading, naked and wetting yourself. The one he had enlarged and stuck on every hoarding in your home town. Work things out on your own. It's not my job, guv.

There have been times when I woke suddenly, and knew that I needed to escape. Once more I would have to wrap up my precious box and get the hell out of somewhere. Mornings when the light hammered and squealed at the window like the scary claws of a famished vampire, and I knew there would be trouble. I can sniff it out. My instincts are good. The hairs in my nose are attuned. Trouble smells like the sluice in an abortion clinic: so many lost possibilities and drippy dreams. With my secret things I can lay it all to rest. Peace, of course, is always just out of sight. I'll tell you something, gratis. A person can easily be deceived in their quest for peace. I had a mouth full of ulcers, big as rosebuds. I thought I could use

my little blade to my advantage; whip 'em out, deftly, lightly.
For my pains I got a mouthful of blood and pus. Ouch. Let
this be a lesson. I learn the hard way. But pain doesn't scare
me. Pain is a rabid dog in a dead-end street. Just take another
route. It's not bleeding rocket science. Pain is the ugly, tangy-
smelling child shut out of the party.

Back to boxics; in another corner is a handkerchief.
Embroidered with a curly P. Not mine then. Some other tart's.
It's tied with a twine knot. Inside: three baby teeth. Milky,
pretty, pearly-barley toothlets. I would have liked more. I've
always been partial to kiddies, but it rarely pays to be greedy.
Well, it does, but you might not be ready to stomach the
wages. Besides, if time is short and the streets are full of
sharp-eyed mothers, it's professional suicide. It would be
dishonest to claim that my knife is always the perfect tool for
the job. In some cases, say, pliers would be cleaner, more
efficient. But hey-ho. I make do. If you need a clue, I'll throw
you a bone; there was a tiny, scarlet mouth in a frothy white
pram, a scream in the street, a fall, a silent, frozen crowd. And,
from yours truly, some ducking and diving, darting and
dodging.

Oh, the satisfaction I derive, the sheer pleasure of my
things, my darling little casket, my receptacle for troublesome
treasures. Here's something else, very pwitty, very nice: an
earring. What could be more charming? I ask you. How lovely,
I hear you exclaim. How enchanting! It's glinty, it's sharp. A
ruby dropper. A heavy exclamation mark. Filigree frippery.
And still looped through an earlobe, like a hook through a
fish's gill. The fleshy lobe now stiffened and pungent. Like a
gobbet of salami. Yum. And so easy, in the dark of the cinema,
from behind, so to speak. Everyone's eye on the iridescent
screen, the inside of everyone's head buzzing to the
soundtrack like a cave when the sea pounds in. And me, black

in the flickering blackness, busy, busy, busy with my blade. Then out and away. A wet witch in the wet night.

Rootling, I've discovered a shocking thing. There are not many items in my box. It's decidedly povvy, positively meagre. I feel the lack. I'll have to go a-hunting, a-looking and a-getting. Fill my box right up. But anyhoo smugness is so unattractive. Smug leads to lazy, lazy to questions, bare rooms, light bulbs, uniforms, tape recorders, peepholes, spread your legs. So then, likewise, pleasure. Always dissolving, like a luminous grey pearl in a glass of coke. It's useless to hope things will stay the same. I hope for nothing. All I know is now, these things I touch now. Hope is the white-coated plastic surgeon who is performing your facelift. The masked surgeon who in real life is a milkman. As you sleep, strapped down, he is drawing around your eyes with his felt pen, fingering his scalpel. His hard-on is monumental. But it's OK. No problemo; chill out. Hope is also the hefty, blessed dose of general anaesthetic you never wake from.

A Crack

Gee Williams

She sat up so abruptly her head bounced once, twice, against the panelling that clothed the gable-end wall. That double bump had Saul instantly alert. The violence of the impact should have been enough to rouse a drunk. But she seemed wilfully attached to her dream. Though her eyes were open and staring, they were in a face set with a sleeper's mask of paralysis. Only the pulling back and down of the corner of her mouth signalled to Saul that any moment now, Julia would wake. But there was still a phase that had to be got through. He saw the huge gulp of breath causing her under-developed chest to swell, the dark nipples leaping on the white skin.

She screamed.

Gathered in more breath.

Screamed again.

No actor asked for agony could have produced a more convincing sound. When first he'd heard it, his own sympathetic system had adrenalised him also. (Sick with fear, is how he'd described it to Julia later, when she'd asked, seeming cool and curious that first time.) Now, as she was about to repeat the process, he took her by one shoulder, not caring whether his nails cut into it.

'Jules. *Julia*! It's all right. You're dreaming. Jules, wake up!'

She didn't turn to him – she never did. Instead she sank back against the wall, bumping her head one last time, while her naked upper torso collapsed into the pillows. Hands that seemed alien to her came up to rub the tightened cheeks. Splayed fingers ran through hair moist with sweat and then back to her forehead. Even in this half-light Saul could see how panic had made a stranger of her. She was a fine-boned, prettyish, terrified woman that he'd never seen before – nor cared about. For an instant, at least.

'Jules. OK? You awake?'

A pointless enquiry. If she weren't, the ear-splitting racket would still be filling the room. It would be rebounding off that high beam at the room's apex. It would be seeping through the inadequate party wall, on the other side of which old Mrs Bellinger had just been catapulted back into consciousness.

Saul leaned across to the bedside table and grasped the plastic mug of water. (Jules had broken two tumblers.) He drank noisily. 'There's some left. D'you want a drink?'

'Um. Yes. If you've got some there.'

'I have. I said so.'

He passed the cup and she clawed for it.

'Thanks.'

'OK now?'

'I'm… Christ. Yes. I'm out of it.'

Interesting. She'd not used that term before. Interesting.

'Was it the same? Same dream? You were screaming again – 'nough to wake the dead.'

'What? No. It's not the same… never the same. I'm sorry. Sorry.'

'That's all right.'

'Sorry, anyway.'

'It's not as if you can help it,' he conceded.

'No. Well.'

They half-lay, half-sat, parallel and untouching. His nostrils filled with the floral scent of her shampoo raised in sweat. There was his own salt-maleness also.

'I'll go and make tea,' he offered.

'No. No, I think,' she slipped downwards and hunched away still further, 'I'll give it another go. What is it now, 'bout six? It feels early.'

He groped amongst assorted objects on his own side. 'Half past five.'

'Fuck.' Just as he was drifting off again he felt her shift abruptly. When he opened his eyes he found he was staring straight into hers – but she was looking past him, looking over his shoulder at something that had become more visible in the few minutes the light had had to strengthen. 'The door,' she said. 'It's closed to. I like it open a crack.'

Saul rolled smoothly out from beneath the covers and into the cool air, as though practised. The lock complained and three floors of the flimsy cottage shuddered as he yanked at the handle. But in the morning the door was shut.

Beyond their garden of wet paving, Culham's village green had been recently doused. Each blade of grass was tipped with a brilliant point – and looking up, Saul found bushes and trees (even those still sunk in dormancy) all zinging with reflective energy. He avoided the grass to preserve his shoes which had the added advantage of giving Mrs Bellinger and mongrel Lotty the slip. The dog was over-friendly and would try to decorate his chinos with its prints but that mattered less than having to own up to hoping *they hadn't disturbed her again last night.* He hurried forward, a sudden interest in the sign of The Lion pub keeping his gaze safely raised. At the very edge of vision he saw Lotty perform an effortless vault into the graveyard surrounding St Paul's church, Mrs

Bellinger's scolding doing nothing to slow her progress over sacred ground. Daffodils were finally out – it had been the latest spring he could remember since first coming to Oxford as a student more than a decade ago. Lotty was trashing them.

The moving air, though delicious, was frigid for April but still a few hardy bees were out working the blackthorn blossoms that draped the hedges. Everywhere it seemed life was making its bid. His bus stop stood opposite the primary school. Already the playground was being crossed and re-crossed by a small posse of children. Reds and vibrant blues in their clothing overwhelmed the strip of washed lawn and surrounding trees. They reminded Saul that his own daughter would be setting out for nursery school about this time. Padded against the chill, but tiny... in her red shoes, tiny shoes... tiny face sparkling with tears – surely a false image? She'd be strapped into the back seat of Kate's car, chattering the drive away through the Cardiff suburbs. Why, in the name of all of the gods, couldn't his ex-wife have just... but then why couldn't he have just...? It was an uncomfortable line of thought and one he needed to snap...

Work, new work, that was the ticket. And, when Virgil was your man, what better for a spring day than... Just get to it, he told himself. *Protinus aerii mellis caelestria* (the bus came into view), which (grinning) he rendered as *Get going with that heaven-sent-honey-thing, dude... Now!* Aristaeus, Virgil's beekeeper from *The Georgics*, duly obliged – though this morning he took the form of a headache. Saul found the myth of Aristaeus had boarded the bus with him and now offered up a series of pulsating niggles. The story was simple enough. Aristaeus, the first ever beekeeper, had lost his bees as punishment from Olympus – sexual indiscretion, what else? Had lost face presumably by having lost his bees. Yet the myth concerned itself mainly with grief and despair... and whining.

A Crack

A lot of whining from bad-boy Aristaeus. He runs after the wrong woman and then it's *Oh mother, my care and skill have availed me naught – and you, my mother have not warded off from me the blow of this misfortune. Cyrene, the mother, the water-nymph...*

The bus crossed the swiftly flowing Culham Cut and then the Thames itself, leaving Culham village by the roundabout route... because, just like Aristaeus, Saul had lost something. He had lost sleep – had failed to recapture sleep after Julia's nightmare drove it off, had dozed perversely around seven and never caught up with a routine that should have ended with a successful boarding of the direct bus into the city.

Sleep was like a bee-swarm... curling darkly through the field of vision, never settling, never stilled... and then as the buzzing... more a droning really... a sustained droning... though a falling one, down and down another octave until...

A scratchy blow, delivered to the side of his face by a woman's shopping basket, restored him to life as a bus passenger. He turned to eye-curse her uncaring back. Tweed coat with a smattering of light animal hair, thick legs in sensible boots, the ancient basket, the paperback emerging from the ancient basket the instant she sat: the woman had professor's wife written through her like seaside rock.

'Oh, hello Dr Prothero!' Someone was addressing him. Someone was pronouncing his name Prother-oo, taking out the Welsh and elongating it to joke-Scottishness. 'Didn't notice you there.' The woman's face became one he knew. It became Maggie's, a 'scout' in his own workplace, Jesus College. *Jesus College, Maggie! HQ of the Oxford Welsh – so what's so hard about Prothero, eh? Eh, Maggie?*

The bus lurched on. The throbbing in his temples settled to a hum.

But now he was safely static at his desk and still the beekeeper maintained his tenancy of Saul's head. *Care and skills have availed me naught* – what was implied here? Knowledge itself is a fickle deity? Don't feel too smug if you've been accepted into that particular cult. The bees, then – *yes*, the bees become peripheral. *Scientia*, itself, is suspect, a tawdry wizardry that leaves the business of life, real human life, side-lined.... Below him, in Second Quad, a girl's train of glowing sorrel hair grabbed at his attention. She was a stranger, a visitor for some lucky bugger who, at this perfect April moment was secreted in his golden-stone cell. As she floated across the face of the latent wisteria, it seemed to stir in sympathy. But it was the same breeze that had set the daffodils jittering and now snatched hold of the girl's thin skirt and blouse, displaying her outline in stirring clarity... between Jules and himself nothing was happening. Her work had always both fulfilled and exhausted her and these sleep problems – or psychological problems – there, he had admitted it to himself, there was some mental thing going on... he didn't know what. How could he be expected to know what? This mental thing was whisking her away to a private underworld whose fumes polluted the daytime. He tried to recall when sex had last seemed like a possibility. Not when it had actually taken place but when the frisson of it had spiced up a morning's lie-in or a rainy afternoon: a hint of chilli on the tongue. Failed. She of the shining hair disappeared into the dark passage that led to Third Quad. Deeper into the college. The gate into Ship Street being locked as a security measure, she'd need to pass beneath his window, would need to display herself to him again if she were ever to get out... life in college certainly had its attractions. Perhaps during the week it would make more sense...?

As displacement activity, he Googled beekeeping, only cancelling the search when Maggie put her head around the door. She was returning a wastepaper basket he hadn't missed.

'Thanks Maggie.'

When she'd gone he typed in *Night + terrors.* Yawned. Waited, finding that sustained note accompanying the yawning process hung on well after the yawn was complete.

'Today's had a theme to it,' he told Julia as they prepared for bed. 'Well, a theme and a sub-theme, to be completely accurate.' He paused for any encouraging signal. She was bending down, placing the belt she'd just detached from a pair of trousers into the lowest drawer. Her bra was a white strip across her narrow back, her panties a pair of white lace shorts pulled tight across a dark cleft. 'There was a sort of basket-thing going on – from bee-skeps, I think. Had this idea about the Aristaeus myth – on the bus.' Even as she was straightening up he saw her shoulders hunch. 'Yeah, I *know.*'

Each vertebra was too well defined, the complete spine sharp as a row of teeth. He walked over, pulled her to him and slipped his hands around her waist... cupping the floating ribs... down across her concave belly.

'I'm really tired.'

'Yes, you must be. I'm...'

'Latham now claims to have found a flaw in the initial protocol.'

'Uh-huh.'

'The original licence was for toxicity-testing. By adding environmental factors... my idea, as you know, I added close confinement of each subject animal, then noise-stress, finally the...'

'Yes, I get it.'

'He says to hold off until he's reviewed the entire series.'

'Ah.'

'It was my protocol,' she said, pushing off from him with enough force to send her cannoning into the pine chest. '*The whole series...* half a million in costs. Two hundred experimental animals in total. And that's not counting all the...' All the not-worth-counting-things, the gesture finished. 'Did I say – I've got to get in early tomorrow?'

Dawn had found numerous small entries into their bedroom, sufficient for him to see her eyes were wide open. They were focused on nothing but whatever she saw was causing her to shriek... to sob. This time there was something pleading in each drawn-out finale, each hopeless gasp by lungs emptied and raw.

'Jules! Wake up.'

The arm he had hold of was slick and she caught him across the bridge of the nose as she fought to pull free. Ohgodohgodohgodohgod – the incantation came up to the threshold of comprehension. But she was easily subdued. For a horrible instant he visioned himself grappling with a child. She fell back, panting. His hand slipped across her breasts and their alert nipples as he let her go... but there was nothing to be felt on that score. Hardly awake himself yet he was depressingly aware of this absence at least. No jolt, no swell of feeling... no swell.

In silence he drank from the plastic mug with its plastic-tainted water, passed it back.

'Drink up, I'll refill it.' If she drank it all he could get fresh, drink fresh himself and wash away the taste. 'Look, I'll – just sit there a minute. I'll be back in a minute. I want to say – something.'

She was upright when he returned and for an instant he was tempted to slide over. But the gathering light showed the set of her features, the way the bones of her cheeks formed a perfectly aligned counterpoint to her dark brows. His heart hardened. A flaw, a lack of symmetry, something to forgive and cherish was what he needed. Was absent.

'We can't have this just going on like – it's been weeks. You have to try and explain to me what's happening.'

'Can't.'

'What are they about? The dreams.'

'I've said. They're not dreams.'

'Nightmares, then.'

'They're not nightmares.'

Licence had been given now for anger. But he reminded himself he'd been angry with her before the questioning and lack of satisfactory response. He acted gentleness.

'All right. You tell me – if you can – what's going on when you wake up like this. What's happening to make you so scared?'

She nodded. But, 'I can't tell you,' she said.

'Why not?'

'Because,' if a lie were on its way now, she didn't flinch from looking at him as she said it, 'I'm not able to. I think I said before, I just... can't... say.'

'But you know?'

'Please, Saul.'

'Please what? I'm trying to help you.'

'But it won't help. I can't do what... I can't do.'

'Is it always the same?' He hoped to catch her off-guard, the way a student's shallow take on his topic could be exposed by a casual observation – something tangential, an innocent remark the poor undergraduate brain lacked the nous to leave alone.

'Sort of.'

'A similar story then – if not always the same?'

'There's no story.'

It was time to take her in his arms now. Saul let his hand burrow out a passage between her burning back and the hot pillow and found how easily she flicked across – how much weight had she lost in these last few weeks? – and settled against him.

'There's gotta be a story, sweetness. Everything's got a story. They say dreams are the stories we tell ourselves. And we tell stories because…'

'Well there isn't. There's this…' she considered for a long while… a very long while. A three-centuries-old structure creaked and settled above their heads. Beyond it the village was so still Saul could hear his own blood's regular progression around his body, through the neck, across the eardrums and back to source. Impossible to ignore once noticed. And then all the wait preluded was '…there's this feeling. Awful. No – beyond awful. There… aren't… words.' Through their joint heat, she shivered. 'No bloody words. I've got no words.'

'But you're feeling things.'

'Yes.'

'Fear?' Curiosity at least could become aroused – with the remembered force of lust.

'Yes. Well, I don't know. *That's it.* There's… terrible things. I can feel terrible things. But no words – I haven't any. I'm me. While it's happening, *I think* I know I'm me. I know it's me it's happening to, at any rate. But I don't have a word, not even for myself.'

'So is that what's so frightening? You do seem *really scared* while you're, you know, shouting out.'

'No.' He felt her chest heave. 'No, there's something going on. Some… things are going on. I'm frightened of these things… happening to me. It's worse than you can imagine. I never knew there could be such…'

'Such what?'

'I don't know.'

She turned on her side, shoved her head roughly beneath his chin and started to cry. He felt the stickiness of tears. The sobs grew in intensity. Saliva he registered now, dribbling as her open mouth tried to drag in sufficient air… and now came snot, oozing from her pressed-out-of-shape nose.

'*Come on.* It can't be that bad. Come on. We'll get through it. It'll stop, you'll see. These things come and go, huh?'

He stroked the short, springy hair back from her ears and felt the skull beneath. He was willing a response, willing her to meet him halfway as he thought of it, to admit that what was going on was unusual, a blip – or blips at least. That soon they'd reclaim the life they'd shared a few months ago: content, undemanding, collusive in a limited range of pleasures.

'Why can't that bloody door stay open?' she mumbled. 'I like the door open.'

Although it was his turn to take the car, he gave it up. Julia's work lay to the south behind wire fencing and threatening signage, a mere fifteen minutes drive. Bus routes north into the city were more numerous, though the journeys longer. But something in her expression had made him hand over the keys, to offer a small easement – anything to slacken off the worry lines. Behind her eyes lurked an atavistic wariness this morning. He'd tried to put a hand out as she swept up her stuff with the briefest of acknowledgements but, tired himself, had mistimed it, fumbled the opportunity behind her back, all his reflexes shot to crap.

…so the bus for him, again…. There was more to this Aristaeus bloke than he'd first thought. The bees, the lost bees, were recovered only following a plot complex and comical as light opera. Inevitably, sacrifice is what's needed – on Aristaeus' part. The valuable beasts (cattle) are sacrificed, the bees consent to return and build in their carcasses. *Yuk*, he thought, the bacon roll resurfacing in his throat like oleum, the jolting bus adding its touch to the suggestion of nausea. Weary, that was all. Lack of sleep always played hell with his digestion – even as a kid it had. (His small daughter had inherited the same tendency: *Heartburn, Daddy! Stop for me!*) Well into his thirties, he was bound to be nurturing those bodily tics that were going to make the downhill years increasingly…

What was up, now? Get a grip! Get back to it!

Aristaeus was forced to appeal to the gods – wasn't that the ancient moral? Beyond the understanding of the pathetic apiarist (still running home to Mummy, please note, when his bees go and defect) he's saved by traditional wisdom wrapped up in religiosity. Everywhere the major theme resurfaces, express it how you will. Don't get above yourself. Defer to the past. Don't break the rules. *You will pay for it.*

Jules had been working on her current project for two years. They'd been together for less than that – up and down. *The environmental stressors… as you know, my idea.* Why had the visitations been delayed, if here was their inspiration? If that's where these nocturnal horrors sprang from? Because what she did, of course, would be enough to give most people the creeps. He'd never say this to her, naturally. What she did was, if not an ethical problem, then… and it might be – yes, it might be, he wasn't sure, wasn't going to let himself think about it for long enough to ever get near to being *sure*. If not an ethical problem, then, an aesthetic one. At the very least it was that. He could never catch sight of her neat, thin hands – red with scrubbing, itchy from that hibi-scrub sensitivity she was incubating – and not feel, well, he had to say it now and, though he was alone amongst strangers on a bus, though he was talking to himself in the privacy of his own head and still it was only just safe to say it.

What Jules did freaked him out.

What Jules did... no, no, *no...* what Aristaeus did, what he was instructed to do, was sacrifice. Four bulls and four cows 'of equal beauty'. Yeah, right, you could imagine that. The Task. Some task. Cattle were so big and bony, with their square frames bursting through skins hung on them like canvas... draping itself into hollows behind the ribs, as though some big important organs had been whipped out... *what Jules did...*

'Maggie!' His mouth greeted her of its own accord. 'I never knew you lived out here.'

'Just the twenty-odd years,' she said without rancour.

Maggie was older, close-to. The roots of her brass-coloured hair were silvery and her jawline just a vague border between face and neck.

'My partner...' he said, 'she works down on the Reading road, at the – a lab. So we live halfway between...'

'That'll be the one where there's been all that trouble?' she offered. Ever helpful, that was Maggie.

'Yes.'

'If this big one, this big new lab, comes to Oxford – you know they say they're going to use the monkeys in it? There's going to be ructions. That's what they're saying. I mean they've had the police to your wife's place again this week. It was on the radio – one of the protestors is in the Radcliffe. And this new one'll be ten times worse. So they say.'

'We're not married, actually. But it's not that simple, the animal question, is it? Obviously people feel strongly both ways. I'm a classicist, of course, so I can't pretend to understand the science but Julia, that's my partner, she…'

'Oh, sorry, Dr Protheroo. There's my friend just got on. We sit together.'

He turned away to find they were passing the well-tended entrance to Radley; it was the school he'd fantasised his daughter might one day attend. In another moment they were amongst fields. An opportunity for trying to spot *beautiful cows*.

Friday. These days they could put off anything like conversation till a Friday evening. Home before Jules – he chopped fresh herbs and vegetables on a wooden board with no clear idea of a dish that needed these ingredients. Beyond the kitchen window and the straggling hedge, Mrs Bellinger had dug a trench the size of a child's grave. Now she was forking in the contents of the huge heap of rotted stuff beside it. Every one of the cottages in the row contributed to the thing. The sweet peppers' innards, woody mushroom stalks and onion skins littering the worktops would be added soon. Mrs Bellinger's heap – there was an element of compulsion about the thing. *I was born in this house. Four of us, there was. My old dad grew enough on this one plot to feed us all. And my brothers were big eaters! When we were kiddies we'd bring the grass from off the green by the barrow-load. My dad cut it for nothing – just to get the clippings. Gets the compost going like nothing else. You can feel the heat coming off it when you walk past!*

Vapour was rising from each forkful. Attent as a robin, Mrs Bellinger examined every deposit, occasionally diving in with bare, stained hands to extract a fragment of yoghurt pot or an indigestible foil top. Lotty the dog was in continual trouble for interference – in fact, Saul decided, the two were a neat tableau of mutual incomprehension. The old woman labouring at a task that surely could have no pleasure in it and no point, the animal's mistaking items of polypropylene or tin as significant rather than the trash they were...

'Hi.'

Jules had arrived in the kitchen, her coat already off, her bag abandoned somewhere. She was all in black, black trousers, black sweater, black boots. Her pink scarf was in her hands, being wrapped around her hands, rolled and twisted, tested: well up to the strain being put on it, though, like gristle.

'Hello. Didn't hear you there. Next door's dog...'

'It's happened! The whole thing. What I said about Latham? We've had a meeting today.' She came and sank onto the stool near to where he was engaged, her look straight out of the window but not on the old woman nor the capering, yapping Lotty.

'He's going to bury the lot.'

'Oh-h. *Infesta hostilis exercitus itinera,*' he said recklessly quoting Tacitus. Julia stared. 'Threatening movements by the enemy on land.' For reckless read *insane,* he thought. Too late. 'I'm – sorry. Very sorry.' Obviously what he must do was abandon the food-thing. Pour some wine, take her into the room which they called the sitting room though they hardly ever sat in it. The next time they caught each other's eyes, hers were suffused with redness and then overflowing. But they fell into chairs across from each other, either side of the empty fireplace. Now he must lean over to pat her knee. 'Don't cry Jules. I know it's easy for me to say. But – look...whatever you've had going on – at work I mean, it's been doing bad deeds to your head, love. These nightmares... call it what you like – you can't pretend it hasn't been crappy. You're exhausted most of the time.' We both are, he knew he mustn't add. 'Maybe it's for the best – for things to come to out in the open like this. Maybe you've been worried about it not going well. Maybe that's what's been nagging at you and now...'

'*What?* I don't know what you're talking about.' Half of
the Sainsbury's best went down her throat in a single gulp,
unnoticed. A bloody droplet fell onto her trousered thigh and
disappeared. She knocked back the remainder. 'There was
never any question of me being worried about work – not
until Latham gets involved, I'm not. Extra involved. He holds
the licence. That's what he reminded us of this afternoon. At
this meeting. *I hold the licence for all animal experimentation in
the whole of this facility. Including this series. Let nobody forget
that. It's my name, my reputation.* Can you believe it?' Saul
could think of no reason why not to believe it but she hurried
on anyway. 'Why would I be worried about work, huh? Until
this week *work* has been really good. Better than good. It was
going great.' Shining eyes added to the intensity of what she
meant to be a parting shot. She got to her feet. 'I'm going to
get changed.'

'No – just hang on. Stay and talk to me.' Why wouldn't
she sit again? He was being forced to lean back, to look up at
her. 'I'm… not so hot myself, as it happens. I'm – I find myself
thinking about Lowri.' Lowri was his daughter. 'A lot. More
than a lot. Really missing her. I need to go and see her. To see
Kate, actually.' Kate, as in Lowri's mother: Jules had met
neither, knew them only as names – but what names! Spoken
aloud, embedded in these sentiments, they must sound heavy
as Yahweh. He had downed his own wine too quickly in an
effort to match her. Certainly the glass, when he glanced at it,
was empty – and on standing, he found the room twitch
across his field of vision. And his head buzzed. But if Jules
had understood all that he intended her to understand, she
chose not to react. He fell back on trying to imagine how she
must feel. Here he was, in her face, close enough to touch but
not touching. Instead he was saying words that couldn't be
taken back. He was hearing them for the first time, himself, so

he knew. They were powerful stuff. Powerful things, words, in any language you liked. 'I'm thinking of going back to Cardiff,' he said. 'Tomorrow, probably. Just for the day – or two.'

'Are you?'

'So if there's anything I can do – before I go…?'

The house became very quiet. But then it was a quiet little place, Culham, with a quiet lane running through it, and they had such quiet neighbours. Even that buzzing in his head had stopped… yes, definitely stopped.

And Jules, she'd taken all this quietly, the mental trouble, whatever that was all about (he supposed he'd never know) and the crisis at work and now this – this pronouncement that he'd sprung on them both. She seemed to be taking it pretty calmly. She was picking up her bag and briefcase, throwing her black coat over her arm in preparation for transferring it to their shared wardrobe. The stairs wound up from the room they were in. Julia halted at the bottom as though about to speak, just as a last glimmer of sun thrust in low enough to drive a bright tunnel through the house, catching her before she stepped into shadow, leaving her dazzled and vulnerable… and all he could think was how this mourning black was doing her no good, how it turned her skin to grey-taupe.

Whatever it was she intended to say never got said. Lotty's muted *yip* came next, sudden as a weapon's report. And when she tried again, *Yip-yip-yip-yip!*

'Jules?'

'You can do something for me, actually,' she said. 'Before you go. That woman from next door? Tell her from me, will you, *to get that dog of hers to shut the fuck up?*'

The Handless Maiden

Richard Gwyn

She comes in through the window, where I am enjoying a game of chess on the floor with Callum (there is no furniture in the squat) as though it were the standard way of entering a building, sidling under the half-open wooden frame and swinging her legs over the sill, before alighting, like a cat, on the wooden floor, within inches of the chessboard. She is wearing very short cut-off denims and a skimpy black vest, and she springs across the room towards Ana, who lives in the house, and in whom (without going into unnecessary detail) I have an interest, before the two of them disappear out of the door and along the corridor to Ana's room, talking in Norwegian.

Callum (tall, Scottish, a slacker) gazes after the newcomer admiringly. She looks as if she has emerged from an illustrated edition of *Oliver Twist*, a saucer-eyed urchin, small and slim, with a mess of short, wheat-coloured hair.

Goril is nineteen, perhaps the most accomplished hustler I have met, and over the next few days, due to her friendship with Ana – they knew each other back in Oslo – I get to see her in action. With her sweet, innocent face, few would suspect that her mere presence in a public place constitutes an immediate threat to any carelessly guarded wallet or handbag, which items, in her company, are likely to vanish without trace. Unlike the other vagrants here in Andalucia, she never begs, nor does conjuring tricks, nor plays a musical instrument, yet she manages to extract money and goods from people with amazing facility; tourists, bar-owners, even, alarmingly, drug-dealers – to the extent that within a week of turning up, she comes to the house one morning with a thick wad of bank notes and offers to take everyone to the seaside. She says she has been given the money by the Norwegian consulate, in order to procure a ticket home before the Guardia Civil incarcerate her for the greater good of the citizenry. I don't know if she is telling the truth, I don't even know if there is a Norwegian consulate in Granada, nor do I care. In the idle way that associations are formed and dissolved among vagabonds, she has become a member of our gang, although Goril is most certainly not a joiner.

The place to which we are headed is an abandoned village on a remote and undeveloped outcrop of land jutting out into the Med, east of Almeria. It is called Las Perdidas, which means The Lost Women, and I should have known better than to go there in the first place, but am intrigued by the possibilities. By which, of course, I include Ana, who looks like a young Björk, and whose feelings towards me are a mystery, due to her reluctance to engage in conversation. There are rumours of natural hot springs and healing mud baths. It sounds like paradise, and as such might provide the ambience for our relationship to blossom.

We take the morning bus to Almeria and have a two-hour wait before our connection. Antonio, along with his friend Pedro, the local boys in our little band, has the idea of buying a yearling lamb, which he acquires off some guy in the nearby market, ready-skinned. Antonio has it wrapped in preserving herbs and sacking for the bus journey to the coast. We have to carry the thing with us, but it's going to be worth it, Antonio says: this is real food. Goril pays for the bus, the meat, everything.

Las Perdidas, it transpires, is way off the beaten track. The bus stops at a nearby town and we walk along an unsurfaced road for an hour before descending a narrow mule-path down the cliff face towards a jumble of stone cottages near the beach. Some of the buildings look as if they were deserted a century ago and are beyond repair, but others even have roofs, and a semi-permanent settlement of hippies and *friquis* have taken over the more robust houses, which are perched at a slight elevation, overlooking the sea. These inhabitants have become accustomed to a drifting population occupying the lower, more ruinous houses, or sleeping rough on the beach, and pay us no attention as we file by, the six of us, carrying our possessions, sleeping bags or blankets, and several plastic containers filled with wine.

When we arrive on the beach, we immediately set about collecting driftwood and scrub for a fire. I make up a search party with Ana, Callum and Goril, and after assembling a small mountain of fuel, we strip off and go for a swim, and although it's April, the water is not as cold as I expect it to be; perhaps the shape of the cove protects Las Perdidas from cooler currents. Afterwards Goril stands naked at the water's edge, vigorously drying herself with a scrap of towel. She suggests we return to the small town where the bus dropped us off, to 'score some beers and tapas'. That's how she talks. Her English, like Ana's, is fluent, but sprinkled with a gratuitous sampling of time-warped hippy jargon. Perhaps it amuses her to talk this way. The treat will be on her, she says, or rather, on the king of Norway. Long live the King, chimes Callum. Ana, in an unprecedented demonstration of affection, links arms with me. She hasn't honoured me with one of her rare and random excursions into conversation yet today, but this, at least, is progress. The four of us move up the beach to explain our plan to our Spanish friends.

The beach fire is going strong but will need to burn down before Antonio can start cooking the lamb on his improvised spit, and it'll be a few hours before the meat is cooked. He and Pedro have a bag of grass and are happy to stay and tend the fire. We have a smoke with them before leaving. By now it's late afternoon.

We're on our fourth round of beers when Goril falls into conversation with a young German, who is drinking on his own at the bar. He's a tourist, rather than a traveller. His name is Kurt. He's predictably blond and red-faced, but seems friendly enough and a little lonely. Goril buys him a drink and Kurt buys us all drinks in return; in fact we can't stop him buying us drinks, even if we were inclined to, he seems so happy to have people to talk with in his faltering English. He is staying at the hotel attached to the bar, and has just driven the length of France and Spain, as he tells us, until the land runs out, in order to get over *heartbreak with a woman*, pronouncing the absurd phrase with such Teutonic sincerity that Callum splutters into his beer (fortunately he is facing me, and Kurt does not seem to notice the indiscretion, although Ana does: she glares at Callum).

Travel, says Callum, trying to make amends in case he has offended Goril also, is a great healer. Travel, and alcohol. Especially alcohol. You are doing the right thing, my laddie. Drink up and forget your troubles. You're among friends.

When Kurt, bewildered by Callum's accent, enquires of Callum and myself where we are from, he seems delighted by our reply: Ah, the Celtic peoples, he says, this I like. Myself I am a *Wandal*. From the Germanic tribe, you know, of *Wandals*.

He beams at us and we smile obligingly. But Kurt is harmless, and generous with his cash, and is obviously enamoured of our blonde Scandinavian talisman, who might be providing him with a glimpse of redemption after his experience with heartbreak woman. So it comes as no surprise that he offers to drive us back along the track in his smart BMW, parking the car where the road ends, and insists on descending with us to the beach at Las Perdidas. The light is fading but the earth is still warm, and there is the edge of a cool breeze from the sea.

The lamb is cooked to perfection, but before we get stuck in, Pedro, who is a connoisseur of plants and wildlife (as well as narcotics) tells us he has brewed a concoction, as an aperitif, he adds, thoughtfully. He seems reluctant, at first, to explain in any detail what is in the drink, but on being pressed, tells us it is made from the hallucinogenic seeds of a plant which grows abundantly in these parts. He passes around a cup filled with the brew. It tastes vile but everyone drinks some; we are a hardened band of psychotropic adepts. When it comes to Kurt's turn, he looks questioningly at Goril. Pedro has given his explanation in Spanish, which Kurt neither speaks nor understands. Goril nods her head, saying something to him that I cannot hear; and maybe I am the only one to notice this, but she turns towards Ana, and she winks. Kurt knocks back the drink and passes the cup to Pedro to be re-filled. Everyone is in a fine mood. Antonio cuts slabs of flesh from the legs and shoulders of the lamb, and there is more to eat than the seven of us can possibly manage. A young French couple, who live in the hippy colony, venture down to the beach with their baby and attendant mongrel, following the scent of cooking. We tell them to go and get the other hippies, but they say that most of the residents are vegetarian, and would not wish to participate in this carnivorous feast. More fool them, scoffs Pedro. How could anyone resist the gorgeous smell of lamb roasting on a spit? Kurt, having demanded a translation of this exchange, agrees. He tells a vegetarian joke, very badly. He tells us we are a great bunch of guys. His words express a touching gratitude for his welcome into this bohemian gathering, this company of druggies and wasters. We help ourselves from the great platter that Antonio has piled high with meat, and tear at hunks of bread and help ourselves to wine, swigging from plastic bottles or squirting the stuff into our faces from the wineskin that Antonio hands around.

Ana, I am pleased to report, is sitting at my side, and she leans close and speaks quietly.

You know, she says, glancing over at Goril, when *she* was about thirteen, back in Oslo, her father locked her in a room and fed her on raw meat, raw reindeer meat. For three months. And someone found out, a neighbour, he heard her howling like a dog, and called the police. When she got out, and her dad was taken away, she wouldn't eat anything else, just raw meat.

Hell, I say, and what happened?

She got sick, says Ana.

Is that it? I ask.

Yup, she says, and smiles, pleased with herself for this little foray into anecdote.

I feel a great affection for Ana, but am startled by her story.

Didn't she have a mother? I ask, didn't she have someone to look after her?

Ana shakes her head. Her mum died when she was small. Her dad was a junkie. He was very bad news. She grew up on the streets. *My* mother, she adds, hesitating, said she was a *handless maiden.*

She did? I ask, curious: why did she say that?

Well, says Ana, it means her father made a devil's bargain, like he sold her soul. In the story, the girl's father is a miller and he makes a deal with the devil, because he is greedy, because he wants more grain from his mill, more gold, and the devil cuts off the daughter's hands and she is left to wander in the forest. That, according to my mum, was what happened to Goril. That's why she's the way she is.

I watch Goril for a minute, sitting cross-legged between her admirers, Callum and Kurt. She is eating ravenously. She consumed several substantial tapas not long ago, but she launches into the meat and bread as if she has not eaten for a week.

Although Callum has the hots for Goril, I am pretty certain he will not make the first move, which is probably wise. Kurt, to her left, is picking at his meat between soulful glances at Goril, then looking around to see if anyone has noticed. While I am musing on this tableau, Goril looks up and stares straight at me. For a split second her eyes spell out an icy, impassive warning, then her face melts into a smile. She makes a little wave at me, fluttering the fingers of her hand, then turns to the French couple and asks them to show us where the mud baths are, the famous mud baths.

We leave the beach and set off up a path through a narrow gorge, Goril walking ahead with the French, Kurt following her like a puppy. It is night now, but the moon has risen and we have no trouble finding our way. In a sheltered spot, a greyish puddle of wet, viscous mud lies below a small waterfall, space enough for two or three to bathe. Goril and Ana take off their clothes and do not need to exercise much persuasion to get Kurt to do the same, Germans will strip off at any opportunity; even so, the girls give him a hand pulling off his pants and the three of them plunge into the soggy bath, falling about and smacking each other with dollops of gloopy clay. I cannot help but notice that Kurt has an erection, which he tries ineffectually to protect with a hand at first, but is soon so covered in wet clay that it barely matters, and the three of them lollop like imbeciles in the pool, shrieking, hooting and plastering each other with sticky mud.

With a jolt, I feel the effects of the potion rise through my body, bubbling through my veins, and I am lifted bodily to a place where everything has the semblance of itself but is undeniably other; the rocks, the cliffs, the faces of my friends, the strange mutt belonging to the French couple (which seems to be sporting an oversize Gallic moustache); everything has been replaced by a simulacrum of itself, and I too, am a new and alien version of me, and all my sense receptors, sight and touch and hearing and smell, are lodged not in me but in this impostor who has occupied the zone I once thought of as my body. *So long as I keep calm*, I tell myself, *everything will be all right*. I glance over at Callum, who, like me, has kept his clothes on. He smiles vacantly in my direction but I can tell, or *think* I can tell, that he is going through his own epic moment, and I decide (or whatever it is that has commandeered my brain decides) that, for now, language is something I might try and avoid. But Callum is edging over to me and is speaking, or rather, he is making sounds I cannot hope to understand, and which I imagine he has little sense of uttering, or control over; like me, he appears to have a problem formulating speech. The three mud-creatures in the pool are clambering over each other, slithering like hideous aquatic lizards through the slime. I notice how long and red Ana's tongue seems, and how it ululates as she makes strange noises in the round 'o' of her mouth, and how that orifice is enveloped by a grey carapace of mud on her face and in her hair and how this might reasonably be expected to diminish my attraction to her but in fact produces the opposite effect; the three of them have grey slimy bodies but red tongues and blue eyes, and the whites of those eyes are flashing horribly in the moonlight. Goril and Ana are kneeling, facing each other, and they begin to kiss, slowly and lasciviously, and Kurt is lying on his belly, flat out in the muck, staring at them, his pupils massively dilated, and then he turns on his side and begins to masturbate, mechanically, never taking his eyes off the girls. Goril looks up and sees what he is doing, cannot help but notice him thrashing away, and she shrieks, reaches for a handful of mud and throws it at Kurt, and Ana joins in, hurling fistfuls of sludge at Kurt, who rolls over and moans, in sorrow or delight, I can't tell, he wears an expression of demented, anguished joy while the two women, who are no longer laughing, stand over him, pelting him with slushy missiles as he cowers and grovels at their feet, and I observe this macabre scene without much concern, and I hear, in the distance, the sound of a conch, blasting a hole in the petrified night air.

As if this were a signal, the assault ends, and someone, it might be me, suggests a swim and we all run back down to the beach, and the three naked mud-people race to get to the sea first, the rest of us jogging behind. The French have gone home, no doubt wishing to protect their child and dog from further scenes of depravity. Then I am very slowly stepping out of my jeans and laughing uncontrollably, which makes it hard to keep my balance, and Ana and Goril and Kurt are standing by the water's edge, caked in the dried mud, and as I wade into the sea, the water closes around me with a lovely cold feeling, like acquiring a shiny new skin, and I am impossibly high, floating on my back beneath the moon and the stars, being swallowed up by the unimaginable vastness of the sky, and afterwards I find my blanket and curl up by the fire and weep, although with no sense of sadness, and Ana joins me and both of us sit wrapped in the blanket weeping and looking at the flames, and then Kurt is running up, also in tears, but his are unmistakeably tears of despair, he is yowling, yelping, running up to us and then running off down the beach, out of his head with grief, as well as simply out of his head, returning and asking us where is Goril and us saying, Kurt we have no idea where she is but Kurt keeps asking us where is Goril, then running off, sobbing, then coming back and begging, pleading with us to help him find Goril, he cannot live a moment longer without knowing where is his darling Goril, and when he has gone Ana turns to me and we kiss, and then a minute, or a hundred years later, I look up, and Goril is standing there, her arm around Callum's waist, head on his shoulder, and Kurt is by the fire, silent at last, but in seething suppressed rage, and we are all tired of this performance and Ana tells Kurt to get a grip, to please, for God's sake, just get a grip and fuck off and go to sleep.

In the morning I make a pot of coffee and decide to look around. Antonio and Pedro are asleep by the remains of the fire. I find Goril and Callum under a blanket in one of the abandoned houses, and there is no trace of Kurt. We spend all morning combing the beach and searching the gorge but do not find him. What more can we do? Ana says she refuses to feel guilty on Kurt's behalf, and Goril agrees. That's life, she says, that's the way it goes, I mean, no one invited him. Callum and I are silent and uncomfortable. The Andalucians mooch, and we all smoke weed.

Later that afternoon we hear that the body of a young man has been washed up on the beach in the nearby town where we went for beers and tapas. Somehow, no one is surprised.

That same evening, I am emerging from the sea after a swim, with Ana, and we see a column of Guardia Civil moving quickly down the distant cliff path, on foot, a snake-trail of green uniforms, six of them. They must have found Kurt's car. We rush back up the beach to warn the others.

We arrive at the house that Goril and Callum have occupied, just before the Guardia. Goril is naked, and as a young officer, a lieutenant, comes into the room with two of his men, she takes her time, carelessly pulls on a shirt, one of Callum's, from a pile on the floor, but doesn't bother buttoning it, sits with the shirt half-open, honey-coloured legs stretched towards the lieutenant, crossed at the ankle, and she talks to him. Without prior agreement, she has become our spokesperson, answering all the questions on our behalf in near-perfect Castilian. The lieutenant is handsome and dark-eyed, interrogates her in a civil, professional manner, scribbling in a notebook as he stands, and smiles at her once, a little too freely, and he tells Goril we were seen by the bar owner talking to Kurt, were seen leaving in his car, and she says yes *Capitán*, we met him, but this is all we know: he was distraught, broken-hearted after a love affair, we tried to help him, we tried talking to him, to comfort him, but he must have wandered off during the night, he must have walked into the sea. She shakes her head sadly. The young Guardia allows his gaze to linger, casts his eyes over her without expression, snaps his notebook shut.

Just Like Honey

Tristan Hughes

On autumn days, when my sister and I were children, we would fill bottles with water and honey to trap wasps. Every year they would invade the small garden behind our cottage, coming out from the green recesses where they'd hidden through the summer to swarm about the hedges and cluster around the deepening red of the hawthorn berries and the dark purple fruit of the plum tree. Often they would find their way into the cottage, drawn there by the rich, slightly fermenting aroma of our own autumnal booty: the bags of stolen apples, the buckets full of blackberries, the bowls of damsons. I remember our kitchen then in a commotion of trembling, fruit-smudged lips, stung fingers, and tears. And so to stop them we would place the bottles around our back door. Any type would do: milk bottles, beer bottles, wine bottles, even an ancient, crimson jar tapered at the top like a demi-john that we'd dug up near the old well, imagining it had once held some strange and exotic elixir.

The wasps were easily lulled by the scent of the honeyed water, buzzing drowsily, almost drunkenly, around the glass lips of the bottles as if they exuded some gently narcotic and irresistible breath. Sitting on the doorstep we would watch as they crept down into the bottles' necks, reckless with the hope of sweet pleasures but also, as I would only realise later, with dying. The first frosts were never far away.

Near the end of the day my sister and I would count their floating bodies, holding the bottles up to the beams of the late afternoon sun, silhouetting them against the different shades of glass where they floated like dark, foetal flecks in a rainbow. My favourite was a cider bottle, whose caramel tint shone golden in the sunlight and appeared to hold the wasps as if preserved in amber, stalled in mid-flight, their stingers sharp yet harmless, the angry buzzing of their wings stilled and silenced. How peaceful they seemed then.

Today I remind my sister about the bottles and the wasps. I'm not entirely sure how they come up, but it must be a thread in some larger and more tangled weave of reminiscence to do with our childhood: about the cottage and the village maybe, or about our parents, or perhaps our years together in the little primary school down the road. I don't know which exactly – each one of them might touch on the wasps. In any case, I believe that what I say doesn't really matter, not specifically, only that I say something. And so I pick whatever subject comes into my head.

Our childhood seems the easiest one. Hasn't it always been? We are so much changed these days, our lives so very different, that to cling onto what we did – indisputably – share feels the safest, least treacherous, option. I won't lie. I have not approved of many of her choices; I have not approved, you might say, of her life. There is much to be avoided in our conversations (if you could call them that): pitfalls to be skirted, prickly, painful details to be skipped, things that are simply best left unsaid. There is no need for either of us to explain how we got here. In fact, I try not to imagine it – for both our sakes! A knock. A door opening. A stranger's face.

The fake, practised grimace of her painted smile, turning slowly to bewilderment and then disbelief and then...

'That crimson jar,' I tell her. 'Do you remember us finding it?' I doubt she does but on I go anyway, rather urgently, even though it is such an inconsequential thing to recall. Yet there is something anxious, almost frantic, in my recollection of it; a grappling towards a less slippery ground on which we can both stand firmly and safely and look around and recognise the view; somewhere we are not strangers. Because blood, as I have realised these past weeks, is rarely thicker than time, all that time we haven't known each other. We have had very little of it to share since back then. And have so little now. The others will arrive all too quickly, I am aware of that. We will not be alone together like this, not for long.

'So, the crimson jar,' I prompt.

You were seven and I was five. It was late in a long, hot August and the fields around the cottage had turned as sere and stubbly as old men's chins. All through the morning we'd played listlessly in the living room at some game or other of make-believe. The point of it eludes me now, but it must have involved dressing up because I remember you were tottering about in mum's shoes and had smeared your face with her make-up. You were wearing her sun hat too: that floppy, wide-brimmed one imprinted with pictures of summer fruits. I wonder what it was you wanted to be back then? An actress maybe? Some princess from a book? Whatever it was I played my own allotted role poorly, so poorly that at last your patience failed and we headed out into the heat of the afternoon.

In the woods by the river it was cool and green in the shadows and that's where we went. There was that tyre that used to hang from the branch of the old oak tree and you started swinging on it, going back and forth through the sun-dappled shade. Mum's too-big shoes fell off your feet and her hat flipped off your head. Leaning against the oak's trunk I watched you, half-intoxicated with the simple thrill of movement, your eyes shining and exultant, your legs kicking out towards the sky. I felt I could have watched you forever then. My pendant heart swayed back and forth with you, sinking down with the fear that you might fall before rising up with a sharp rush of relief as you soared once again into the air. Every time you made it. You could defy gravity. You could go anywhere.

Only we weren't supposed to go near the well, were we? Looking back I find it strange that Mum and Dad called it that. It didn't look like those picturesque wells in story books – with the neat slanted roofs and the winch for winding up wooden buckets; it was really just a hole in the ground, covered with a piece of corrugated iron and ringed with rusty strands of barbed wire. But then again they called the cottage a cottage even though it was little more than a dilapidated bungalow. It was a sort of kindness, wasn't it? The way they did that for us? Trying to hide the ugliness in our lives as if all that was needed was a sugar-coating of words.

From the corner of my eye I spotted it, through the sagging strands of the wire: a red glimmer in the earth, like a jewel, like a ruby. It seemed to draw me towards it until without thinking I was on my hands and knees and crawling under the wire. From up above on the tyre you watched me.

'You're not supposed…' I heard you call. And the rest was lost as you swung backwards.

The jewel grew as I dug the earth with my hands. It turned into the jar. You were standing inside the wire too then, with your hands on your hips.

'Let me see it.'

'No,' I said. 'I found it.' I was cradling it in my arms as if
it were a treasure, a magic potion. 'I found it.'

'Let me see,' you said, but I wouldn't let you.

'Fine,' you said. 'I'll find my own.'

Wasn't that always the way, sister? Thinking you'd find
just what you wanted around the next corner, thinking the
world would give you jewels if you only looked hard enough
for them? As you knelt by the well and took off the covering
I felt my stomach flutter. This was going too far. We weren't
supposed to.

Can you hear me now, I wonder? Are you listening? Look at
you! How distorted and misshapen your features have
become: your cheeks swollen and scraped; your nose shattered; your entire skin a bruise of different colours – purple and
yellow and red. Look what your life has done to you! The
policeman said it was lucky I found you when I did – lying
crumpled and broken on the floor of that room – before it
was too late. I try not to picture that room: its curtains – on
which the pattern of vines and their clusters of grapes had
grimed over to resemble a dirty spider's nest hung with sacks
of dead insect eggs; its filthy, tobacco-yellowed walls; the
nauseous, over-ripe warmth of the gas heater. I wish I'd never
gone there, had never followed you back there.

But what else could I do when I saw you on the street? I
didn't even know you lived in that city. None of us knew. After
you ran away we heard nothing, nobody did. I knocked and
when you answered I hardly recognised your voice, it had
become so low and coarse and tired; the false syrupy promise
of it sounded cloyed and heavy as if your tongue could hardly
carry it anymore. Come in, you said, as though I were another
one of them. Come in. And when I did, the first thing I saw
was the bin by the bedside – its wicker frayed, its bottom

heaped with pink translucent sheathes, the discarded skins of snakes. I said nothing then. And you looked right through me as though I were a ghost. For a second you closed your eyes as if maybe I'd be gone when you opened them. You, you said, pulling your arms about your body as if to hide yourself. You. What are you doing here? And I wished I wasn't there. I wish I had never seen you there. After I left I closed my eyes and pretended I hadn't.

'What can you see?' I asked as you knelt by the edge of the well.

'Nothing,' you said.

But suddenly the jar in my arms seemed a paltry thing and what lay down there an Aladdin's cave. Throwing it aside I knelt beside you and could see the thin strands of down on the back of your neck, all soft and golden. And then I looked below.

It was ten – maybe fifteen – feet deep, with sides of sheer, smoothed earth. Here and there, near the bottom, old roots poked out and made a kind of canopy, above the tangle of webs and dead, wet leaves that covered the bottom itself. It was too dark to see properly but I thought I caught the twinkle and glint of riches down there and craned my head greedily forward.

'Get back,' you hissed, pulling hard on my shoulder and leaning out further over the edge. I couldn't tell whether you meant to keep what was down there from me or stop me from falling; either way, the next instant I was sat on the ground and you were gone. When your voice came it was whispered like you were calling me from far away. Does mine now sound the same to you?

Creeping back to the edge I could barely bring myself to look. I thought the well had swallowed you forever, had drawn you down into depths so terrible that we would never retrieve you. But there you were: your painted face staring up at me; your hair covered in webs and leaves; your eyes wide with panic.

'Help me,' you cried. I said I'd go get Mum and Dad but you said no, no, no, you can't tell them. Just like you did later. Only I didn't know what to do. I didn't know how to help you.

'Help me,' you said and your face was so twisted and ugly with fear that I couldn't even look at it. My stomach felt sick and my arms and legs trembled. I couldn't look and I couldn't think properly and I thought if I could just think properly for a second and not see your face then I'd know what to do. So I reached for the covering and began to pull it back over the hole. It slipped over your face like an eyelid.

'No, no, no,' you cried. And then I couldn't hear you any more.

Under the oak tree the solitary sounds were the buzzing of insects and the slow trickle of the river. A heavy, breathless stillness had fallen over everything – except the tyre, which continued to rock, gently, back and forth. Mum's shoes and hat remained lying on the ground and I picked them up as I trudged by. It was like the scene of a kidnap, where only the missing piece tells you it's a puzzle. I tried to figure it out. Sitting down beneath the tree I cupped my hands over my ears and buried my face in the hat. But eventually its soft, worn fabric and its colours must have lulled me into a sleep of sorts, where I dreamt I was cushioned in a pool of warm, sweet-smelling water which I never wanted to leave. And then the trickle of the river returned to my ears and grew as loud as a cataract and I was swept away with it into a cold, grey, underground sea. When I opened my eyes I thought I saw your pale, naked body suspended in its freezing waters, your mouth opened wide as if to speak. But instead it was just the tyre, still now in the cool, fading light of the evening. Shivering and frightened I began the walk back to the cottage to tell Mum and Dad how I'd left you there, how I'd done nothing.

By the time I got back it was almost dark but I dreaded going in. I lingered, still shivering, near the door, trying to postpone the moment of my confession. And then, to my dismay, I saw a sliver of light widening across the garden. The door was opening and from behind it Mum emerged, calling out my name, and behind her – framed in the light of the hallway – there you were. You must have got out on your own. You must have got out on your own and not told me. And that's what I always thought afterwards: that you could get out of anything on your own.

It's warm in here, isn't it? Not too warm, but not cold either. They keep the temperature the same through the days and the nights; you would hardly know the difference between them if it were not for the sunlight that filters through the window shades, coloured that orangey-brown that institutions favour. Yesterday I noticed the leaves were beginning to fall from the row of sycamores at the edge of the car park and the first nip of autumn bit through my clothes. But in here the seasons aren't felt at all. They are nothing to you now, I suppose, only pictures behind these windows, images blurred by the transparent bags of sugared water they feed you with. And this darkness, my sister, it will not last long, not this time. It will be no more than a short, feathery blink, I promise. It is better this way – that I don't see your face or hear the murmured protest of your breath. Through the glass walls of this room I can hear the buzz and cry of alarms and the footfalls of the people running. But not to worry. They are further away than you think. They cannot touch you. Safe in this amber light you are already in another place.

The Epilept

Cynan Jones

I shouldn't be telling you this. I swore. She said: 'If you don't tell anyone, I won't come back.' Tell no one. Not a soul. And here I am telling. There we go. We promise a lot, don't we? But then, do I believe in God? No I don't believe in God. So it doesn't matter then. I just think it's better I write this all down, so you know. Because it's going to happen again anyway. I can feel it. Anyway, they say it's better to write it down.

It hadn't gone well for us, Dad and me. We lost Mum more or less when I first got there and then Dad hit the drink for a while but got over it but had a big problem believing in things. Work. Getting up for it and taking the hassle when he'd seen it can all be snuffed out like that. But I think it was a mistake to take her in. Just like that. I didn't see it would solve things.

They pay a great deal for a foster child. Depending on the badness level. But it's always a lot, really. Given that mostly you don't have to do much. Just treat them okay, and get them to school. Whatever. Still, it meant Dad didn't have to work, and got most of the day to himself.

I shouldn't call him Dad really. But names are so impersonal. I don't know how much they got paid for me. I had a 'capacity', they said. I remember that word. I was fostered, so maybe it was a natural step for him to have her in as well. An easy way out.

Where am I? I'm getting confused. I shouldn't write that down should I, how I am feeling doing the writing. The teacher told me that, but I like to do that because it helps, like I'm talking. I'm trying to tell you what happened. Well, I woke up because I was too warm. I couldn't sleep. I was really unnaturally warm. You know when you're bothered and all little things start to get to you – and then you're cold. It makes you feel odd and scared of normal things – you know how it is on your own, when you're scared – every crack of furniture relaxing, every sound a house makes when it gets left in peace for a while. They all matter. And then when you get up you're heavily tired and cold, but the rest of it's hot and thirsty and you need the toilet badly. I got up. Had to. She was just sitting in the lounge in the dark, staring. She really frightened me very much. It was just after she arrived with us. I didn't do anything. I think she might have been asleep. I saw her through the door and she didn't move and I got a glass of water and went to my room. It freaked me out though.

It was a few weeks after that, 'it' happened. I call it 'it' because I can't think of a proper thing to call it. Just thinking gives me this itch, this horrible sick-feeling driving little itch like a hair growing the wrong way in your face. *Deal with it.* That was one of the lessons I got from somewhere I don't know about, can't remember. They reckon I was too young, or I blocked them away or something. Well. I hope writing it *deals with it* like the teacher said.

We lived a pretty much okay way, and it was loads better than how it had been for me. We did normal things. Watching the television, sharing the washing up, going to school. Dad was never right after Mum died, but who is, once you get to a certain age? *We all have our cross to bear.* He used to say that a lot in this way that was like he was cheering himself up but you knew it just made him sadder. Like there was a come down from gulping in okayness like that, like drinking too much Coca Cola. 'We all have our cross to bear.' That was his phrase.

Looking back, some things. I think it is better if I just write things down and I can try to make them sound better as written-down things after, otherwise I am going to get lost.

She was okay, but she walked a lot in the night. We got used to that. We had two cats and one dog. The dog was killed on the road just after she came. That was weird, like a sign.

And another night I found her, sitting asleep. Her eyes were open then and very obvious in the black room, but she was by the window. They picked up light, made more of it. Like ice seems to catch moonlight even on sort of dark nights, and throw it back at you. I was frightened because she'd been there and I got a glass of water and went to bed. But I thought her eyes looked at me. Then when I checked back, they weren't. But I was sure they'd watched me pass the room. That's what being scared can do.

Another time – sorry this is a list, but *work it out* I'm thinking – she was just in the corridor peeing herself. She was tuttied down in her nightdress just peeing herself onto the floor. Christ, it smelt sharp. Really sharp. She stared until she finished, like she didn't know I was there but then she kind of grinned at me and laughed and moved her hands through the cold stream of pee on the corridor tiles. In this kind of trance.

Then there was in the bath. I got really scared then. She was supposed to be in the bath and it was always a difficult one about watching her because there was only me and Dad and she was at that age, well, you know. Getting boobs and things and a little bit of hair which I saw that day and which, even though the rest is horrible, I remember looked silly and joke-like and odd, like someone had stuck it on for 'dressing up' or some game. I was in the house on my own then, Dad had *popped out*. We still don't know what she did. She was in the bathroom and there was just this noise. This terrible noise – a far away-sounding, hollow sort of thing, like a crunch. Except, a crunch is a 'coming in' sort of sound, a sound of things smashing together. This was like a crunch going out. I don't know. I can't write it down. When I got to the bathroom – I was there like a shot – she was lying under the perfectly still water of the bath. All the tiles were off the wall in the tiniest pieces. Smithereened. There weren't any tiles in the bath. Not a bit of them.

It was always warm when she did these things. So warm like it felt my head was boiling up.

There are other things. Like we'd find her a lot with her feet in the toilet, or on her bike asleep in the house, driving over and over into the wall. But it was like those were little things. Now I should write about IT. That big it. What happened. I'm writing this down because I saw on the telly an ape going crazy and that was what it was like a bit. So it all came back to me. I'm going to just try and write it down, the bits I really remember, like it was, without too much describing or me saying the things I thought at the time, so it's like a science thing, because otherwise it will be like writing a story – I'll try and join it up after.

Sitting in the lounge watching something on telly. Dad was somewhere else in the house. Her coming in with blood on her, me getting up, she just went for me.

A low growl. I hear it before she comes into the room. At first I thought it was a cat purring – like they do if they sleep on the end of your bed: with the warm, the sense, the comfort of people.

In the kitchen, Dad's special bottle – its lovely light blue metal top that caught the light – all broken standing on the unit spilling down the doors, still spilling even though it should have run out. Like it was just making itself from nowhere. She came into the kitchen chasing me. Screaming for Dad.

Pulling out drawers, smashing up things, kicking the floor – her. Dad coming in and just looking really scared and kind of frozen and I remember him very clearly then. 'Oh my God, oh my God,' and then all of a sudden he was all cut up and I didn't know how and she was still standing there smashing up things at the end of the kitchen where he wasn't standing. It was like he started to tear. He was so frightened.

The horrible noise of the cat. Battering itself at the window in another part of the house, trying to get out. Battering itself over and over into the wall. It killed itself, it was so frightened. They said they found that *difficult to believe*.

Dad shouting: stop stop. I was dragging her out of the room where all the tins were – the pantry thing. Her arm had just come out through the half-open door, unnaturally long, stretched, like a joke arm, holding, making fun, a thin useless chain, like a bathtub plug chain. Then: trying to hold her wrists together and drag her. Christ, she was so strong, so fucking strong. The sound of water. A bath running, Dad shouting and I don't know what above the din. She was kicking and screaming and all unshaped and her face. Her face had just gone. She was laughing like she did that time she peed in the hall. (She was wearing the same nightie.) Just her teeth lashing and snapping, her head flicking at me uselessly. Flick. A little desperate, like when you drop a worm into water and watch it wriggling. (I tried to make a sort of cross with my thumb and first finger while I grabbed her, and touch her arm with it. I don't know. It was a pretty stupid thing.) She was groaning. A dull, achy groan like the drawers of old furniture make.

We got her into the bathroom, both of us fighting together and unlocking her fingernails and things out of the door, trying to get through. There were sounds everywhere. Dad shouting. The water crashing into the bath. Then something just changing. Dad looking at me really sadly and then I was backing out of the room. I just let her go.

Before I left I saw her split his ribcage in two and pull all the stuff out, like the inside of a bird.

When I went back she was sitting in his ribcage. She was small, had gotten tiny, and was coiled up into his body like a cat curled on a chair. She looked happy but upset at what had happened. Happy it was over. She was getting smaller which she looked sort of sad about.

When the police came she had gone. I was trying to tell them things. To explain.

(You know what it's like when you dream. When you remember a dream? When you wake up it's very clear, bits of it, and you are very clear and awake. But somehow you can't remember the story, the whole thing, just bits of it, like when you fast forward through a film.)

They didn't believe me, but while I was in the cell she came to me and made me promise I would never talk about her again. But here I am. Perhaps she'll be back now. Now I've broken the promise again. By telling you. I'll hear her say: 'I'm back. I'm back,' and then I'll know I don't dream her. You will know it too. They said to me in court I was an *accident waiting to happen*, talked about my '*capacity*' lots. Sometimes it makes me feel special. Like Jesus Christ. That I have a 'capacity'.

Really, it's you who dream. You dream her impossible. That's what's different between you and me. I know she's there, but you want her not to be. There needs to be a world, for you, where these things do not happen, so you dream one up, all of you. But isn't it a little warm there? Sniff. You see, you know. She's very, very close.

The Lovers

Matthew Francis

They were not of an Age but for all Time, the motto says in English and Greek on the stained-glass window adorned with images of six writers of each nationality: on one side the heads of Chaucer, Malory and Johnson surmounting full figures of Spenser, Shakespeare and Milton, on the other, Aeschylus, Euripides, Sophocles, Plato, Homer, Aristotle. The fifth-formers sit in the front row, the sun shining through Shakespeare's brown scalp into their eyes, while the head-master declaims from the stage with the sixth form massed behind him, twisting his hands in his gown behind his back and staggering slightly as he always does, even when standing still.

'I am very sorry to have to tell you.' He has a way of saying words one at a time, so the announcement sounds like: 'the (death) of our (much-valued) (friend) and (fellow)-(pupil) (David) (Nisbet) in a (bicycle) (accident)'. There is a little gasp, more for the sake of politeness than anything. It's Monday morning, and Nisbet died on Saturday; most of the people who know or care who he was have already heard about it. The only part that's news to anyone is the bicycle accident, which is embarrassing, the sort of jolly, innocent death an adult would make up for a schoolboy. Did he even have a bike? None of them has ever visited his house on the other side of London so they have no idea. There is a minute's silence so the school can listen to the rustles of its own discomfort, the squeaks of chair legs on the floor, a squawk of wind in one of the organ pipes.

Sam Gregory, the fixer, neat and sandy-haired, looks across at Millgreen, sitting half a row away to the right, taller than the boys around him, an expression of suitable but not excessive emotion on his face. He is a classicist, who believes that man's natural instincts are dangerous and need to be kept in check by social constraints. He also has what he calls a betrothed back home in Chiswick. Next to him is Walfisch, the hierophant, who looks, with his heavy-set body and large stubbled face, like a man in his forties, and is sometimes taken for one of the masters. Walfisch says he's above sex and his only lust is for knowledge. The three of them must have been the nearest thing to friends that Nisbet had. None of them could be said to feel grief, but it's still hard to believe. He wasn't serious enough for death, surely? It makes you think: if Nisbet can die there is no minimum qualification.

Millgreen feels that the day should be marked somehow; he has already decided not to attend choir practice this evening. He will be taking the day off to go to the funeral on Friday, as the whole form has been given permission to do, but he is not looking forward to it. He knows he will have to talk to Nisbet's mother there, Ursula, as he must call her. He imagines her as tall and stately, her face whitened and stiffened by grief so that it looks like a bust of Athene; he doesn't think she will cry, judging by her voice on the phone to him the other night, but if she does, it will be in an unconvulsive, sobless way, the tears slipping out and down in spite of herself. This he can stand. What worries him is the thought that she will come up to him and clutch his arm, kiss him, draw him to her body in an embrace that he will be too courteous to detach himself from. And then it will be too late – she will believe for ever that he was Nisbet's friend, may even want to see him on other occasions, and he will never be able to tell her, yes, I knew him, we played chess sometimes, he used to phone me every Sunday night at eleven to find out what the English prep was for Monday morning, but that is all. Millgreen believes in telling the truth, but the time to do that was on Saturday when he was too shocked by the news, by the whole situation. From the moment his mother called him into the hall to tell him there was a lady on the phone for him, he knew there was something wrong.

'Is that Gideon?'

'Yes.'

'This is Ursula Nisbet speaking. David's mother.'

Already, his mind was struggling to catch up, to remind him that Nisbet carried on existing on Saturday nights out there in Grove Park with his full name and his mother, leading his un-uniformed life. And this cool, milky voice was part of it, flowed round Nisbet all through his off-hours. The thought was so unnerving, he hardly noticed what she was saying.

'I'm afraid I've got some bad news. David died suddenly today.' The way she said *died suddenly* made it sound as if it were one of those things that happened in life, like one's voice breaking. Which David were they talking about again? 'I thought you would like to know.'

A hint that he was supposed to reply. 'Yes, thank you, that's very kind of you.' He tried to put a warmth in his voice to show how grateful he was.

'I found your number in his address-book,' the voice said. Millgreen's reply had obviously been the wrong one, because it had become slighty harder and more formal, explaining itself. 'So I decided to call you.'

'Oh yes, thank you.'

'Would you let his other friends know for me?'

'Of course, um, Mrs Nisbet. I'm sorry. I really am very sorry.'

'Ursula,' she said. 'I know you are. Thank you, Gideon. That means so much to me.'

She rang off without giving him time to explain that the number was in Nisbet's address-book because of Sunday night prep. And now his supposed friendship with her son is some kind of bond between them. Millgreen is pacing up and down the cloisters, trying to think. Although the playground with its screaming first-formers is just a few yards away, no one is allowed to run here. He queues at one of the drinking fountains, and crouches over it thirstily, ignoring the piece of chewing gum stuck to the nozzle; the water is ice-cold, chlorine-tasting, piped, according to an age-old rumour, from the swimming pool. He wonders if he is ill – isn't excessive thirst supposed to be a symptom of diabetes? Standing, he puts his hand on his forehead. It feels hot, but then, as he reminds himself, if he did have a temperature it would affect the hand as well as the head. He might use that idea in the English essay he's writing: to see the individual as the source of moral values makes as much sense as trying to take your temperature with your hand. Values can only come from a community. He looks round the cloisters and sighs. Not the kind of community he would have chosen to take his values from, assuming that the choice, paradoxically, had been up to him. Being large, he has always been selected for the rugby team and the athletics throwing events, both of which he hates. While he excels in class, he receives from the masters an almost subliminal message that his particular brand of excellence has something unsavoury about it. It's as if they secretly want him to charge around the corridors knocking people over, to forget his prep from time to time, even to answer back. How do you conform to an institution that demands insubordination?

There were no such problems for Nisbet, who was in detention every Tuesday and Friday without fail. Millgreen couldn't help admiring the barefacedness of his approach: no lies about leaving the prep on the train, just a straightforward Ah, sir, there you have me. 'Why don't you just do it, Nisbet?' he asked him over one of their chess games.

'Er, good question.'

'It wasn't a rhetorical one.'

But Nisbet only smirked and crouched lower over his battered pocket set where two of the black pawns had been replaced by matchsticks. If he could be said to be serious about anything, it was chess. He carried magazines in his pocket, and would produce one in the course of a game to check he was following the opening correctly. When Millgreen pointed out that this was cheating, he protested that the openings were all known anyway, so there was no skill in playing them. The real game began once you were *out of the book*. Millgreen knew nothing about chess beyond the moves, and the notion that anyone should read books on it seemed criminally frivolous to him.

'Ponziani's Opening,' Nisbet announced. 'It's not very sound.'

He believed that he had one great game in him, and always at some point raised a finger in the air and said Aha! under the temporary delusion that this might be the one. He was quite prepared to have his brilliant winning sacrifice reclassified as comedy when it turned out not to work.

Millgreen wandered round Room 27A thinking about Heraclitus and Anaximander, eating an apple, stopping sometimes to pick up a dictionary from the bookshelves so that he could look up the etymology of some word that had taken his interest, and only coming back to the board when it was his turn to move.

'And if you're not going to do it,' he persisted, 'why go to the trouble of phoning me to find out what it is?'

'So I'll know what I haven't done?' Nisbet looked up at him hopefully to see if he had made a joke.

'The masters set the prep to help you to learn. Plato says that every man finds pleasure in learning. It is the nature of humankind. Apart from which, they just give you a detention when you don't.'

'Tell me about your fiancée.'

'What about her?'

'Well, has she got a name?'

'Her name is Rachel. We've known each other since childhood.'

'And you really are engaged?'

'I intend to marry her when we reach twenty-one, yes.'

'Does she know it?'

'We have, an understanding.'

'And do you kiss her and,' Nisbet squirmed over the chess set, 'feel her up?'

'I don't want to talk about her in that way, if you don't mind.' Millgreen regretted sounding so prim, but what else could he say?

'Is she pretty?'

'No, but she is beautiful. To me.'

'Don't you ever fancy other women?'

'You mean do I ogle the secretaries in Pyramid House? Do I press myself against blondes on the Tube during the rush hour? Do I keep copies of *Mayfair* in my desk? No, I don't. Because it's only pampering the animal in yourself, which will never be happy until it has consumed your reason.

I intend to get married, Nisbet, because marriage is an institution specifically designed to give the animal a neat and well-tended pasture to graze in.'

'If I had a fiancée,' Nisbet said, 'I don't know what I'd do with her.'

Or did he say, 'I know what I'd do with her'? Now that it might be important, Millgreen isn't sure. And he remembers with a shock that Nisbet actually met Rachel shortly after that, the night she came to hear him sing in *Elijah*. They were walking arm-in-arm here in the cloisters, which had been turned into a refreshment area for the occasion, with trestle tables laid out with ham and cheese sandwiches, pink and green marshmallows and tall frothing glasses of ice cream soda. In the archways, diagonal streaks of rain showed bronze in the lights, and sometimes a gust of wind would swish some of it inside, causing shrieks and giggles from the girlfriends and mothers. Millgreen was off-duty now, tired and triumphant from the singing, Rachel in a flowery dress pressing softly against him as he steered her through the crowds. And suddenly, there was Nisbet, in a suit, shaking hands with Rachel, putting his head on one side to smile at her: 'Charmed to meet you, madam.' And Millgreen pulled her away sharply, calling out a quick goodbye over his shoulder. He could hardly have been jealous of Nisbet. But he had seen a flash of something pass between them that he felt, obscurely, he must protect him from.

Now he knows it was too late. He pictures Nisbet in his room, an attic one, surrounded by chess books and unwashed clothes. (No doubt he refused to allow Ursula in there more than once a week.) He must have lain on his bed, staring at the cobwebs on the beams, dreaming of Rachel's white arms, straight nose, long, almost-blonde hair, thinking up jokes he might have told her if they had been allowed to talk to each other, that he might still tell her if he ever managed to meet her again. Hopeless. At least if Nisbet had been Keats or Shelley, he could have written poems about it, pernicious ones in Millgreen's opinion, but it might have saved his life. As it is – what is the romantic's way to commit suicide? Not slashing your wrists in the bath: that would be too heroically classical. No, he reaches for a bottle on the shelf, paracetamol, untwists the cap, takes out the cotton wool from the neck...

And Rachel has no idea of the deed she has inspired. He can never explain, and she would probably not understand if he tried to. As a matter of fact, he hasn't seen Rachel for a couple of weeks, not since she was so offhand when he asked her to come to the Palestrina at the Royal Festival Hall. Chocolate and earrings and the activities of various friends from her school, some of them male, seem to be her principal interests these days. There are times when he wonders if they do have an understanding after all. But he hasn't talked to anyone about what's happened, unless you count Ursula, and he feels the event ought to be marked in some way. If he's not going to tell Rachel, perhaps he will drop into church on his way home, and say a prayer for Nisbet's soul. There is no God, but at times it is necessary to behave as if there is, for the sake of a well-ordered mind.

At lunchtime, one of the secretaries in Pyramid House, the massive office building on the far side of the playground, breaks her kettle and shouts down to Sam to ask if he can fix it. He has had his eye for months on a girl who works on the same floor, the one who wears the blue sweater, so he shouts back: 'Sure, why not?' She lowers the kettle carefully on a string, past window after window where other secretaries and their managers must be looking up from their desks to see it go by. Halfway down, the lid comes off; it doesn't fall straight, but spins and tumbles like an unbalanced frisbee, taking the wind and spiralling off to land with a clang about fifty yards away in the middle of a football game being played with a tennis ball. (School rules, to encourage ball-control skills and minimise breakage of windows.) He takes hold of the kettle and the girl looks down from her window, a face fringed with limp hair. 'Probably a broken element,' he shouts, and the hair nods, then withdraws. I'm in there, Sam thinks gloomily. What's her name? Gemma, isn't it? There was a time when he knew most of the girls in Pyramid House, at least to shout to and gesture at, but that was when they were still a challenge. It has been getting him down recently, the thought that all the fanciable women in the world are older than him. They're called girls, even he calls them girls, when they have jobs and bank accounts and cars, and most of them are taller. You can kiss them all you want, but it doesn't take away the fact that you have to wear a black blazer with a gold badge and a black and red stripy tie, and that hair is to be worn short of the collar. Maybe that's why he fancies the blue-sweater girl, who has never asked him to take a look at her brake pads or sell her a quarter of an ounce of Moroccan hash. If he's going to be a schoolboy for another two and a half years, he might as well find a woman who treats him like one. Though, to be fair, she's never taken any notice of him, so can't be said to be treating him as anything.

Sam is in the cellars by now sorting through a pile of old kettle elements, trying to find one that fits. Nobody knows this space like he does, certainly not the school caretakers, who confine themselves to a little corner of it underneath the kitchens. He has rigged up a lab-cum-workroom of his own here, complete with a buzzing, unsteady electricity supply run off from the school's main generator, and his own power tools. It is here he does the repair work that helps keep him in drugs and cigarettes, making a charge for all customers with a Y chromosome.

He'll say one thing for Nisbet – he was easily impressed. Sam remembers him standing here, gazing round with his dull green eyes, trying to think of something clever to say.

'Aha!' he said in the end, raising a forefinger, 'an electrical current!' And opened and closed his mouth several times. He was trying to work out a pun, but was too pole-axed to manage it.

'What a shock?' Sam suggested, trying to put him at ease.

'Ah,' Nisbet agreed. In the undiffused bulblight, his cheeks looked redder than ever as he turned slowly round looking for something to sit on, failing to find it then turning round all over again. He would have carried on revolving indefinitely if Sam hadn't found him an unopened catering-size cardboard box of teabags that bowed under the pressure of his buttocks but didn't split. Nisbet was the first person Sam had ever brought here. He didn't even bring his girls – Pyramid House provided plenty of after-hours office space to cavort in, and it always gave him a thrill to look up from the warm neck of a secretary and see the gothic bulk of the blacked-out school on the other side of the glass.

Everyone else was too cool or too embarrassed to ask Sam, 'How do you manage it?' Nisbet took his time getting there, though. He started coming up to him in Room 27A when no one was about, waving his forefinger and saying, 'Mr Gregory, I presume.' Sam had no idea what he was after. And then one day, 'What a gay dog you are,' Nisbet said, and while Sam was wondering whether it would be necessary to punch him in the mouth, added with a triumphant little cough and a flourish of the forefinger, 'I don't mean that in the vulgar modern sense, of course.' It turned out Nisbet had been staying late, watching what he got up to in Pyramid House.

'You are, ahem, something of a ladies' man, I think.' The funny thing was, Sam had never thought of himself in those terms; Nisbet wanted some tips and tricks, and as far as he knew, Sam didn't have any.

'I don't know, I just kind of, wave at them.'

'Wave at them?'

'And you know, shout.'

'Shout? What kind of things do you shout?'

'Oh, anything. Lovely weather we're having, like the new hair, what you doing later?'

'All three things at once, or one at a time?'

'I don't know, Nisbet. It doesn't really matter what the words are. Anything will do. You just talk to them. Only louder, because they're a long way away.'

Nisbet's lips moved, practising the lines. Just be yourself, Sam was about to say, and then it occurred to him that being himself would be fatal in this case. Imagine him standing at the form-room window waving his finger in the air and shouting Aha! at the sweater-girl, or even at Gemma. You are something of a lady, I presume. If he was going to act naturally, he was going to have to be taught.

'Listen,' Sam told him in the cellar, 'the first thing you have to do is sort out your appearance. I've got a mirror here somewhere.' It was a round dressing-table type with magnifying glass on one side, still in its box underneath a pile of stereo equipment, and when he finally found it, the dim, harsh light of his bulb was hardly adequate for Nisbet to see the extent of the problem. All the veins in his cheeks seemed to be broken, as if by some catastrophic embarrassment in his past. The nose, similarly, had a broken look, and gave the face a permanent sadness which the smirk of the mouth turned into a parody of glee. You could at least change that. 'Try not to smile, Nisbet, OK?'

'I'm not smiling.'

His hair had probably never been combed, and when Sam produced his silver-plated comb in its leather sheath, sharp enough to draw blood, he didn't know what to do with it.

'Do you have a parting? Do you have a fringe?'

'I have hair,' Nisbet said.

The clothes were worse: the blazer that was so big he looked as if he had a second, higher pair of shoulders inside the first, the un-ironed shirt with one wing of the collar up and the other down, the tie with the narrow end protruding six inches below the wide end.

'All girls want from a man,' Sam told him, 'is to look as though you happened on purpose.'

Now, sitting in his cellar with the kettle at his feet, he has the depressing thought that maybe nobody does happen on purpose. Does he have any more control than Nisbet had? The only thing those lessons achieved was to make Sam feel superior; they did nothing for Nisbet, who didn't get his hair cut and carried on dressing the same way. So why had he asked for them – did he actually want to feel worse about himself? Or did he want to be reassured that there was an alternative mode of being, if he could only be bothered to adopt it?

But then there was the night when Sam came into Room 27A and found him staring across at the blue-sweater girl. It was that peculiar time between the end of after-school activities (detentions, play rehearsals, Combined Cadet Force, Fencing Club) and the locking of the main gate. Elsewhere the early evening news was starting, but here it was already midnight: the lights were turned out in the nave-like corridors and the form-rooms were shadowy and smelled of disinfectant. He opened the door and saw Nisbet sitting on top of a desk by the open window, his feet drawn up, staring out across the darkness at the girl, who was not wearing her blue sweater tonight, but a crimson blouse. She looked as if she was about to go out on the town; standing unnoticed in the doorway, Sam couldn't see down far enough, but the way she was moving suggested high heels. She was alone in the office, busy with what was probably a last-minute tidy-up and put-away. He knew how prosaic the doings were in that building, monthly sales figures and cost-effectiveness studies, but some magical property of glass turned her movements into a solitary druidic ceremony. Nisbet never took his eyes off her, and his face, for the first time ever, wasn't wearing that smile. We both love her, Sam realised – even he knows this is not just another lady. And at that moment, the crimson-bloused woman turned and stood full-on, facing the window. She looked, not at Sam in his corner, but straight at Nisbet. Then, with a semicircular sweep of her arm, she waved at him, once, twice, three times. Sam's eyes went straight to Nisbet to see what he would do, wave back, jump up and open the window, shout something. But he stayed motionless, his expression unchanging. There was no one else she could have been waving at. Maybe he thought she was getting back at him for staring. No, her eyes were wide and serious and the wave was too purposeful, heavy with semaphore-like meaning. Sam had been on the end of a few signals himself, could remember the first time he'd received one of those looks, the way his stomach had turned over. He almost went up to Nisbet and shook him, screamed in his ear, she wants to meet you, you arsehole, go and get her – *almost*, that is, in the sense of *not at all*. The girl's wave had paralysed both of them, Nisbet on the desk and Sam in the doorway, and she seemed to be satisfied by that, because she gave a little nod, then turned away, got her coat from a stand by the door and left the office. And Sam slipped away too, leaving Nisbet

staring into the illuminated space as if he thought there was
still a person in it to look at.

Every day Nisbet had to sit in class knowing that she was
there on the other side of the playground, cool blue or hot
scarlet, whatever, waiting in that glass case for him to go
across to her. In his stripy tie and his non-fitting blazer. It
must have driven him mad to have the adult world staring
right back at him, out of reach, and this weekend he just...

Crap: he's knocked a whole stack of Japanese microwaves
onto the concrete floor. What's he wasting his time for? He's
got a job to do, hasn't he?

Nisbet will never make a ghost, Walfisch thinks. After all, if
everyone became a ghost when they died, the world would be
overpopulated with them. It takes intense spiritual and mental
focus to qualify for the afterlife. All that stuff about headless
horsemen and the spirits of murdered women crying out for
revenge, that's what causes the confusion. There is nothing
sensational about ghosts. Usually they don't have bodies, and
when they do there's no dripping blood. For the dead, the
material world is as vague and wispy as their world is to us,
and a lot less interesting; the only reason they deign to appear
here at all is when they have a message to pass on. Another
common misconception: that they come back to tell us where
the buried treasure is, or that we mustn't get the number 14
bus to work tomorrow, or even that they still love us. They
have different priorities now. Love and money don't mean
anything to them, and as for warning us we might be about to
get killed, why should that seem a problem to someone who's
dead already? Walfisch has had dozens of messages from the
dead, and none of them made any sense.

So he is not worried that Nisbet's ghost holds him
responsible. Nisbet has dissolved into the Aether, his red

cheeks and green eyes just part of the swirling patterns in the universal fluid. Walfisch realises that he has been staring at the blotches of light made by the stained-glass windows on the rows of blue plastic stacking chairs down below, inadvertently projecting his thoughts into the shimmering colours. He is sitting in the organ loft above the Great Hall, the place where he gives his tarot readings. Apart from morning assembly, it is only ever used for organ lessons on Thursdays, so he can be sure of privacy here, and he finds the vertigo and echoing space conducive to a spiritual atmosphere. Not that it had that effect on Nisbet.

'The Fool! How dare you, sir!' He gave a waggle of the finger, as if thinking of stabbing Walfisch with it.

'The Fool is your Significator. He represents your innermost self.'

'Ha! Insult me, would you?'

'Do not underestimate the Fool. He is Jesus and Dionysus, the incarnation of our highest and most self-sacrificing nature. He smells a rose even as he steps over a cliff. His mind is on immaterial things.'

Looking back, Walfisch tries to remember if there was any clue in the cards. Nothing obvious, certainly, like Death or the Ten of Swords. But The Lovers turned up – he remembers Nisbet getting excited over the naked figures: 'Oh look, a lady in her birthday suit!'

Why did he ask for a reading in the first place if he wasn't going to take it seriously? He must have been after something, but it didn't seem like it at the time. The reading was never finished – instead, Nisbet grabbed the cards when the Tree of Life was only half-laid-out, with a shout of 'My deal!'

A shame, because he had the makings of an acolyte. There was a pained look in the eyes that suggested spiritual depths behind the frivolity.

'You know, Nisbet,' Walfisch said, 'there are other worlds than this. What happens here is only a reflection, a shimmer on the surface of the universe.'

Nisbet put down the cards. 'Can you do magic?'

'Indeed. I can hold converse with the dead, and with what you would call Angels. I can foretell the future, at times. I can fly in my sleep. I can make myself invisible when I choose.'

'How do you make yourself invisible?'

'It is not a party trick. It takes years of study and practice.'

'But when did you start? You're only...'

'Fifteen, of your years.'

'And people can see right through you?'

'It's more that they don't look at me. It amounts to the same thing.'

'What about these angels you talk to?'

How to explain to someone like that the orders of Angels and Daemons? There is so much that even Walfisch doesn't know, and far more that he knows but dare not reveal. But however it was, he told Nisbet too much, one evening a few weeks later, when they got talking in Room 27A and he found himself explaining about the succubus. 'The name comes from *sub*, under, and *cubere*, to lie: a spirit that lies under, a female spirit that has sex with men. There is also the incubus, a male spirit that has sex with women.' Walfisch has always thought it significant that -*us* is a masculine ending in Latin – the succubus is not really female, for it is not alive.

'You mean, you can do it with a ghost?' Nisbet said.

'Believe me, you wouldn't want to try it. It's pleasant at first, but... The succubus is a sort of psychic disease. You catch it, if you're very unlucky.'

'What from?'

'There are spirits which lie around waiting to be picked up. There's a story, for example, of a nun who swallowed a

Daemon that was sitting on a lettuce leaf. There may be a succubus in this very room, lying on a shelf, or in a dusty corner. Then again, Eliphas Levi tells us that there are succubi that live in books. Read a certain word on a certain page and the succubus slips in through your eye into your brain.'

Nisbet was redder in the face than usual, breathing hard, too excited to say anything flippant. Perhaps he was infected already, with the desire to be infected. It was harmless enough, surely, to tell him about it? After all, what were the chances of him actually encountering one?

But if the succubus feeds on sexual desire, where better for it to lurk than in the midst of seven hundred and fifty adolescent boys? The psychic energy in this building is immense, with only a handful of human females to channel it or, more probably, intensify it further: three or four teachers whose breasts get stared at irrespective of their age or looks, and two girls who have been allowed into the sixth form to do Greek A level, one small and plump with frizzy hair, the other small and plump with straight hair. If you walk down the sixth-form corridor during break you will see the entire sixth form crammed into one or other of the rooms, standing or squatting on the desks, with the two girls holding audience in the middle. (The frizzy-haired one, to judge by her expression, is enjoying herself, while the straight-haired one isn't.) Open any desk, and you'll find, nestling among dried sandwich crumbs, dead insects, set squares and protractors, a dirty magazine or two, or a novel called something like *French Undressing* or *Heavy Petshop*. Most of them are new and trashy, but occasionally you come across an old book with stiff textbook-like covers and sprightly little line drawings or black-and-white photographs from the era when women always looked like cakes, even when naked. Lust has been building up here for a hundred years. At night when everyone has gone home, the form-rooms and corridors flicker and crackle with it, a liquid, purplish light that only Walfisch, who has passed beyond sex, can see. Sooner or later, something had to ignite.

Nisbet must have found the secret. Perhaps it was in one of the pornographic novels, or in one of those leather-bound, gold-tooled books locked away behind glass in the library. He could have stolen the keys and stayed late reading, night after night, until he reached the fatal page, and the virus took root. Or perhaps the succubus just smelled his need and made her own way to him down the corridors.

She would appear at first as a dream, the courtesan dancing for the sultan, or the leather-clad strippergram, or someone quite innocent, the girl who sits next to you in the cinema and accidentally drops her choc ice on the front of your trousers and then tries to wipe it off with her fingers, and you think, that's funny, ice-cream is meant to be cold isn't it, and then you wake up with the alarm clock showing three-thirty and a lot of mopping up to do before you can go back to sleep. Nothing unusual about that. And then, after a few weeks, you reach the stage where the dream becomes less like a dream, and the girl less like a girl, when every time you go to bed, you know you'll be lying in the arms of that plasma that hasn't actually got arms, or breasts, or vagina, shaking and coming till there's nothing left to come but your vital substance, your soul. And all the time he must have carried on going to school, pale, flushed and listless, and nobody noticed the difference until the life in him was used up.

Everyone knows fifteen-year-old boys don't have bicycle accidents. At fifteen, the only thing that can kill you is love.

Sing Sorrow Sorrow

Anne Lauppe-Dunbar

She watches him as she moves through the thickening crowd, tequila glasses slung snug against her belly, her eyes offering the possibility of more than just a shot.

She sees him fumbling with his trousers for the right change, shows him the smallest glimpse of her tight nipple through the coy slits in her dress. This is, after all, her hallowed ground.

The city crowd is twitchy from a day on padded seats, fast bucks, number punching, and that elusive killer deal. Their laughter (initially inclusive) will soon turn derisive, laced with venom and a need for sex. Their eyes follow her as she makes her way through the crowd; she is their evening's wet dream. Lean closer, she dares, smell my perfume, let yourself be taken to a wild forest where owls grow and trees fly.

It is her eyes that demand attention. They sing of black fathomless places, a place for them to enter and push to a shuddering greedy bliss. She pauses, eyes drifting here and there, her mouth an endless painted smile – as endless as the Tequila bottle. She collects clean shot glasses from the bar, jokes with her colleagues as she places each one in their small holder on the outside of her leather belt.

They know to laugh, to take care, to back away if she gets too near. They call her Tinker on account of her being so vibrant and small, so perfectly formed, so electric to watch as she works the crowd. But her face can change from light to black. One moment she's there, the next she's the green moon or a predatory night owl.

The city suits tremble with anticipation, they sidle up, brushing so near she can feel body heat as she pours another shot, another layer on sour beer. They think of girlfriends waiting at home, legs spread, eyes shut. Mission. Position. She could give them so much more.

The moment draws out slowly, blissfully, she pours – such anticipation is the best. He must be ripe for picking, soft fruit ready to drop. Caught in her headlights. A rocking hard on. A willing sale.

She will take him because of there is an empty space in her birdcage. Deep in the catacombs under the city floor she has been busy – the wide rounded arches holding cage after cage of swaying death. Only small pieces, she has no need of the rest.

Tinker works the crowd, waiting to catch his eye, to gently remind him that he, for tonight, is the chosen one – the lucky one. He quivers: big bones under loose skin.

She has everything carefully prepared, clinically laid out; from the razor knives snug in their tight plastic sheaths, to her long blades that will slice tendon from bone. They hum a silver tune, a metal thrum that soothes her when the waiting becomes long – *he will come, he will come.* Against her skin the tequila bottle hums with the murder song – *sing sorrow sorrow.*

The night is darkening; heavy with drink the herd is let loose, only one will be penned. Dazed he waits. The pack spews out into the sharp night. He wavers, but her smile is ready and she pours him a glass of a different mixture, a golden liquid that will calm him, and as he drinks, low in her belly, she feels a hot burst of wet delight.

He stands shaking his head like a dazed bull as she hangs up the leather holder; the glasses glint once, twice, then are hooded.

They leave through the back door. He reaches for her, clumsily unbuttoning his shirt – the promise of her small breast making him twist with desire; pinpointing her as the only thing in his universe. She leads him down into her world, allows him to rub her nipples until they hurt, to push his penis hard against her tiny form as he grunts, pushes, pushes then sways; hands falling useless to his sides mumbling, dribbling and moaning, as he tries vainly to hold on to what he desires so much.

She is gentle with him, placing him tenderly on her special chair, straddling him as he groans, eyes wide and frantic. She sings to him, stroking his hair, his mouth and, as she touches his penis, he tries to arch. His eyes, now red with fear, look up then sideways; his mouth offering up white muted moans – high above her he can see wicker birdcages on metal hooks swinging in silence, rocking in the slow breeze; shadows spidering from one domed ceiling to the other. He moans once more, and then is silent.

The task begins. Her silver tools are awake and humming. She sees his eyes are still open and because he is brave, because he was once strong, she kisses him gently; slipping her tongue deep between slack lips, tasting beer and the remains of the drug. She notices, when she moves, she is so small that even standing full height to his sitting, her head is level with his. This makes her laugh with childlike delight.

He watches her fill a clean syringe with pink liquid, tries to speak when she holds his arm to find a vein, but he can't, he can't even hold his head which now lolls against the chair sides. If he doesn't close his eyes she will have to cut them out. Tinker wonders if she should tell him, but decides no, she has so much to do that any interruption is best avoided.

She works fast, placing the now empty syringe next to her blades, collecting the black, red, and yellow buckets from their resting place across the room. She croons to him singing *sorrow sorrow* as he watches, eyes frantic and white. She closes them as his bladder empties – a long wet gush that spills, stinking, dripping onto the floor. She laughs again, turning to pick up an old white towel, dropping it on the thick plastic sheets around his chair, mopping the liquid with quiet efficiency. Wringing the towel's yellowed water into the first bucket, she leans against the counter to look at him.

He is so beautiful, pale pink skin unblemished, young. She feels a tug in her belly, a long-ago memory of motherhood perhaps? Too long and too distant, but then he opens his eyes again (she notes admiringly he is still able to see). She takes the smallest knife, the baby of the family, a fragile blade, delicate, almost see-through, pulls back his head using the thickness of his hair to hold him just so, then straps the belt across his neck holding everything in place. She slices, delicately at first, through the eyelid until she feels the connection gently snap, then she lifts, pulling out one weeping eye then the other. Each peeping tom is placed in the yellow bucket, along with his urine.

Then she begins her real work, her natural calling. Choosing a slice of his back – she hasn't seen such a clean sheet of skin in years, she strokes the length of it with gentle fingers, moving the fine hair one way and then the other before she cuts.

His last breath gasps out as she severs the right arm, more likely a heart attack than the drugs and she pauses, wishes him a fair journey, telling him kindly that a part of him will always be here, in the birdcage that he will fill.

Now she has to tidy away all the waste, efficiently slicing through skin, bone and marrow. After each cage is filled she has her knives sharpened by the one who has always served her, making sure she stays safe, whispering to her *it is time,* when a new hunting ground must be found – as it is now.

As the night moves, Tinker slices until she is blood red and all that remain are three full containers. These she carries, with a little difficulty, to where she found the well, a dark, endless hole that eats their contents without a sound.

She tips each bucket, noting the thump and splash, then builds a fire in the huge hearth, burning plastic along with all her clothes and the chair; she has no more need of it.

Finally Tinker showers, washing away his blood with a glad heart, her fingers touching deep inside her as she whispers out a gentle moan.

The skin she crafted is now ready and dried by the fire. She strokes it then, lowering the last empty birdcage, places the final small square inside. As she pulls the rope to re-hang the cage she sings to all her skin birds, her darlings, her children. *Sorrow sorrow* little ones, *sing sorrow sorrow.*

Absolution

Mary-Ann Constantine

It must have slipped in while I was taking the bags out to the car on Friday. I imagine it blowing round the house, in and out of rooms, whipping the curtains, pushing itself up against the window panes. I imagine it testing the blocked-up chimney, being baffled by the woodburner; I see it vortexing up and down the stairs, increasingly anxious, increasing in velocity, until finally, in the back kitchen, it burst open the double doors of the French window and escaped, buffeting the little flowering cherry before twisting, flipping back on itself like a huge salmon to take off up the hill and away.

As soon as I got the front door open on Sunday night I knew that the cold air was different in kind from the retracted cold of the house left alone for the weekend. I walked through to the back, cautiously turning on lights with an outstretched hand, to find the doors wide open to the wet night and a scattering of black leaves on the tiles. I left the leaves and pulled the doors to, locking them this time. I did a quick, brave, scout for burglars in all the other rooms in the house, and then put the heating on for an hour, because it was cold and I wanted to hear the boiler's chunter. I made tea and toast and put the radio on. After a while I unpacked my stuff and went to bed.

Rain woke me early. I padded peacefully around the house in my pyjamas, reclaiming it, inspecting the rooms for traces of the wind's incursion. There were none. That picture had probably been skewed for a while; there were the usual piles of paper on the desk, nothing underneath. The dark chocolate petals of the tulips on the windowsill had fallen gently around the vase. Nothing even to hint at that prowling, nervous presence I imagined turning anxious circles in the sanctuary of my clean, bright house. Of course, being reasonable, and with some respect for the laws of physics, I knew that the gust would have been instantaneous, straight in and out. But I kept half-looking for signs as I headed back upstairs to get ready for work. The swirl of coloured clothes on the floor in the girls' room was not new, either. I picked up a few socks automatically, and stood there, missing their morning fuss and bother, planning treats for their return. Then I woke myself up properly with a shower, got dressed and drove off to the office. I wondered if he would have sent me an email.

He hadn't. I worked stultifyingly late, hoarding hours to make time for the girls when they came back from their father's later in the holidays. The migraine came on as I drove home, eating away at the edges of my vision, turning the windscreen into an abstract splatter of drizzle and light; the car had to find its own way for the last mile up the hill through the dark lanes. I swallowed painkillers, more tea, and went to bed early, sleeping deeply under a mountain of stratified quilts and blankets. I find it so hard to keep warm.

What happened then? What happened? I was suddenly awake. An animal leapt across me from out of the bed. Grey-brown, shorthaired, larger than a rabbit, smaller than a deer. Neither cat nor dog. Did I cry out? In seconds I was out on the landing in the shocking cold air of two in the morning;

then I was in Alice's little bed, curled over in fear, desperate for a child to hold. I groped around until I found one of her rag dolls and pushed it hard into the space under my ribcage where the shock felt worst. It took several minutes, I think, before I started to breathe again properly. For a long while I lay in the tiny bed and suffered the lurching sensation of trying to hold two wholly incompatible states together. Like the other Alice, I thought briefly, and with sudden compassion: grown so big so fast, poor thing. But was she this frightened? I gradually quieted my breathing so that I could hear if the creature downstairs was trying to get out, but the rain was hammering on the skylight and pouring off the eaves, and I could hear nothing except the sound of its ferocious cleansing. It must be running off in streams, I thought. And then there was no way of avoiding the thought of them all, pathetic little scraps, buried for surreptitious baptism under the slate skirts of church roofs; *nameless me*, they cry, according to tradition, to bloody superstition, *nameless me*.

It had been an exceptional day. As good a reason as any, we agreed, to make it the last. At first I had been tense and resentful. The food in the posh pub was nothing special, and we did not seem to have much to say. But afterwards we walked by the river, and, after a month of rain, the late February sun came out cold and bright on fierce brown water grown to twice its normal size. It was almost at the top of the old bridge, pushing against the stone and through the drowned arches, too fast, I thought, and too powerful. But we were hypnotised; I relented, relaxed. He took my cold hand.

Come on, he said, I'll show you a secret.

We climbed over a stile onto a footpath that led away from the river, all elder and brambles and mud. After about half a mile we came across a building with a copse of ash trees to one side. There was a raucous rookery in the trees; the birds, the clumps of nest and the thin branches were all sharp and dark against the washed-out blue sky. Naturally I wasn't surprised when the building turned out to be a little church, tucked into a damp mossy graveyard littered with snowdrops, celandines and early primroses. Most of our days out involved a visit to a church. Neither of us has much time for Christianity, and I actively disapprove of God, but after what happened I suspect we were both inclined to some sort of penance; and we both love churches, at least the right sort. This small plain building with criss-crossed glass windows looked like the right sort.

He held back, deliberately of course, taking pictures of gravestones. I felt that I already knew what this place would be like: simple, with polished oak pews, Sunday's flowers, a plaque or two for the war dead and the local squire on the whitewashed walls. Perhaps it was a decorated font he wanted me to see; a leaping hare or a little grinning creature carved into the misericord. There was always something. I pushed at the thick door several times before it gave. When I did get it open, it took a long moment to understand what I could see.

The thick curve of stone pillars; the uneven floor and walls, paint flaking off them in the warm burnt reds and yellows of an Italian fresco. I moved forward as though into a wood, unable to grasp its shape: everything curved inwards. A Virgin and Child carved on a wall were so worn away that they too were just curves, protective curves round a blank little head. I could not look at her, and turned my face upwards to the windows. The cold clean squares of the criss-crossed glass made the pale bright world outside look fluid: underwater rooks, the snagging twigs like weeds, like a lost alternative version of the ones I had just passed. I think it was the loss, the loss of the alternative, that hurt. It felt as if all of time had been compressed in there. It took the breath from me. By the time he came in I was helpless, crying.

We sat outside on a grave-slab, snowdrops at our feet, and he put his arm around me. I buried my head in his winter coat and found after a bit that I could breathe again. Words came back to us one by one, until there were enough to make a bridge, a thin and rickety bridge at first, but firming up quickly, first to consciousness, and then to affection, and then – safest of all: dry land – to wit. When the wind bit too sharply we headed back for the car in search of tea and cake, and found the perfect place, all doilies and black-and-white waitresses. The rest of the afternoon we were our funny, ironic selves, and even our last goodbyes at the station were so *Brief Encounter* we could only laugh.

The girls came home. School started again and the days got warmer and busier. The creature, like the wind, must have found a way out; it didn't come back, or at least I don't think it did. For several weeks, with the headaches, I had this sense of something colourless and formless moving just beyond my line of vision. I stopped trying to catch it, and eventually I was bothered by nothing more than a ripple and a shadow, rather like the effect of looking through old glass. I always lock the back doors now, but have taken to leaving the kitchen window open just a crack, in case.

It was a good while later that he sent the map, marked with a scattering of little black circles. The scrawl on the attached yellow post-it said, *I'll be in the visitors' books; look me up*. And I thought, you know, I might do that, over the months, the years, if ever I happen to find myself in the right place.

Herself

Zillah Bethell

This was his big chance. He'd written letter after letter and now at last a reply; and not just a reply but an invitation. An invitation to dine with Miss Amber Imogen and friends, 25th of September, black tie if you please. He did please very much as a matter of fact and he smiled to himself as he put on his cravat and brown silk cummerbund. His face shone with anticipation and soap water and it looked, he reflected, so scrubbed that she might very well see in it her own reflection. His whiskers were trim and had the length and breadth, he flattered himself, of a man just entering his prime. He was altogether satisfied with his appearance and taking his black umbrella from the hatstand, he said to himself, Orlando my lad, a lick and a spit here and a dusting off there and you're done. Quite done. He snorted in delight at the 'if you please' of the invitation, now folded up in his pocket. Why, wild horses, he thought, pinning a pale pink buttonhole rose, wild horses wouldn't keep you away!

He approached the house delicately, like a suitor, fancifully imagining that an Irish setter strode at his heels, perhaps for courage or perhaps because the Orlando in *her* book had possessed one such fine and noble companion. He felt that he wanted to come upon it from all angles, all at once, to catch it unawares in its slumbering beauty from the northside, the westside, the southside and the east; and thereby lay some sort of claim to it. He stopped now and then to admire the grey stone, warm grey he thought, almost honey coloured in the sun; and to pick a cobwebbed blackberry from the bushes that clambered and clung to the long, thin forgotten path, unvisited by bicycles or cars. The house itself was shielded from afar by a clump of willows, overgrown in the rich alluvial soil and close by a dimpled, trickling stream where he imagined a black swan lingering, a sentinel throughout the year. The willows stood like great green waterfalls reaching up almost to the topmost of windows, austere little skylights from which to peep at the moonshine. He half expected to see her there, dangling her Rapunzel gold hair and waiting to slide down those great green waterslides but the windows were empty and the house, close to, had the look of a long-forgotten ghost, the air about it silent and still save for the peaceful buzzing of flies and loudness of grasshoppers. He shaded his eyes to the field beyond where a pair of ink-splashed ponies cropped grass and intermittently swished their tails; and beyond that to a bizarre topiary of bent and whispering trees. The whole place, he decided, had an air of cosy reverence about it, like a pair of slippers outside a confessional. Quite fitting, he thought, for a reclusive writer of romance.

Wiping his stained fingers he knocked at the door – a brass lion's head on purple peeling paint – and stepped back to wait. It was opened almost immediately, as if she'd been peeping at the keyhole, by an old woman with grey hair and a pair of pince-nez on a beaky nose. No doubt the great aunt, he thought, handing her his folded invitation.

'You're early,' she said shortly without bothering to look at it. Orlando refrained from retorting that the invitation hadn't specified a time and, bowing low, said graciously: 'I couldn't resist the temptation, I'm afraid, having been so long an admirer... I tell you... I can't tell you the honour.'

The great aunt gave a thin smile so that her beaky nose dipped, and beckoned him in. He followed her through a cold, narrow, stone-flagged passageway into a dim, shuttered kitchen lit only by creeping chinks of daylight and a solitary spirit lamp in one corner. He wondered momentarily whether they had electricity or simply chose not to use it. The lamp sent light-glancing fragments into the room, illuminating stray objects and dust, while dark pools of shadow collected untidily behind things, making the place seem emptier and yet more cluttered than it might have been. A young woman sat almost invisible beside the lamp, sewing and humming fitfully to herself.

'That,' said the great aunt meaningfully, 'is Dolores.'

Orlando bowed and greeted her but she made no reply, her head bent against them. He noticed for the first time, as a fragment hit the bright yellow blossom of its centre, that a patchwork quilt lay spread across the table at which the girl was working. The great aunt motioned him to sit and he sat himself carefully down at the far end on a little wooden chair while she rummaged in a drawer for candles and went out the way they'd come, to see – as she put it – if Miss Imogen was ready to receive him.

He felt somewhat abandoned when the great aunt left and he sat uncomfortably still on his chair, trying not to be put off by his strange new humming companion, the darkness of the interior and the unpleasant smell he caught in whiffs now and again and which he located somewhere to his left. He hoped fervently that it had nothing to do with supper, though supper, he reflected, in this establishment seemed a most improbable event. Although it may be, he argued to himself, that the kitchen is reserved for the humming Dolores and nothing whatsoever to do with Miss Amber Imogen. He felt a faint sense of relief at the thought and, relaxing a little in his chair, hitched his black umbrella to the back of another he could just make out in the gloom and decided to try to engage his new companion in conversation. His mind roamed from subject to subject before finally settling on the one he thought most likely to elicit a response.

'What a marvellous quilt,' he began quite charmingly. 'Such autumnal hues.'

The girl raised her head in a movement reminiscent of a startled gazelle and said quite simply, 'It's for Aunt Ursula. She can't get warm some nights.'

'How very kind,' murmured Orlando, pleased that he had been correct in his supposition that the old woman was an aunt of some kind and Dolores an unfortunate cousin they no doubt kept out of compassion. He went on, after a pause, to remark that the house was very lovely and would he be correct in assuming it was something of the Elizabethan period; but the head was bent again and humming and he got no answer. He mused a little while on Dolores' darkly parted hair and the gloomy room and felt a sudden mixture of delight and disbelief, almost absurdity, at being there. For how long, he asked himself, had he been an admirer of Miss Imogen and her work?

'I've read all forty-four of your cousin's books,' he said in articulation of the thought. 'I'm an enduring fan. *Sycamore* I believe to be her finest, though I do, to some extent, agree with the critics when they say that *Confiscating Abel* is the one that will, perhaps, best stand the test of...' he tailed off, faintly embarrassed that his words fell on deaf ears and thinking, moreover, that these were remarks he should address to the authoress herself. Poor Dolores was too wrapped up in her quilt, so to speak, and he didn't believe she had a clue as to her cousin's reputation.

He fell back, in the humming silence, to looking about him; and as his eyes became accustomed to the light he perceived that the room was not so big nor so cluttered as he had imagined. There was an Aga upon which two grey Persian cats lay entangled in quite unhygienic proportions and a sideboard where a great many unwashed dishes stacked up and a collection of tins, like hatboxes, stood. A clumsy wood carving of a horse decorated the lonely mantel, and a large and labelled egg collection displayed itself in a glass specimen case above an untidy rack of spices whence Orlando felt, perhaps irrationally, the unpleasant smell must emanate. He was about to get up to investigate when Dolores spoke in a loud and strangely accented voice, 'I love ze music. Bach, Strauss, Rachmaninov!'

Orlando sat back in his chair as if pinned by the sound.

'Oh yes indeed,' he smiled politely. 'Bach I love particularly. *The Goldberg Variations* must be amongst the most wonderful things ever invented, don't you think? So sad, so beautifully poignant... They say, do they not, that Mozart comes from heaven but Bach... Bach leads you there.' He paused to give her room to intercede or to agree but she had resumed her work with such an intensity of devotion, it was as if she'd never spoken, and Orlando feared he had imagined it. He eyed her suspiciously for a few moments, thinking the while that she was really quite decidedly unattractive. She had a goitre on her neck as large as the largest egg in the glass case and her fingers roamed over it now and then. So busy was she with her flashing needle and so intent did she seem that he was half afraid she would prick it accidentally, causing it to burst and shed its contents, if there were any, all over her precious quilt. He twitched nervously at the idea and leapt up to dispel it and with it his sense of irritation at the girl's oddness. He went over to the rack of spices in pursuit of his earlier mission and the grey cats slid and sidled into the shadows as he passed them. He soon discovered, upon careful inspection, that the odour arose not from the rack but from a morsel of rind and decomposing vegetable matter lying folorn and despised even by the well-fed Persians, on one of the unwashed plates. He tried to convince himself, in the event that Miss Imogen did rule the kitchen, of there being something splendidly Gothic in the idea of things rotting under lamplight, but he wished all the same that the great aunt would come and fetch him and, spinning round with a degree of agitation, asked Dolores quite abruptly, 'Am I the first?' To which the girl threw back her head with a laugh and, jumping up with a gesture that scattered templates and coloured thread and might just as well have been an instruction to Orlando to follow as to remain, ran out of the room.

He decided to follow, having exhausted the possibilities of the room, and the great aunt being nowhere in sight; and thinking, too, that when in Rome, however eccentric, one did as the Romans do. The stone-flagged passageway, he now saw, had several connecting doors like a warren, and through one which stood ajar he glimpsed the bright blue petticoat of his disappearing Alice. He called out to the girl to halt but all he got in return was the sound of echoing footfalls on marbled floor and snatches of dying-away laughter. He stumbled after her, sure that he was being led to Miss Imogen herself and wondering at the same time where on earth the great aunt had got to. It was a house, he reflected, of doorways and disappearing tricks like one of those weird and wonderful fairground attractions that are made up of shiny facades and machinery with nothing of substance behind; and he half expected to come out on the other side into a cardboard field or velvet-painted sky.

The room he now entered was in fact quite bare and unfurnished with light streaming in from all directions; and he passed through it with barely a glance for it was hardly the sort of place he imagined Amber Imogen. She, surely, would be awaiting her guests in the sibylline splendour of her library, surrounded by dusty volumes and a copious notebook to hand should a thought come into that exquisite auburn head. *Orlando, is it? How good of you to come... I felt sure that you would...Your letters, you know, quite gave you away as a man who keeps his word... a man of integrity... the sort of man who understands, who feels, who sees through to the core, the very heart of things.* A slight pause, a nervous flutter, the delicate pressure of soft ardent fingers drawing him in, welcoming him in to her small circle... *This is Orlando, my very dear friend.* That special light in her eyes for him, just for him like a piece of invisible string connecting them, and her at the end of it, a dainty butterfly in swirling chintz, moving amongst them, quite the hostess with her plate of hors-d'oeuvres. Modest, shy, a little frostily self-effacing perhaps but with hints of fire beneath. Oh yes, he thought, remembering a passage from one of her books, there would be fire beneath; and feeling his pulse quicken with his feet he fairly tore through the empty rooms and along another winding corridor until he came quite suddenly upon a large palatial hall with a curling oak staircase, perfect for sliding down, and a multitude of artifacts on the walls like scalps or trophies of a long-ago, more primitive age. Dolores, he saw, was standing at the far end beside a dark studded door, in the disinterested pose of a gaoler. He paused a moment to collect himself and then began to step across the grey and black squares of stone, his pace as measured as if he moved on a chessboard; and sharply contrasting with the tumult in his breast. This is it, he kept saying to himself. This is it!

Ignoring Dolores, he knocked at the door and a familiar voice invited him to enter. He went in and the room, dark and candle lit, its deep-green velvet curtains drawn against the soft September light, seemed to breathe him in like the prelude to a sigh. There was a subtle fragrance of conifer and pine in the air, and he thought fleetingly that he might as well have been in an impenetrable forest for all he could make out of the gilt-edged frames filled, he supposed, with images of dead pheasants and mellow fruit, the secret mahogany panels veiled by tiger skins and tapestries of leaping unicorns; and the solitary figure herself glittering red beneath the candelabra. Amber Imogen stretched out her arm in a rather imperious gesture towards him.

'My Sir Lancelot,' she said in greeting. 'Come.'

'Oh... very dramatic,' laughed Orlando excitedly and, entering into the spirit of the thing, he rushed over to the outstretched hand which looked almost dismembered in the half light and, bowing down so low he almost doubled up, kissed it profusely, quite extravagantly, murmuring at the same time in rapturous tones, 'My Guinevere, my Guinevere.' He gazed up with adoring eyes into the long sought-after face and as he did so the words died on his lips and he started back, almost falling over himself, in horrified astonishment. He stared open mouthed, unable to do anything but hang on grimly, for dear life as it were, to the hand which now seemed cold and loose fitting in his own. It was a sight, he would afterwards recall with slight exaggeration, too horrible to contemplate. The face was a ghastly sheer-white, the mouth a bright red seeping wound and the profusion of amber curls so askew that wisps and tendrils of grey hair came creeping through around the temples and protuberant ears like a barrister's wig on back to front. It was, however, he decided, quite recognisably the face – minus the pince-nez – of the old woman who'd met him at the door, the great aunt Ursula. He squeezed her hand even harder to compensate for his embarrassing lack of self possession and, getting up like a man after a punch up, went over to the drinks tray and helped himself to a glass of champagne, tossing it down in one fell swoop and tottering off a few paces, his senses reeling. Was it some sort of monstrous practical joke? Could this really be Amber Imogen, this gumless old wonder? If it was, then he had assumed, well, he had assumed too much. He had never imagined her to be old, he had thought she was merely prolific. She must be fast approaching eighty, he said to himself, hovering uncertainly in front of her until his initial feeling of repulsion gave way gracefully to one of renewed admiration. What a feat, after all, of the imagination. At her age.

'I do so admire your work,' he said into the silence.

Miss Imogen, who'd been eyeing him keenly, snapped her fingers as if she gave 'that' for her work and stepped forward on cue, her arms open wide to embrace him. 'My Caesar,' she said huskily. 'My dear dear Antony.'

'Now now,' said Orlando, stepping back a pace. 'Let's not get carried away.' He pretended to look into the bottom of his glass and then, seeing she was not to be put off and rapidly closing in, wildly at the walls for inspiration. 'What magnificent decor,' he remarked with poorly mustered enthusiasm before hurrying over to the mantelpiece where he put down his glass and looked up at a painting, quite invisible in the dark. 'Mmm,' he began, fingering his chin with an air of profundity, 'mmm... I do think art today has lost some of its... oh... what shall we say...'

'Come on,' whispered a voice suddenly close and horribly intimate in his ear. 'Get your clothes off!'

Orlando wheeled round. 'I beg your pardon,' he stammered nervously, trying to evade the grip of Miss Imogen which was sudden and surprisingly strong about his waist. He could feel her breath hot and foul against his cheek like the breath of some monstrous basilisk hatched no doubt, he thought, shuddering, from one of those kitchen eggs.

'I know you want me,' she grunted, almost on top of him. 'Don't fight it.'

'I'm not fighting it,' gasped Orlando, trying to extricate himself. His foot kicked over the fender and in the clattering distraction he managed to duck free from a hot press of glittering red sequins, and made a dash for the other side of the drinks tray. 'It's a mistake,' he said agitatedly, tossing down another glass of champagne. 'Some sort of frightful mistake...'

'Fiddlesticks,' said Miss Imogen coming towards him with a purposeful gleam. 'Let's get down to it while we've got the chance!'

Orlando felt himself breaking into a cold sweat and he reached for his blackberry-stained handkerchief which seemed, now, to belong to an aeon ago.

'I tell you, you've got the wrong man,' he said feebly, edging back to where he thought the door might be. 'I'm interested in your mind not your outer b... bodily form. It's a cerebral thing,' he added, getting a table between them.

'Stuff and nonsense,' Miss Imogen declared, waggling a finger at him. 'You don't fool me. I know what makes men tick.' And she did a little caper as she came towards him.

Orlando watched in dismay as she lifted her ruby red gown to reveal what looked to him like a gartered chicken's leg. The passage that had so tickled his fancy such a short time ago came into his head and a shudder went through him. Dear God, the idea was monstrous! He lunged backwards, almost losing his nerve completely, into the darkness and his fingers collided thankfully with the doorknob. He yanked and twisted but the door wouldn't budge an inch. He bent down to shout for help through the keyhole but the faint sound of a little humming voice on the other side stopped him in his tracks. It dawned on him then that he had been locked in, that he was at their mercy; and the thought held him almost transfixed for a second in the oncoming path of the thundering great aunt, her dress in disarray and the wig half off her head. She's a raving nut, he said to himself and the silent articulation galvanised his mind and body into action so that he sprang away from the door as Miss Imogen lumbered up to it, and darted off into the middle of the room where he began to circle a gold-threaded chaise-longue as if he were at a merry game of musical chairs.

'My dear Guinevere,' he began, skipping around with crafty steps. 'My Cleopatra, my Queen of the Night.'

'Yes, my dear,' came an eager panting voice close behind.

He thought desperately of noble knights and courtly suitors.

'I have plighted my troth,' he went on lamely at first and then getting into the swing of it, 'to die rather than dishonour you. To brave the slings and arrows of men rather than suffer a single hair of that precious... er... auburn head, a crystal drop of that pure untouched vessel, a blossom of that fair damask rose flower of y... youth, to be sullied, besmirched, muddied or stained in any way. Whatsoever.' He paused a moment then and with a sweeping gesture took the pale pink rose from his buttonhole and offered it up to Miss Imogen, wafting it about beneath her nose in the hope, perhaps, of transporting her into nobler, gentler realms; but the rose seemed to act like a red rag to a bull for she tossed it aside with a shake that quite dismantled her wig and, making a determined grab for the region around his brown silk cummerbund, cried out, almost beside herself, 'Stop prevaricating man and get your trousers off! Dolores'll be here in a minute with the supper tray.'

'Supper?' echoed Orlando faintly, wondering what else was in store for him. A nostalgic image flashed into his mind of his old granny knitting and baking cakes, and he sighed in dismay. This one, he thought savagely, would give her fanny away for a scone and a boiled egg. He wondered vaguely if it would be classed as conduct unbecoming of a gentleman if he were to wrestle an old lady to the floor, and was about to conclude that the circumstances were quite extenuating enough when Miss Imogen herself pinned him to the chaise-longue with a supremely muscular grip and clamped a hefty bottom on top of his legs.

'Stop playing hard to get,' she reprimanded with an angry waggle. 'It's enough to make a girl insecure.' And using her one free hand she started to undo the top of her gown which sat like a frilly doily about her neck and said in a voice suddenly soft and demure, 'Well, what are you waiting for?'

Orlando, feeling almost ashamed of himself, pleaded a headache. 'I feel quite frightful, I'm afraid... I think it must be the champagne... I'm not used to such hospitality,' he babbled, shifting uncomfortably beneath her weight.

'Bah!' cried Miss Imogen, smoothing her wisps of grey hair with an air of wounded dignity and getting up off him in slow, old-womanly movements. 'You're all talk and no action!'

Orlando gave her a look.

'Well, I do beg your pardon,' he said a little sarcastically and not a little put out.

'Oh you're a fine one,' she went on in a querulous tone. 'It was "At your service Miss Imogen" in your letters, oh yes, you can't deny *that*, Mr High Falutin Fancy Talk... Coming round here dressed up to the nines,' she added, fishing a pair of pince-nez from somewhere about her person and sticking them on the end of her beaky nose. 'What's a girl supposed to think?'

'I never meant,' began Orlando, not quite knowing what he did mean and thinking, after all, that he had better shut up. 'I am sorry,' he said a little more contritely and then, wondering what on earth he was apologising for, straightened up on his chaise-longue and cried, 'Now hang on a minute!'

'Well I should say so,' muttered Miss Imogen, quite ignoring him and hobbling over to the tray where a bedraggled little wig straddled an empty wine glass. 'I used to make 'em pant,' she informed him suddenly, picking the wig up and twirling it around on the end of her finger, the faintest of glimmers behind her glasses and a self-pitying edge to her voice. 'I was quite a little firecracker, believe you me.'

'I dare say,' said Orlando, still too ruffled to be moved by *that*. He fingered his cravat and smoothed down the cummerbund which had got a little crumpled in the struggle, before going on with a stern look, 'But it's no excuse for going about wigging yourself and carrying on like some sort of femme fatale. And what's all this "girl" business anyway?' he added with a dry laugh. 'It's not on, quite honestly. At your age.'

'It's the only way,' sighed Miss Imogen, flopping down onto a little chair beneath the candelabra, her red sequins rippling like fish scales, 'to get them here.' And taking a little handkerchief from the sleeve of her gown, she began to fan herself with a truly woebegone air.

Orlando, looking at the garish face, felt a sudden burst of sympathy, and was about to go over and comfort her when a thought struck him. *Them*?

'What, have there been others?' he asked sharply.

'Oh, hundreds,' said Miss Imogen with a dismissive little flutter. 'Thousands even. But alas, no Prince Charming.' And she blew her nose and with much violence into the small lace square.

Orlando's pity turned to disgust. He was just one in a long line of her conquests. He had not even the distinction of being singled out. It was too much! He got up, smarting with indignation and righteous anger and went over to where she sat.

'It's been quite delightful,' he began with clipped courtesy, almost grimacing, so that Miss Imogen shrank away from him a little. He put out his arm. 'But I'm afraid I must be going. I promised, you see, to pay my grandmother a visit....' He had, in truth, promised no such thing but the idea now appealed to him with such force and tenderness that he thought, at that moment, he might very well have done. 'It doesn't do to be late,' he added, tapping his watch with mock severity. 'She worries so... the littlest of trifles and she imagines some terrible thing has befallen me... you know how it is,' he finished with a slightly envenomed dart.

Miss Imogen looked a little hurt and confused and she started up out of her chair. 'But you'll stay to supper?' she cajoled. 'Dolores'll be here in a minute with the supper tray.... ah,' she broke off happily as the door opened and a little trolley came wheeling in, 'here she is!'

Orlando eyed the trolley and its attendant.

'I couldn't possibly,' he said quite firmly, 'stay for that.' And he began to march off towards the door.

'I'm about to hum an aria,' announced Dolores invitingly, crashing down the plates.

'Poor Dolores,' whispered Miss Imogen, hurrying close at Orlando's heels and making vain little attempts to clutch at his arm. 'She thinks it's a game... we do our best, you know,' she stammered, 'Dolores and I, with our books and our music but... the last one was nearly ten years ago.'

Orlando stopped and turned to look at her.

'Perhaps another time,' he said coldly, holding out his hand.

'Is Mr Orlando off?' piped a little voice from the tray. 'Or would he like a lump or two?'

'Shut up dear,' said the great aunt sweetly, without taking her eyes off his face.

Orlando paused with his hand on the doorknob and his eyes swept the softly candle-lit room.

'My name is not,' he said scathingly to no one in particular, 'never has been and never will be "Orlando".' And with that he strode off with his nose in the air as if he were leaving a nasty smell behind him; and as he crossed the chequered stone floor of the hall a little voice could be heard shouting after him, 'Rimsky Korsakov!'

I was pretty lucky, he said to himself as he made his way along the lane, replaying the scene in his mind in greater and more grotesque detail each time, to escape with my life! They're both of 'em mad as hatters. That Dolores doesn't know if it's Christmas or Easter and as for the great aunt... well... she must surely be way past the menopausal age. He wondered, then, how many other poor sods they'd got hold of and he pulled his jacket close and picked up his pace a little. He had determined, in his dash for freedom, upon the course of action he'd excused himself with – that of visiting his grandmother; and so it was that he made the small detour round, moithering, as it were, on his lucky escape, to Apple Tree Cottage.

The hour was late and the night shone happily with twinkly new diamonds; Orlando felt a great desire to be in his grandmother's kitchen where the light was warm and the old tabby stretched out on the hearthrug. There was a soothing predictability about her ways and he would have betted his life that at that very moment she was in the act of making cocoa in her silver melting chocolate pot and letting the cat out for the last time. She would at any rate, he felt sure, be glad to see him despite the hour and her not expecting him because in a funny way, he had decided, she was always expecting him. That's what grandmothers did, what they were supposed to do; and the assurance of things in their right order buoyed up his spirits as he trudged a little wearily along the deserted roadside, irritated not least at the thought of having left behind his new black umbrella, which had been expensive, and buttoning his jacket up against the soon-to-be chilly air.

He could see already the dim silhouette of his grandmother's orchard peppering the hillside with darkened lollipops and the house itself rising above like a gingerbread loaf, its stick of rock on top puffing away in mad little puffs just as if his grandmother were down on her knees by the grate, her appley-dappley cheeks going in and out like bellows. He pressed on, feeling suddenly hungry and very tired. The hill was steep and he panted feebly as he went up it, thinking all the while that it got steeper every time. As he rounded the corner he saw that a little light shone from one of the downstairs windows like a birthday candle and he remembered how, as a lively minded child, he had thought it was a house fit for Hansel and Gretel. He clipped in through the bright white gate and ran quickly up the path, nearly stumbling over the rotund figure of his grandmother who was watering the clematis in the front porch with her old green watering can.

'At this time of night, Grandmother?' he said by way of greeting, giving her a big bear hug. 'You are a late bird!'

'Giles!' she cried, dropping the watering can with such a clang that the old cat who'd been cleaning his whiskers by the door shot back into the house with a startled miaow. 'Dear boy, what a lovely surprise. Come in, come in, you must be quite exhausted.' And she hurried him in with her no-nonsense charm to her cosy, warm-as-toast kitchen.

Orlando took a deep breath as the old familiar tea and biscuity smell hit his nostrils. He looked at his grandmother's face, into the eyes so blue you could row across them in a little boat and, hugging her again, said, 'It *is* good to see you!'

She looked at him in surprise and remarked upon his oddly extravagant dress.

'You're not in some sort of trouble, are you?' she asked. 'You would tell me, wouldn't you, if you were?'

'Dear Grandmother,' he cried, pretending to be shocked. 'What can you be thinking of me?'

'You're a rascal,' she laughed. 'Like your father. Make no mistake about *that*.' And she bustled about merrily, chafing his cold hands, telling him how much he'd grown, how like his father he was and getting out her china pot and cups and spreading the table with bread and scones and home-made jam. Orlando sat himself down where he always sat on the chair beside the grandfather clock and he felt a great calm settling over him like a blanket. He watched his grandmother, empress of her domain, busily attending to the kettle and the fire and the old cat, her twisted paper curlers catching the light and the funny whistling tch sound coming through the gap in her teeth, and he gave a faint sigh. This was how it was meant to be. Everything was where it should be, right down to the old marmalade jar and the mothballs beneath the settee. All was safe and reassuring and warm. There would be, he thought gratefully, no surprises here and getting up to give his grandmother a hand, he said to her tenderly, 'You sit yourself down now there by the fire and I'll bring over the jug.'

'You're a good boy,' she replied, obedient as a child. 'You'll make a fine husband one of these days, whatever your mother says.' She looked at him eagerly. 'We'll have a game of racing demons afterwards shall we?' Orlando nodded. She peeped at him a little shyly from the corner of an eye. 'How's that sweet young lady Mabel then?'

'I don't know, Grandmother,' said Orlando, bringing over the jug and not wishing to remind his grandmother that Mabel had been a little girl he'd thrown a stone at more than twenty years ago. 'We went our separate ways.'

She sniffed reprovingly. 'Your father was a bit of a heart-breaker, too, you know. Did I ever tell you about the girl he...'

'Yes, Grandmother,' he said quickly, not wishing to hear that particular story again. 'How are your artichokes?' he asked to distract her for she was always having trouble with her vegetables.

'Had to have him doctored,' she replied. 'Wouldn't keep away from his lady love down in the village. Pert little Siamese with black points. Can't really blame him, poor old Archie. Now he's gone all hairy.'

Orlando looked at the snoring old cat by the fireside, and seeing that the subject was close, you might say pressing, to his heart he felt emboldened to ask: 'You don't, do you, Grandmother, still have physical er...' he almost mumbled it, 'urges?'

'Good gracious, you're a rascal,' she cried. 'Just like your father! Orgies? What orgies?'

Orlando made a gesture for her to turn her hearing aid up and she fiddled attentively with her ear for a moment then gave it a fierce bash.

'Ring ring ring,' she shouted. 'That's all it does. What?'

'Urges, Grandmother. D'you still have physical urges, you know, like Archie's urges?'

'Archie's urges?' she cried. 'What the devil are you talking about? I told you I'd had him neutered.'

'No, *you* Grandmother. Do *you* still have urges?'

'Giles, dear boy!' she exclaimed, throwing up her arms. 'I gave all my urges up, thank God, when your grandfather died. Messy business,' she added, pouring herself a cup. Orlando gave a great sigh of relief and, relaxing completely, took a long sip of tea.

'All I do now,' she went on, her eyes taking on the look of boiled sweets or a child stealing them, 'is take an Amber Imogen to bed with me!'

Persephone

Dai Vaughan

It was the way my mother stood there with a slight puckering of the brow and a frown of distaste and said, 'You don't still want Persephone, do you?' Spring cleaning time; and she was holding what had once been my favourite doll, a quite big one, flaxen hair now ratty. Unnoticed by my mother, sawdust was trickling from somewhere under her skirt onto the carpet. Being nearly fourteen, I was no longer interested in dolls; but all the same, I half wished she could simply have said, without the puckering and the frown and the hint of drama, 'We can throw this old doll out, don't you think?' To call her 'Persephone' she must have been prompted by some residual respect for what I and the battered old thing had once meant to each other. Still, I just said, 'No, you can chuck her.' So Persephone's eyes closed for the last time – well actually I think only one of them did, the other was stuck – as Mum laid her back in a box too short for her, so that her sandalled shiny feet flopped over the edge, and hauled on the rope to lower her down the service lift: the wooden lift on which, every morning, we lowered the ashes in pails which were then re-filled with coke by the caretaker and pulled up to our third-floor flat to fuel the Ideal boiler. (Mother always swore the caretaker diddled us over the coke.) And then, like the gates of the underworld, the doors were closed on that draughty shaft. The boiler was horseshoe-shaped, with a knobbly blue enamel surface. Stove enamel – of course. Dr Jones is a great believer in free association.

It might have been easier, it seems to me with hindsight, if she hadn't been called Persephone in the first place. As it was, however, after six months of not thinking anything about it, I suddenly found myself wanting her back. What actually happened was that I woke up distraught from a dream about Pluto – Walt Disney's unaccountably yellow hound, that is – who'd been circling the outer reaches of the solar system stretching his scraggy neck and howling miserably with the intensity of the cold and the blackness of the sunless regions. It was all nonsense, of course; just different shadings and degrees of nonsense. At first I put it down to all those hormonal changes. The first big crisis was a recurrence of the periodical argument about the practicability of keeping a dog in a third-floor residence. I'd had this brainwave, you see, that everything could be put to rights if I were to buy a dog and call him Pluto and somehow, through extremities of kindliness and devotion, let him know he was loved. Then, in the long dead hours between getting home from school and Mum's return from work, I took to idly dropping melon pips down the graveshaft – pomegranates being in those days too exotic an item to be stocked at the corner greengrocer's – from which rose on the chill airs occasional strangely distorted scraps of human speech, as if severed from both source and meaning, drifting and slowly turning on the currents with the insubstantiality of pale flakes of burnt fabric. Down there, somewhere, Persephone patrolled her domain. I would listen compulsively whenever I had the flat to myself, awaiting some intimation of... what? The brickwork of the shaft was unpainted, coated with grey grit, smelling of wet coal sacks, so that the phrase 'sack-cloth and ashes' persistently leapt to my mind. It's strange how some phrases retain their force when the things they allude to have lost all currency. Lodged in the speaking-tube alongside the door was a whistle, polished, lathe-turned from some hard, dark wood – *lignum vitae?* – the sort of thing you'd expect to find now in a heritage museum. The caretaker would blow it in the morning to signal that he was ready to dispose of our wastes and replace them with fresh fuel: the squeak of the old pulleys; the dead thump of heavy ropes against the walls. It surprises me in retrospect that a man blowing into a tube four storeys down could activate a whistle to a piercing shriek whose peremptory intrusion into breakfast I used as a child to dread. You'd think the pressure would somehow dissipate on the way up; but it didn't. And now, when alone, I began half to expect a summons, the unplugging of the whistle to release to my ear not the wheedling voice of the caretaker but a dry-husky female plaint, scarcely audible: 'My eyes are still open. Please take me back.'

I had long forgotten all this. It was Dr Jones who coaxed it back from the nether psyche. A howl rending the blackness of the cavern, the cavern where I'd run amuck when my lights failed and only the discipline of my companions, ignoring my flailings and random blows, had saved me from drowning, and, as the yellow object swam into my ken, the realisation that this was not the inner blackness of a cavern but the outer blackness of the universe, and that what was mournfully orbiting so far from the solace of the sun was a dog with floppy black ears and oversize paws and a tip-tilted nose like a pickled walnut and a tail like a lavatory brush. That was the fourth session, the one where the localised symptoms of a pot-holing trauma began, within his terms of reference or rules of engagement, to reveal their linkage to forgotten states.

It was also the session when, emerging from a sort of reverie or hypnosis, I became aware that the good doctor was himself not averse to a little exploration of moist, dark places. I asked him whether he did that with all his patients, and he began very briskly to point out firstly that it would have to be a female patient, secondly that it would have to be the last appointment on a Thursday, when his receptionist had to leave early to attend her yoga class, and thirdly... Then he just smiled and said, 'Do you have any objection?' I asked if it was part of the treatment, and he said it would only be possible to assess in retrospect what had or had not been part of the treatment. Then: 'The point is, I need to know for next time – I mean, to know whether you mind.'

'I don't mind,' I said; 'but there is one condition.'

'What's that?'

'That you remove all those certificates and diplomas from the wall.'

'What on earth have they to do with it?'

'I just don't like being seduced amid testimonials to your expertise.'

'They're not testimonials to my expertise at seduction.'

'So it's not part of the treatment. OK, I still don't mind. But it's still a stipulation that you get rid of them.' He said nothing, and showed me out very formally. But next time the walls were bare, patched only with rectangles where the paper was unfaded; a strange, austere exhibition of absences.

We changed into our wetsuits in the van – the boys first, then the two 'ladies'. Then the five of us clambered up the rock-strewn slope to the skewed fissure, half concealed in bramble and whinberry, which gave entry to the system. Dr Jones used to tax me with the suggestion that the adoption of a wetsuited pastime betokened a desire to adopt a new skin in preference to shedding an old one, and that the new skin was primarily characterised by its want of bodily orifices; but I suspected this emphasis had more to do with his own preoccupations than with mine, and he graciously conceded the possibility. The particular adit we now approached was one I had come across in my days of solitary fell walking. Seeking cover in order to relieve myself, I had become aware of a strange, negative energy emanating from this cleft in the rocks, something comparable to the roar of the ocean supposedly generated by the ever-diminishing subdivisions of a seashell's spiral when brought into resonance with the eardrum in its own curly lair. Peering between the near-upright slabs of the opening, I had noticed the unnatural smoothness of the rock surface, evidence of others having squeezed themselves through; and with curiosity I edged a little way into the gap: just far enough, a few feet only, to be clutched by the morbid welcome of its chills.

Later, after eating my sandwiches on a springy heather bank, I entertained a daydream in which I edged a little farther into the stone passageway until, even with arms outstretched, I could no longer touch the walls to either side of me. At that point I hesitated, and looked back for reassurance to where the pale halo of the light of day was still clearly discernible. I told myself that there was no need to worry so long as I could see that light; and I moved slowly forward, checking the safety of the ground ahead before putting my weight on it, glancing behind me every so often, gaining in confidence. Then came the moment when I glanced back and saw nothing. I quickly suppressed an impulse to panic and told myself that, provided I were to turn through 180 degrees and walk back in exactly the direction from which I had come, I must inevitably come again within sight of the entrance within a short time. So I turned and, as

I imagined, retraced my steps. I walked for a minute, two minutes, three, refusing to accept the evidence of the obvious: because to accept that I was walking in the wrong direction would leave me with no rational strategy for re-establishing my orientation. Fear threatening to engulf me, I grasped at a desperate parody of geometrical reasoning. I would turn ninety degrees to the left, proceed for five hundred paces or until I met a wall (in which case I would follow it to the right), then reverse and take one hundred paces in the opposite direction or until I met a wall (in which case I would follow it to the left). I met no walls. I saw no glimpse of daylight. I could only conclude that I was in the middle of a vast cavern where all directions were alike. Then I felt a hand on my shoulder, and a voice dry as old tobacco said, 'I want you to take me home.' If I screamed, the darkness sucked the sound from me faster than I could utter it, and I heard nothing.

I woke from my doze with the sun on me. But the fear persisted. It was far from clear to me what I had experienced; but after a few weeks, during which the very thought of falling asleep at night filled me with anxiety, I realised that the only way of dealing with this, extreme as it might appear, was to tackle the problem at root by joining a club, forking out for whatever gear might be needed and, in a word, mastering the disciplines of speleology. That, before the days of Dr Jones, was my idea of a cure.

So we squeezed one after the other into the tight, stony mouth, switching on our head-torches with the unquestioning orderliness of a parachute platoon queueing up for the jump into the night, and proceeded along a passage which, though not oppressively narrow, would not have allowed the errors of navigation envisaged in my one-time fantasy about it. There was nothing to be frightened of at all. Even the wetsuits, we had been assured, would be needed only for a stretch of thigh-deep wading, plus about thirty seconds' total immersion as we wriggled through an underwater arch. Though we'd all dutifully listened to the weather forecast, this was not one of those deep systems where a storm on the surface might raise the water level with life-threatening abruptness. Still, it makes me smile when I reflect upon the dank airs and icy waters and the perpetual discomfort of walking along cobble-littered corridors, to think how long it took me to disabuse Dr Jones of his compulsion – a trifle old-hat anyhow, in my view – to link potholing with sexuality.

We'd been walking for about half an hour, and were passing through a relatively broad gallery, when Andy drew our attention to a low shelf formed by a slanting slab of rock, beneath which was a jagged gap about a foot at its highest.

'Rex Bishop was the first to penetrate that,' he said. 'Folks had often wondered if it was a passage to anywhere, or if it just shrank to a close. Some had tried with candles, and fancied they saw a trace of air movement, but it was obvious that if you wormed your way in and it didn't go anywhere there was no way you'd be able to worm your way out again. You'd be stuck for good and all. It was Rex who had the courage to risk it and found his way into a whole new labyrinth. All it needed, you see, was for someone to conquer the fear. That's what it's all about: conquering the fear.'

'But it sounds from what you say as if fear was entirely justified,' I said.

'No, that's the point I'm making. It turned out not to be justified once Rex challenged it.'

'Well, OK; but it wasn't exactly an irrational fear.'

'Makes no difference whether it's rational or irrational. What I'm saying is it's the fear itself you've got to overcome.'

The others were beginning to give me impatient looks, so I nodded as if he'd now made it all clear to me. Then, just as they were moving off, I thought I heard something.

'Wait,' I said. 'I think I can hear voices.'

I knelt in front of the heavy low lintel as Andy paused. 'It's quite possible. Rex discovered a vent from the parallel system high up on the cliff face. High, but not inaccessible. Groups sometimes enter it from there.' He grinned. 'You're not hearing cries for help, are you?'

'No.'

Andy turned away. I didn't know what I was hearing. The voices, if they were voices, were ripped and shredded, child-like and plaintive, fluttering at me like bats escaping at dusk from under the eaves so sudden and evasive and dusk-coloured that you can't be sure whether you've seen them or not; or rather, you can't ever be sure you've seen an individual bat, yet you're in no doubt that you're observing a flight of them. Realising the others had reached a point where a narrower passage led off from the gallery, I rose and hurried to follow them. I moved too quickly. I slipped on the moist stone and fell forward; my lamp smashed against something, and I was in total darkness. It was only for a couple of moments that I was out of sight-contact with my companions, but in those two moments I lost control. All my hard-learned procedures deserted me as the voices, now inaudible if indeed they had ever been audible, chased me like multitudinous, veering, skittering pipistrelli, and I ran shrieking in one direction and another, making for wherever I imagined I might have seen an exit-way, until, with the fricative rub of rubber on rubber, the group crowded round to restrain me. It was after that that I was placed under Dr Jones' supervision.

I have heard the shades whispering their jaded secrets, I told him, in their sibilant slack voices; and I explained to him that the dead run out of secrets in time. I have given as good as I got – or tried to – I told him, I have wept beside subterranean rivers; I have leaked from the womb and the source of all sufferings; I have challenged the gods to wrestle; I have fasted at the funeral; I have traced the flight of bats with an alert finger and accounted for every one of them, and I have short-changed Charon in pitted black pennies. What, I asked him gruffly, did he have to say to that?

'You said Charon...'

'A joke. The sort potholers make when they come to an aqueous impasse: "So where's old Charon, then? Skiving as usual – have to report him this time...."' So then he changed tack and asked about the orbital dog, and I said, 'You mean Laika – wasn't that the name?' and he said, without a trace of irritation – God, how it annoyed me the way he always kept his cool, – 'No, you know what I'm talking about, I think. You told me once about a dream you'd had....'

'Oh *that* dog: the Disney dog.' And he said, 'How many heads did it have?' And I said, '*Heads*? Well how many do you think? How many heads do dogs usually have?' Then I told him how I'd always wanted a dog but Mother had said you couldn't in a third-floor flat, it'd be cruel. Dr Jones often came back to this question of the dog, I'd noticed. He was sharp enough to spot that it was somehow important; but he hadn't yet sussed it was the name that mattered. I said Mum had frowned as she grumbled that the ferryman had nicked half our coke, and Dr Jones said was I talking about cocaine or Coca Cola; and I said neither, just the fuel of that name, and then he picked up on what I thought he'd missed and said, 'Hang on, did you say the ferryman?' and I said no, not the ferryman, the caretaker, whose name was Berryman; quick thinking, but the damage was done and he'd made that link with Pluto, and now it could only be a matter of time and he pounced like a cat on a sparrow and said, 'You say you lived in a third-floor flat. How was the coke delivered?' and I said by lift, and he said, 'Describe it to me.' And suddenly I realised I was in denial, and it was a relief to be able to say that – to use a bit of his jargon without sniggering at least inwardly – because we hadn't found much to share up till then. And after all, I'd never been trying to be uncooperative. Not really.

I don't know what I'd expected his flat to be like, his studio flat which he called a pied-à-terre, his actual 'home' being a converted tithe barn in a district whose limestone has such a warm glow that you think the sun's out when it isn't. Or so he said; but I've never actually known him visit it. Maybe there's a marriage on the rocks; but I don't ask. I suppose the understanding was established from very early on in our relationship that he was the one who asked the questions. I seem to remember reading somewhere that Freud kept a collection of tribal figurines amid the fust and dust of his consulting room. Dr Jones' equivalent, in a living space otherwise as utilitarian in its furnishing as an air raid shelter, was an accumulation of ten-by-eights of mortuary statuary: angels or wights or cowled, wingless creatures displayed in attitudes admonitory, desolate or cringing, their bronze robes hung over urn or headstone with all the gravitas of slowly melting tar. He explained to me that he was trying, so to speak, to prune back the profuse growth of symbolism, the confusion of parallel and intertwining mythic systems which had, after all, developed quite by historical accident over the centuries, and to arrive at something akin to an Esperanto of allegory, a system of archetypes so compelling in their relevance yet clear in the differentiation as to supply everyone, regardless of culture, with a lexicon for the articulation and hence potential resolution of his or her psychic conflicts. Seeing me unconvinced, he led me to a bookshelf from which he took a small, silver-framed image which seemed to be a cartoon snipped from a magazine.

'This,' he said, handing it to me, 'is what launched me on my quest.' The cartoon represented the familiar character, instantly recognisable from his stubbly chin and lolling tongue, of the thirsty man in a desert. In this instance he was shown crawling up to a notice board on which was nothing but a dot and an arrow, pointing to it, with the legend *You Are Here*. 'Do you see?' Dr Jones said. 'I mean, do you resonate to the essential truth of it? We can stumble across the truth in the most unlikely places. But as soon as I saw this unassuming little drawing, I knew... yet it conceals its true profundity. Look how cleverly the dot has been placed not at the dead centre of the notice, but as if its precise position were of some significance. In the absence of other landmarks, or even of any indication of scale, there can be no possible significance to the eccentricity of the dot. Nevertheless that is a perfect replication of our experience of life, where we all devote so much effort to persuading ourselves that it matters where our dot is in the emptiness. So all I'm doing, or hoping to do when my system is perfected, is to make the position of the dot more meaningful by populating the vacant space with figures, figures that will enact for patients the dramas of their solitude. Up till now, psychoanalysis has had to work in a briar-patch of inherited mythologies. With my system, we shall be free to cultivate our neuroses as if they were new roses.' (The unconscious, he once told me, is very partial to puns.) In my own case, nevertheless, he stuck to the tried and tested.

The eventual revelation was theatrical, if mutedly so. Following a chaste meal of spaghetti al burro accompanied by a Bulgarian Cabernet Sauvignon, he produced from the fridge, with a flourish that might equally have been a waiter's or a conjuror's, two small silver platters, each bearing a crusty, flushed yellow, spiky-crowned dome. I turned mine over, and there they were: the pips all clotted in their gargle-pink jelly. We were sharing a pomegranate; and it was my first ever.

When Dr Jones had asked me to describe the service lift, I'd come up with a genuine forgotten memory: namely, that as a child I'd always envisaged it as descending into a realm of utter darkness. Of course, whenever I peered down into the false cupboard I did discern a blur of light; but I'd somehow managed to interpret that as spillage from our own, upper storeys: a glow that would spread no more than a yard or two from the bottom of the shaft. This was all in spite of the fact that I knew perfectly well what the bottom of the shaft looked like, having watched through the railings as the caretaker went about his duties in the service area.

'Doesn't make any sense, does it?' I said, to which Herr Doktor replied with one of those smirks they all keep in readiness for such occasions, 'It's dreams that make sense – dreams and language. Reality doesn't. You mustn't expect it to. That's a category error.' What I think had clinched it for him, though, was when he asked me about my mother, and I told him how, before we'd moved to the city, she'd managed a smallholding somewhere out in Essex. He immediately cast her as the goddess of abundance, of corn, of the Earth's bounty. The abundance in question had mainly been root crops which, as the fields lay adjacent to an arterial road, had had every opportunity to concentrate the lead from the soil into their fibres before receiving a final dusting of sulphur dioxide on the wayside trestle tables where they lay in wait for passing custom. No one bothered about such things in those days. No one knew. But Dr Jones saw that as no reason to resist weaving a sub-theme about food-as-mortality, or perhaps food as emblematic of desire for mortality, into the splendid tapestry of narrative with which he now presented me, all loose ends neatly knotted. Digging his silver spoon into the pomegranate pulp, he said light-heartedly as one whose task is finished: 'Consider this your cure. Melon seeds would never have done it.'

Well, I suppose it had to happen sooner or later. Some time earlier, Dr Jones' receptionist had come back unexpectedly one evening and found us *in flagrante delicto* – a term which, as a teenager, I always privately translated to myself as 'delicious flagrance' and found decidedly alluring. For a while it looked as though nothing was going to come of this, and life went on as normal; but evidently the receptionist had at some point summoned the resolve to report him to the governing body of whatever professional association he belongs to – belonged to – and the body in turn decided to take 'steps': which meant, in a word, that he was hauled up before a tribunal of his peers and, no doubt, competitors. I volunteered to confront these people myself as a sort of character witness; but he pointed out, truthfully enough, that anything I might divulge about our relationship could hardly fail to show him in an even worse light by the sort of standards the tribunal would be applying. I suspect, in fact, that I am not the only person to have been accorded the benefit of his idiosyncratic methodology, and that this played some part in his reluctance to have me around at the hearings. Not that I'd have cared a hoot. I have always been of the view that what does not affect me need not concern me.

Anyhow, the upshot was that Dr Jones was struck off – his licence revoked. From that point on, he would have to rely for his living on hole-and-corner work. But even holes and corners take a while to find; and in the meantime he was hungry. There was no more talk of tithe barns, which, whether real or fantasised, cannot withstand calamities of such an order. Naturally enough, I felt myself in part responsible for his loss of livelihood, and saw it as my duty, at the very least, to feed him. At first I would buy such items as rice, parsnips and raw fish and leave them at his flat for him; but it soon became apparent that he was too despondent to cook, and I often found the food untouched at my next visit. It occurred to me then that pies offered the most conveniently portable form of nutriment, and before long I had settled into the habit of baking blackberry tarts, apple turnovers, steak and kidney puddings, Cornish pasties made with corned beef – a throw-back to my days of word association, that one – all in a gratifyingly successful attempt to keep him fit and well. The potential symbolic significance of myself as a source of provender seemed never to cross his mind. Sometimes I would pile into bed with him to stop him brooding.

Gradually he began to build up a new clientèle, mainly of hoodlums troubled over their guilt. I said I'd thought the whole point of hoodlums was that they didn't have any guilt; but he said no, nobody lived by bread alone, and for many of his patients – indeed, he suspected, for most of the criminal community – guilt and its suppression were of the essence of their life's project: 'These, you see, are people whose selfhoods were founded upon defiance of the prevailing norms. Now, just as they are reaching that hazardous mid-life passage, they find that society's dominant values have moved so close to their own that they no longer have anything much to feel guilty about. They are at a loss, disoriented, drifting... What's that tune you were humming just now?'

'Tune? I think it's called "The Girl with the Flaxen Hair".' Well of course I knew it was. He gave me a puzzled look, seemed about to say something, or at least to think something, but then dropped the matter. I've been forced of late to recognise that he's lost interest in me as a conundrum. I'm just the woman who makes the pies. To be fair, I know he assumes my treatment completed. But it shouldn't be a question of being fair to the man you go to bed with. He ought to be more observant than that. It's his job to be.

Oh yes. I went along with his little narrative which identified me as Persephone. It was flattering, it was comforting, and it explained many things whose understanding made life easier for me. Figures in a landscape; a symbol among symbols instead of a dot on a bare board; distances and scale established in preference to the featureless relativism of a vast and unlit cavern: yes. But for all that, he didn't get it quite right, did he? Like a cowboy builder, he left the work unfinished. And I didn't see it was up to me to tell him, though I've kept on nudging him with clues. And as I say, it's not that he's failed entirely to notice them, but rather that he picks them up as one would pick up a pebble on the beach only to give it a glance before tossing it aside again. That's why I think he's lost interest in me – or in my narrative, which in his terms, at least, amounts to the same thing. He does not want to know that Persephone is my daughter, my doll, and that I still need to find out where she went, whether her eyes – or just one of them – are open, whether her hair casts off sparks in the darkness or whether it has all fallen out, and above all if she has anything to say to me. Did she, as one laid her supine, croak Mama as some dolls do? I have no recollection of it.

Looking at the pastry lattice on a cherry pie I have just baked, I am reminded of bars on a prison window. If a rational fear is no more legitimate than an irrational one, if only in hindsight, then – and this is an understanding that I don't owe to Dr Jones – an irrational state may be no less fruitful than a rational one. Time to move on, then. Dr Jones has failed me. It is time for new new roses, and perhaps – who knows? – a more fertile myth.

Rhiannon's Bird

Imogen Rhia Herrad

Rhiannon lies in her swaying bed in the dark, listening to the hum of the motor. Every now and then the lights of a passing car flash through the camper van like ghosts, and are gone again. Jeff has just left, but it feels as though his hands are still on her, his fingerprints; as though he's marked her. Rhiannon shudders, but she can't shake his hands off. She feels grubby. And something else she hasn't got a word for. A nameless feeling swells inside her until she can't breathe, almost chokes. Before he went, Jeff straightened up and stretched out a lazy hand into the upper bunk, where Buddug sleeps. Rhiannon heard bedclothes rustle and then a surprised little sound from Budd, and Jeff's voice laughing and saying, 'Night-night, little one.'

He went after that, not even looking at her again.

Rhiannon has been lying stock still ever since. All she's been able to think of is that he's going to start on Budd now, who is only six.

And that she'll have to do something to stop him.

The bed sways with Rhiannon in it, the wind whistles in her ears, and she's cold and exhilarated and dizzy every time she looks down and sees the ground below them, sheep like balls of cotton wool, trees like broccoli and streams glinting in the sunlight. She's not in her bed at all, she's sitting on the back of a huge bird that's carrying her through the sky, and there's another bird by her side with Buddug on its back; her long chestnut hair is streaming in the wind like a blood-red banner. The birds open their beaks and begin to sing and Rhiannon knows that they're *her* birds; she called them to help her and they have come.

They're camped by the sea when Rhiannon wakes up. She opens her eyes, glad that the night is over. She's not liked the dark since Jeff has begun to come to her bunk to say good night, and play games. It's sunny outside and the camper van is full of a greenish-blueish light as though they're actually under water. Rhiannon can hear the gulls screeching.

She lies still for a moment and listens. There's Budd's breathing from the upper bunk; she's still asleep. From beyond the curtain, muffled a bit by the thick velvet, come Annie's breaths, regular and slow and a bit snuffly because she's coming down with a cold.

And.

And nothing. No Jeff. Rhiannon lets her breath out with a whoosh. It's all right. She's all right. Budd is all right. Jeff's not there.

Probably afraid he'll catch the cold off Annie, Rhiannon thinks, full of scorn; brave now.

He must have left the van before they started out for the sea. Sometimes he takes off for weeks, alone with his motorbike and his tent.

Rhiannon scrambles out of the narrow bunk, punches her pillow down and arranges the blankets so that when Annie comes to look it will appear as though she's still in there, burrowing under the covers. She pulls her jeans and trainers on and an extra sweater because it's windy by the sea.

The hinges of the door used to creak, but they don't any more because Rhiannon put some oil on them from the kitchen, so now she can slip out whenever she wants, and Annie won't hear her.

The wind nearly tears the door out of her hand, it's strong and she has to pull against it hard to keep hold of the door, and to shut it softly behind her.

Annie told her that she's seen the sea before, that they lived on a campsite by a beach for a while when she was small and Budd just a toddler. She and Budd used to build sandcastles, Annie said, but Rhiannon can't remember. She's only ever seen pictures of the sea.

But now as she's struggling up the dune and through the sharp-edged grass that grows in the sand, the fishy, salty smell and the whipping, stinging wind seem familiar. And when she's reached the top of the dune and sees the beach stretch away in front of her, wide and flat and empty, it's like she's always known that it was here. Like it's been waiting for her.

Rhiannon slithers down the dune and breaks into a run as soon as she reaches the hard-packed sand. She runs all the way towards the flat grey water of the sea. She feels like a kid, happy and excited, and everything else flies out of her head. She can see the thoughts stream after her on the wind, and dissolve like the smoke of Jeff's stinky cigarettes. It's a long time since she's felt like a kid, without the weight of the thoughts and the worries and the responsibility on her. She feels small compared to the hugeness of the sea. Small and alone, but in a good way.

Rhiannon walks along the beach, as close to the grey splashing waves as she can without getting wet. The water is company, it's like a dog that runs alongside her. It doesn't want her to do anything in return.

There are shells on the beach. If she collects some and

takes them back, Annie might put them in an empty jam jar and stand it on a shelf to take away with them as a memory of the sea, when they move on. Rhiannon wants something to remember this beach by. It's hers. It's been waiting for her.

They're on their way to a big fair where Annie will pitch the colourful tent and do her storytelling. She's said that she hopes the weather will be good because that will bring more punters, and more punters mean more takings. They could do with more takings, Annie's been taking coins out of their emergency jar and it's only half full now. She keeps giving it worried looks. Rhiannon has seen Jeff helping himself to coins from the jar as well, but she's not said anything. Who to? Annie won't believe her, or if she does, she won't stop him. She used to laugh off things like this, and that would annoy Rhiannon; but at least she laughed then, she would tease Jeff and talk back and disagree with him, and she and Rhiannon and Budd were together in a way they're not now. They were a unit. A family unit, thinks Rhiannon, who's heard the expression somewhere and liked it. But they're not a family unit now. Annie and Jeff are a unit. And she and Budd are another. It's like they're on opposite sides.

She doesn't know when the fair is, nor how far away. Maybe they're only staying the one night here by the sea. Maybe they're going to go on today.

She needs something to take away from this beach.

Something to remember.

A weapon, she thinks, and immediately unthinks it.

Something.

Something glints in the grey-brown sand. Rhiannon looks up to see whether the sun has come out, but it hasn't. But there's still something glinting on the beach. She goes to look.

A creature lies on the sand and looks up at her, and it's like a thing from a dream or from a nightmare. It has a long fierce golden beak and big black empty eyes, and its skin is like glass, like a jellyfish, so that Rhiannon can see through it; can see its red snaking veins full of blood and its coiling purple intestines, its pulsing red heart and lungs spread like butterfly wings; and its delicate golden bones.

It looks at her out of its bottomless eyes. The golden beak clicks.

Rhiannon backs away. She wants to turn and run, further along the beach or back to the camper van, away from this thing; but its black gaze holds her and won't let her go. It's like the creature is pulling strength out of her, as though it plugged itself into her and is powering itself. Because now its movements are growing stronger. When Rhiannon arrived a moment ago it was just lying there on the sand, barely breathing. But now it's raising its head, with those bottomless eyes still staring into hers, unblinking. Its body is palpitating and then, and with a flash of gold, it is stretching what Rhiannon realises are its wings: stick-like golden bones covered in a clear membrane. And then it begins to struggle to its legs, beating its wings and stretching its golden bony neck and clicking its beak at her more insistently.

Rhiannon whirls and runs, runs back along the beach, claws her way up the dunes somehow and tumbles down them on the other side. Her throat is raw and her breath comes in almost-sobs when she reaches the camper van and flings herself inside, not caring that she will wake Annie and Budd.

'There she is,' says the voice she hates most in the world. Rhiannon stops as though she's run into a brick wall. He speaks softly, silkily, like a cat would; no, not a cat, thinks Rhiannon, a snake. That's what Jeff is like, he comes up and slithers around you and then, before you even know he's there, he strikes.

Rhiannon swallows. Tries not to show that she's nervous. That she's flat-out scared.

But he's already seen. He smiles at her for a moment, while he has his back to Annie so that she can't see. Smiles, and winks, and Rhiannon can feel her heart stop beating. Just for a moment, her chest feels like it's empty. Her mouth is dry and she can't swallow.

And then something else crashes over her, a feeling like a wave of crimson, hot and red like blood. No, not a wave: a flash of lightning, because it's already gone, so quickly that Rhiannon can't even say what it was.

'Your mother was worried about you,' says Jeff's voice, still in that soft, silky tone.

The cold seeps through Rhiannon again. She is filled with dread.

'I was just out on the beach,' she says, and although she tries to speak like she has confidence, it comes out in a whimper. 'I wanted to see what the sea looked like, Mum,' she says, lifting her head and looking at Annie, as though that would do any good.

Annie has put the shutters up on her face. She won't say a word unless Jeff speaks to her first. She's always like that when he's around.

'Go on then,' says Jeff. 'Help your mum with breakfast. Lay the table, whatever.'

'What about you?' says Rhiannon. She hadn't meant to say it. It slipped out. *Cheek*, Jeff will say, and add it to the list of reasons why Rhiannon needs taking down a peg.

But he just laughs. 'I'm taking Biddy for a walk on the beach,' he says. He never calls her Buddug. Says he can't pronounce Welsh, even though there's nothing to it. 'You went gallivanting off before she was even awake, poor kid. She wants to see the beach too, you know. So now I'm taking her.'

His eyes bore into her. He wants her to get the message. His back is turned to Annie, she won't see. Buddug is standing by the door, tugging at his sleeve. She's eager to go to the sea. She doesn't know what's going to happen.

But Rhiannon does. Jeff is telling her, here, under Annie's nose. He's going to start on Buddug, now, when he's got her alone on the beach, and he's telling Rhiannon that it's her doing. Her fault. All of it.

He gives her a last smirk, grabs Buddug by the hand, and they're gone with a slam of the door.

'Mum!' says Rhiannon. '*Mum!!* You can't let him! You must stop him. Please! Not Buddug.' Her words trip over each other, her tongue is too slow, too clumsy. She feels dreadful. It's like trying to run in a nightmare but you're rooted to the spot. Like trying to scream but you can't even open your mouth.

Annie gives her a look out of eyes that are as empty as the pebbles on the beach. 'Stop it, Rhiannon,' she says. 'I really don't understand why you don't like Jeff. Stop behaving like a baby now. I won't have it.'

'But Mum! He's going to hurt her. You must stop him, you must!' Her voice has risen to a scream. If this was a nightmare, she would be safe now. But it's not.

It's worse.

Something explodes in front of her eyes. Something red and bright lights fill her head for a moment.

It's Annie's hand. She has slapped her, so hard that Rhiannon's head snapped back and hit the wall behind her.

'Shut up!' Annie hisses. 'Shut up, shut up, shut up! I won't hear another word about this, I won't!' Her face is screwed up and twisted with fury. The dead pebbles that were her eyes have cracked across, and through the cracks Rhiannon can see a glowing anger as red as live coal.

The realisation hits her harder than the slap did. Annie already knows what Rhiannon has just told her. She doesn't want to hear. She doesn't want to do anything about it. She doesn't want – what? To confront Jeff? To lose him?

So she slaps Rhiannon for telling the truth and leaves Jeff to put his hands on Buddug.

She must have known, Rhiannon thinks, numbly. She must have known what he's been doing to me, too. Must have known, and didn't stop him.

A sound fills her ears, a tortured shriek. She thinks it's the kettle boiling, but it goes on and on and Annie doesn't make a move to stop it.

The song of the Birds of Rhiannon, who could wake the dead. She hears the words in her mind as though somebody has said them.

And then she knows. The golden bird.

Rhiannon turns and runs to the door, outside, back to the beach. The shrieking is still in her ears, but it is she now who's making the sound, answering it, maybe? A high, keening wail comes out of her throat as she runs up the dunes and back down towards the grey water, towards the place where she saw the golden bones of the bird glinting on the sand.

It comes flapping towards her, answering her call. It is monstrous, golden and beautiful and deadly. Has it awakened her or has she awakened it? It flaps towards a spot in the dunes and Rhiannon runs after it. It knows what she wants it to do. She knows where it's going.

There's a dip halfway up the dune, sheltered by clumps of tussock grass. Buddug is lying there, looking startled, while Jeff lies beside her, stroking her cheek with one hand and crooning to her. His other hand is inside her jeans, which are unzipped.

Rhiannon wants to yell at him, to shout, to rage, but all that comes out of her mouth is a keening shriek.

Jeff turns, startled. He sees her, and for the briefest moment a look of guilt crosses his face, then it's gone and fury takes its place. And *then* he sees the Bird with its bottomless eyes and its thrusting beak, its blood-red heartbeat and purple guts and its golden bones shimmering through the clear skin.

'What...' he says. It's his last word, *What*, because now Rhiannon flings herself at Buddug and wraps her arms around her and presses Buddug's head against her own chest.

And the bird flings itself at Jeff. Rhiannon almost wishes she could avert her eyes, press her face against Buddug's hair and not see what happens.

But she wants to see. Now it's his turn to suffer.

The bird launches itself at him, digging into his shoulder. Six small red marks appear on Jeff's white T-shirt where the claws dig into his skin and draw blood. But that's nothing. The bird pecks at his forehead, his cheeks, his mouth. His eyes. His eyes are bottomless red holes now, streaming with blood. Finally, he's crying for what he's done.

He puts his hands up, frantically scrabbling, swatting at the bird, and it pecks holes into his palms, snaps off fingers.

He screams, but the keening call of the Bird of Rhiannon is louder.

He's still alive when the bird is done with him.

The bird has swollen with all the blood it's drunk. Its bones shine brighter than ever through the jellyfish skin. It unfolds its bat wings – golden bones glinting – and shrieks, once, like a cockerel crowing. It's big enough for Rhiannon and Buddug to scramble onto its back.

'Hold tight,' Rhiannon says to Buddug. She is sitting behind her little sister, with one protective arm around her.

'Where are we going?' Buddug asks in a small voice.

The Bird unfurls its wings once more, leans forward, testing the wind.

'Away,' says Rhiannon.

The City

Lloyd Jones

1

It happened during that terrible autumn when the northern lowlands were flooded by sudden violent thunderstorms. Many of my relatives died – I still have their possessions in the attic, in boxes, unsorted.

I have a clear memory of the city's arrival in my consciousness: I was walking on the shore one evening in a pale milky light; hardly any form was visible – the islands offshore were merely a smudge and the hills above me had dissolved in mist. But I saw the city clearly. As I moved across a gangway from one dimension to another I entered its gates without fear, yet I stayed for but a short time during that first visit. To remain there I had to concentrate in a way which was new to me, and it took a while to get used to it. I soon got tired during that first day and returned to my own little world. But it was there from that day: the city. *My* city. Huge and silent, sheer and simple yet seemingly impenetrable – bolted together and layered neatly slab after slab.

The place was on a huge scale. My first impressions were of enormous metal girders, each as wide as a house, rearing vertically into the sky. Each bolt was as big as a car. These stanchions were mechanically perfect in every detail. I lay on my back and looked heavenwards, up the side of a metal strut; without interruption or adornment it went upwards and yet upwards for an inestimable distance – I have no idea how far – until it disappeared into a bank of fluffy white clouds. Each girder was spaced equidistant from its neighbours, which marched onwards as far as the eye could see. Ranked in military rows, they were painted a dull olive green and stood on a smooth stone floor which looked like marble cut in enormous square slabs. If there was an inner part to the city, such as rooms and cafes and offices and streets, I saw no point of entry anywhere. In fact I spent some time among the girders trying to find a door or any form of ingress. But eventually I got tired and gave up.

Days passed, weeks maybe, before the city appeared to me again. As I crossed over to it I saw the same vista: mile after mile of massive metal stanchions propping up a layer of clouds. This time, however, there was a slight difference. At the base of the first stanchion, I encountered an ice-cream van with a colourful blue, candy-stripe awning which fluttered optimistically in the breeze. The van was playing a peal of music to attract my attention – a verse from the nursery rhyme Three Blind Mice. It was a typical scene which I had seen many times before at dozens of British seaside towns. Outside the van, on a white plastic chair, sat a personable young man in shorts and a light-blue short-sleeved shirt with epaulettes. He unclasped his hands and rose to his feet in an act of welcome when I walked up to him. He was clean-shaven and well groomed, in contrast to the people who normally operate these vans – youngsters with beer on their breath, nicotine stains and just-got-up eyes. We exchanged pleasantries and he entered a door at the rear of the van, which rocked briefly until his head popped out of the central serving hatch.

'Ice cream? Or maybe a lolly?' he asked pleasantly.

I looked at him, lost for words. Yes, as it happened I really fancied an ice cream. But I had no money. I told him so.

'Oh, never mind about that – the first one's always on me,' he said with a glittering smile. 'Anything you like – a 99 perhaps?'

Within a few minutes we were both sitting on plastic chairs, eating ice creams. I felt most relaxed, taking in the sunshine and licking my vanilla cone. He allowed me to finish my 99 before quizzing me about my visit to the city. Eventually I shared my thoughts with him. I told him how mystified I was by the city's overall appearance. Highly unusual, I said. Did anyone live there – and if so, where? He laughed lightly and replied that many millions of people lived there.

Where *was* the city, I enquired.

He indicated above us and below us with his thumb.

'Everywhere,' he said.

'And where are we now?' I asked. He looked at me quizzically. 'What part of the city is this?'

But it was clear that he didn't understand me. He shrugged his shoulders.

'This is it – all of it,' he said.

I pressed him further. 'Where do you live in the city?'

He thumbed downwards and grinned broadly.

'Down there, my friend!'

I asked if I could go down with him to visit his neighbourhood.

He scratched behind his ear and mulled this over.

'Perhaps. You'd need a Basbo.'

He lurched into his van and came out with a small contraption, about the size of a mobile phone, then moved towards me. Cradling the back of my head with his left hand, he moved this device towards my left eye before I pushed him away and said something like *whe-hey*! He looked surprised.

'What are you doing?' I asked.

He laughed out loud, raising his eyes upwards towards the clouds.

'I'm scanning you, twitto. Can't get a Basbo without being scanned, can you?'

He sat down again and turned his face towards the sun while I considered this latest development.

'Will it hurt?' I asked.

'No,' he murmured.

'And what will happen then?'

He looked at me deeply.

'Same as usual, of course.'

'And what's that?' I asked.

'I'll take the scan to the Office and they'll visit me when they're ready. OK?'

I lapsed into silence and sat in my chair until the breeze began to raise goosebumps on my skin.

'OK then,' I said. 'You can do it if you like.' Again, he looked perplexed. Perhaps he was a bit simple. 'You can scan me if you like.'

Because I wanted to visit the city. I wanted to see where he lived. I wanted to see what was down there, under the huge marble flagstones.

Having eventually understood what I meant, he fetched his device and repeated the operation, this time allowing the scanner to nestle in my eye socket until it beeped gently and a green light lit up a screen on its fascia.

'No probs,' he said. 'I'll get that seen to then.' The day was dwindling, so he started to pack away his gear. 'Another ice cream perhaps, before I go?'

I smiled reassuringly. 'No thanks,' and then realised I

didn't know his name. 'By the way, my name's Ben,' I lied. 'And you?'

He looked at me with a level gaze, then smiled wanly.

'We don't actually give our names at the first meeting,' he said. 'It's not the custom here. We give each other names when we've got to know each other a bit better.'

'What's that all about?' I asked. 'Something to do with names giving us preconceived ideas about a person? The Adolf factor?'

'No, nothing like that,' he said. 'Just habit, I think. Call me F2 or something like that for a while – *you* choose what you call me for now.'

'OK,' I said. 'I'll call you F2, if that's what you want.'

I was getting irritated because I could see problems with calling someone F2 and then reverting to another name. To me, he would always be F2.

2

I go to the mountains on Sunday with Erika. We walk past an isolated homestead, up through the heather until we reach a group of rocks – the place looks like a tumbledown giant's house because we can see traces of a building with a doorway and an apron of smooth green grass in front of it. We watch the landscape below us – it's immense and brooding today, smoky and mysterious, almost sinister. The invisible sun filters through the clouds in beams of weak sunshine, which strobe the fields below us with pallid light. The distant land looks like Mordor: I half expect hobbits and orcs to appear at any time.

We talk about our lives, the usual stuff. I take a picture of her falling off a boulder. We feel far away from humanity, then, out of the blue we hear an ice-cream van in the distance. We can't see it, yet it seems to be very close, just below us. We laugh because it seems so out of place here in the mountains. The sound must be coming to us on the wind, though it's not particularly breezy. The ice-cream van moves on and silence returns, then Erika notices a pall of blue smoke rising from a farm in the middle distance. It mingles with the murk and rises slowly to blend in with the clouds. I tell Erika about the ice-cream man in the city. *My* city. She doesn't seem surprised that I've had this fantastic experience. I tell her about the enormous girders reaching into the sky, the car-sized bolts and the marble floor, vast and smooth.

The ice-cream van starts jingling again, further away now. We laugh. Quite a coincidence, she says. Then another fire starts up, on the other side of the river, and we joke about the ice-cream man being a crazy arsonist. It's just a coincidence, we know that. But it seems a bit strange, and the nature of the day, with its bluey-grey half-light and otherworldly silence adds to the mysteriousness of the experience. We walk back to the car, past the homestead. She takes me home.

3

I entered the city again roughly a week later, when I was in the right frame of mind. Or the city entered me, I'm not quite sure. Crossing over to the metropolis again I found the ice-cream man sitting in the same position as before, on a white plastic seat in front of his van. Greeting each other, we seemed to mimic our first encounter: yet again he was dressed in shorts and a light-blue shirt with epaulettes; yet again he rose to his feet in an act of welcome when I walked up to him. I noticed that he had a shaving scrape on his neck, and he looked tired, otherwise everything was the same as before.

'How are things with you, F2?' I asked. 'Is everything OK in your life, F2?'

He ignored the gentle sarcasm, smiled, and spread his arms wide in a rather Italian gesture.

'Sure,' he replied. 'Everything's great with me, why shouldn't it be?' He mounted the back of his van and his head popped out of the hatch. 'Same as usual?'

'Yes please,' I replied, 'and I've got some money this time.'

He laughed. 'No need for that,' he said as he handed me the cone. 'You'll not be needing money around here my friend.' Seated in our chairs, he asked me where I came from and I told him. 'Never heard of it,' he replied laconically. 'But geography never was my strong point.'

He sucked around the chocolate finger in his 99 and we lapsed into a comfortable silence as I studied the mile-high stanchions disappearing into the clouds. We sat in the same sort of sunshine as before – it never seemed to rain in the city – and I licked away at my ice cream while he reclined in his chair with his head cradled in his cupped hands. He watched me in silence.

'How's your week been,' I said eventually, to break the silence.

'Good, thanks.' Then he slapped his right leg in a gesture of remembrance and leapt to his feet. After moving his chair aside he opened the passenger door and scrabbled about in a wad of papers, found what he was looking for, and waved it in a celebratory manner. 'Got it!' He jammed whatever it was between his teeth, closed the door, rearranged his plastic chair, and sat down again. When he handed it to me I noticed that the envelope had an imprint of his teeth in a crescent on one side. 'No need to open it,' he said. 'It's your Basbo.' He thumbed behind him in the direction of nowhere in particular, and said: 'We can go any time you like.'

I looked at him steadfastly. 'Into the city?'

'That's right. Into the city. Whenever you want.'

It seemed all too easy to me and I was a bit suspicious. 'Anywhere?'

'Oh no,' he laughed. 'Certainly not. But you can come to my part of it. Is that good enough for you?'

I didn't reply immediately. But by the time I'd finished my cone I was in the passenger seat and we were weaving our way through the stanchions in a cavalier fashion, as if F2 had been watching too many road movies. Then he sobered up, levelled out, and drove in a straight line for a while. He seemed to know where he was going, though it all looked the same to me. I felt a small thrill of panic. Would I be able to get back to my country?

I asked him what the score was.

'Dunna worry old pal,' he said mockingly, 'I'll take you back when we've finished.'

As we careered along I asked him about my status in the city. Was I a guest, and did I have any rights? Driving with his arms extended rigidly in front of him, like a learner, he continued to stare straight ahead while he replied, 'It's hard to explain. Did you ever have one of those transfer books when you were a kid? You know, the ones with footballers or actors, and you bought transfers in a shop and stuck them over the pictures in the book.'

'Yes, I remember having a footie book, I think I filled it completely,' I said.

'Well,' said F2, 'you're the equivalent of a transfer while you stay in our city.' I was dumbfounded. I had never felt *unreal* before – but now I felt a panicky sweat begin to prick out on my skin. Not real? A transfer? I heard F2 gurgle rather maliciously by my side. 'You're still yourself, as it were, but down here you're just a symbol,' he continued.

'So you've sort of bought me in a shop and now you're going to stick me in a transfer book,' I said.

'Not exactly,' said F2, but he didn't elaborate.

Chilling news, and I felt a judder of fear pass through me. Would he ever let me go? He must have sensed my fears because he added with an attempt at reassurance, 'Don't worry. Some day soon you'll understand everything.'

Eventually we stopped and he turned off the motor. The view looked exactly the same as before: mile after mile of bolt-upright metal stanchions rearing up in the air, without a single sign of life or habitation. Then, without warning, we started to sink below ground. It was a strange feeling, like the beginning of a fairground ride when the carriages come to life unexpectedly and off you go on your mad journey – except there wasn't a jerk, and our descent was as smooth as a ride in a modern lift. Within a minute we'd stopped; he restarted the motor and drove away along an underground subway tiled all around in the same sort of stone. It was underlit and good on the eye – for one thing, there wasn't a single mark of graffiti anywhere. I looked round and saw the platform we'd descended on rising slowly upwards again, blocking out the light.

'I'm taking you through the city – it's on all sides of us now,' he said. 'But we're not allowed in the other sections, only my birth section. This subway goes straight to it. Won't be long now.'

The drive was just beginning to make me sleepy when we passed through a ring of bright light – some sort of sensor I think – and then we parked in a vast parking lot; F2 drove his van into the only available spot, which was clearly his own. Again, the place was spotless. He guided me along a walkway to a booth and presented his eye to a machine in the wall; it gurgled like a baby in response and he laughed also. F2 indicated that I should do likewise (my paper Basbo was obviously just for show), and when I did so the machine made its baby noise again. F2 thought this very funny, so I too tried to be amused.

Passing the machine, we walked on for a while and emerged into a small park in which people were engaged in the usual activities: children were playing, adults were lying around gossiping in the grass and birds were flying from tree to tree. Looking upwards, I noticed that the sky was an illusion created by lasers which projected a summery scene of blue and white and yellow onto a man-made roof above. Soon we were scuttling through alleyways, weaving our way through crowds of people who were busy shopping in a seemingly endless mall of brightly lit shops. Then we cut off down a side street and entered a much quieter area made up of huts. We seemed to be in a shanty town, because on either side of the narrow alleyway I saw shacks made up of tin sheets, canvas, wooden boards and plastic sheeting.

'This is amazing. So you live in a shanty town – I didn't expect anything like that in the city. I expected...'

But I stopped short, because I noticed that F2 had halted and was looking at me in an odd way.

'Shanty town?' he said reflectively. 'You're not the first to use those words. To be honest with you, I don't know what they mean. This is my home, and I'm proud of it. I love it here. But if you think that there's something wrong with it – you said *shanty town* in such a strange way – then I'll take you home straight away.'

I noticed that he was looking hurt, so I walked up to him and spoke to him reassuringly. 'No, please don't be offended. I didn't mean to be rude in any way. It's just that I wasn't expecting it.'

Mollified, he led me away up a side alley and we arrived at a shack with a bright blue door, though it hung slightly awry on its hinges.

'My favourite colour,' he said. 'Like it?'

'Beautiful,' I replied truthfully, because it's also mine.

He went through to a tiny side room and I sat myself down on a rickety box which had once been used to hold vegetables.

'Tea or coffee – or maybe something else?' he asked me through an aperture.

'Tea for me please, white with no sugar, if you don't mind,' I replied.

He carried on clattering about and I took this opportunity to look at his home. It was tiny – about ten feet by ten feet – and contained little more than a sofa bed and a few bits and bobs. There was a TV in the corner but that seemed to be it. F2 appeared to be living in the equivalent of the slums. But then I noticed something odd. Since I was so close to all the components which made up his shack, I could see every part of them – and it became clear to me that nothing was old or decrepit. Every tin sheet, every wooden board and every plastic sheet was new. There wasn't a spot of rust or grime anywhere. The shack was brand new. And the materials hadn't been salvaged or looted; they were purpose made. The shack was constructed from pristine materials chosen specially for F2's habitation.

Over tea he talked to me about mythology, as if it were the only subject we'd ever discussed. He said his people had constructed an effective mythology of their own but they had failed as yet to construct individual mythologies. *Personal* mythologies. That's what it was all about, I realised. Perhaps he wanted my own personal mythology for himself. Sitting there like a political agent, with an unnerving grin, he said, 'I want to write your biography.' He said it enthusiastically, but I felt a cold finger of fear touching the back of my neck as I squatted in his tiny home with its bent (but shiny) nails and its clean window panes, all cracked in exactly the same corner. 'I want to know all about you!' he said with a sly grin. I was beginning to mistrust him; a little worm of doubt had crept through the door of his unconvincing little home, with its beaten earth floor, as perfectly spotless as the rest of his ersatz city. But could I escape my own creation? And did I want to?

4

It's five weeks later. I'm sitting in a jazz cafe with Erika in the Akasaka district of Tokyo, near the Shinto shrine of Hie-jinja. I can smell the incense still, I can even hear the babble of the crowd, but my mind is on other things. Inside the temple there's a fortune-telling device and I've been foolish enough to read the thin scroll of rice paper with its Japanese characters on one side and English translation on the other. The English is execrable but two sentences fill me with foreboding. They say: *Do not Travel. Go to the Dentist Soon.*

The bit about the travel comes too late – I'm already here. Superstitious fool that I am, I say a fervent prayer to the gods of the temple, asking them to still Mother Earth's shaky hand (I dread earthquakes) and to guide my plane home safely across the Siberian wastes when we leave. But the bit about the dentist floods me with prickly heat again. It reminds me of F2. So far he's given me only a handful of facts about himself – and one of them is that he's a trainee dentist. *The perfect occupation*, he said nonchalantly. *Allows you to relieve pain or to increase it, according to your mood.*

Chilling. And there's another thing. Strolling – slightly lost – this afternoon we passed a gigantic metal door whose huge concertina flaps were still squashed in the open position. Beyond it I see one of those miniature cities within cities which you see occasionally in vast metropoli like Tokyo: a shaded subterranean avenue surrounded by identical condominiums, all under one roof and self-contained. Restrained, and removed from the main city, it has a secretive existence of its own. No sign of life; I imagine this gated area is inhabited by quiet people who share little of themselves with the outside world; they are neat, well-organised professionals who come and go in the metro-gloom according to their own patterns of time and meaning. Here, in this concrete forest of shadows, with its cool canopy of balconies, I imagine F2 would feel at home.

He has started to colour my thoughts, as sunlight tinges newspaper yellow... no, as the night leaves shadows. I feel as though I'm stumbling around in moonlight. The light has weakened since he came. What did he say in his tailor-made shack? He wants to introduce me to the sacred animal. Where? Somewhere in his city. What can it be – a unicorn? A white cow?

5

I decided to visit the city as soon as I got home. I think I was trembling slightly as I left the house. I headed as usual for the shore, towards my transference spot. I wanted to confront F2. I wanted to ask him if he was indeed a creature of my imagination, or whether he was real in some way and had insinuated himself into my life. Was he some ancient spirit which wanted to invade my mind? A dark afflatus? I have never believed in such things, nor disbelieved in them either. Like ghosts, they have avoided me so far. But enough of my sane and rational friends believe in ghosts – or have seen them – to make me unsure in these matters. Age has taught me not to be sure of anything. All these points I wanted to discuss with F2. I intended to be quite firm with him: I wanted to know if he was real. I wanted his name and some personal details. Some of his past. I wanted to know what made him tick.

I stood on the shore, trying to pass over to the city in record time, without making much effort. It didn't work, neither that day nor the next. For weeks I tried to pass over to visit F2, but nothing happened. Nothing at all. It seemed that my 'experience' was over, and the city was no more. So I gave up and resumed normal life, or as normal as it could be. F2 remained in my mind; I seemed to see him in the shadows whenever I visited the major cities of the world; either he was a figment of my imagination, stirred into being by ferro-concrete, or he was a small god of urban areas. Something like that anyway – I never associated him with the wide-open spaces and greenery of the countryside.

When I'd almost forgotten about him, he came back into my life. One minute I was walking on the shore, the next moment I saw the city's leviathan gleams and its metal spires. Instantly, I was there again. The huge stone flags felt cool under my feet (I always seemed to arrive bare-footed, like a castaway). And there he was to greet me as usual, sitting in his plastic chair by his gleaming ice-cream van. It occurred to me then that being a trainee dentist was at odds with being an ice-cream man, but I let that go for now. I suspected that my angry state of mind a few months previously had restricted my access to the city and to F2; it was only when equanimity returned that I was allowed back in. F2 was friendlier than ever and popped a 99 into my hand as soon as I'd sat in my chair. He was in expansive mood, laughing and joking as if we'd never been parted.

'It's all about dimensions,' he said to me conspiratorially. 'Other dimensions are swirling around us all the time, but humans rarely visit them. As for the people of the city, we spend most of our lives outside our own time and space. Today we can share the same dimension again – and it's nice to see you.' He chattered on without a care in the world, or so it seemed. 'We must do it more often.'

I finished my ice cream and contemplated asking him if we could revisit his home. I wanted to see more. And as if reading my mind, he suggested just that. In no time at all we were waltzing between the huge metal struts. Was it my imagination, or did we follow exactly the same zigzag pattern as before? On the way he revealed his motive. He really did want to write my biography, urgently.

Of course, I was wary. Why would he want to do that?

'Who needs a reason?' he countered breezily. 'Your life story is as good as anyone else's, surely!' We sank down below ground and the roof closed over us. 'Besides, it'll be a rather unusual biography.'

'In what way?' I asked.

'It'll be the story of everything you've forgotten,' he said.

'But isn't that impossible?'

'Hah! Thanks to the sacred animal and your Basbo scan, we can compare your version of events with what actually happened,' he said. 'The discrepancies constitute your own personal mythology, and that's what I'm after!'

He explained what he meant over a mug of tea (which had authentic-looking tannin stains) in his shack.

'Humans are delightful,' he said. 'You take a basic scenario and change it gradually and subtly in your minds, little by little, until it suits your purpose. You can turn black into white if necessary. You can edit a scene time after time until it runs exactly as you want it to run. Brilliant! We can't do that, you see, so I want to enrich my life. Surely you can't object! I merely want to borrow your own story, to fill a void as it were. And it won't hurt one little bit!' We looked at each other over the small strip of tatami matting between us. 'Besides,' he added with a forced little grin, 'you *do* want to get back to your own time and place, don't you?'

I sipped my tea, feigning calm. He was beginning to threaten me. There was a sardonic gleam in his eye when he spoke to me, and malice in his voice. I felt trapped. So I used a little guile to extract myself from the situation; it was a trick I could only use once – I played the *sick relative card*. I had to go back to be at someone's bedside, I said. But I would return to be examined – for my forgotten memories to be transferred to my new friend, F2. Perhaps he wasn't that clever after all because he fell for it like a child. Afterwards, as night fell around the giant stanchions, he returned me to my own dimension in his rocking ice-cream van.

6

Through the window I can see the hulks of three huge high-rise flats in the distance, only just visible in the smog; tiny orange lights show the course of the M93 as it disappears over the hump of Aluvadora. It's quiet now, except for the bleep of a transfusion machine plugged to a neighbouring patient. I'm at the hospital with Erika. She's been brought here as a precaution, and she's sleeping. I'm still holding her hand, as I did in the ambulance. We better play safe, said the doc when I called the medical centre. Sitting here, I have plenty of time to think dark thoughts about F2, to wonder if he had anything to do with this latest development. But now that Erika's sleeping, I have no one to talk to. And only Erika knows that I'm not cracking up, that all this is really happening. At least I think it is. Her sudden illness is just a coincidence, surely. But maybe I better get back to F2 in case he had anything to do with it. Has he taken Erika hostage?

7

F2 grinned at me when I got back. When I told him about Erika he said, 'Nuffin to do with me guv!' He was cradling a mug of coffee in his hands, squatting in the lotus position on the floor of his shack. Outside the open window a colourful candy-stripe awning rippled gently in the breeze. He was anxious to complete the transference of information from my brain to his, so that he could let me go, as he put it, but in the meantime he was telling me a bit about his own dimension.

'Humans think they're so marvellous,' he said sarcastically. 'With their *massive* brains and their *wonderful* imaginations. But that's where we score over you. Because you lot don't actually have any control over your precious little imaginations do you? And that's our mode of entry. Your imaginations are like power points to us, my friend. We plug in and enter. Easy peasy lemon squeezy. And once we're in, you're completely powerless, because humans care so very much about what other people think of them. For instance, my friend, you yourself won't tell anyone about this experience, will you, because they'd think you were mad. Bonkers. Absolutely potty. Or eccentric at the very least. They'd avoid you or they'd lock you away.'

He fell silent for a while as he finished his coffee. Then he raised his fingers to his lips and emitted a piercing whistle. It was so loud it hurt my ears. Afterwards, a deep silence fell over the shack, over the whole street. Not until then had I realised how quiet it was in F2's neighbourhood. In the shadows of every city there are small points of absolute silence, the trig points of eternity, remaining there forever despite our clutter. Then, almost imperceptibly at first, from somewhere in the distance came a series of noises which sounded like a huge rusty crane or a tank on the move, without the sound of an engine.

'Here boy!' said F2 in a comical – or was it manic? – voice. He looked at me, and by then I could see only the whites of his eyes, like an animal's, in the gathering gloom. 'I thought perhaps you'd like to meet the sacred animal,' he went on quietly. Somewhere at the far end of the street I could hear a squealing noise as the animal's claws or tracks gripped the tarmac and swung around the corner towards us. Distantly, as if in a dream, a jingle floated towards me on the wind. I knew it from my childhood, and I knew it also from my first day in the city. It was Three Blind Mice. F2 smiled at me. 'If you concentrate in a certain way you'll be able to keep it at a distance – but never more than a street away. And then, unless you're different from everyone else, you'll ask it to come to you. Eventually you'll want it all to end. It's a very special moment. That's when you find out a lot about yourself, very suddenly, my friend. Personally, I quite enjoyed the experience. I can tell you one thing for sure. You'll never be the same again.'

Being a Digression Regarding the Dangers of Excessive Hospitality

(and the Legendary Unpredictability of the Wasp)

Euron Griffith

The noble and esteemed Salaam-el-Duur (eloquent and vivid demographer of the Arabian peninsulas) describes in the fifth volume of his *Histories of Persia* how the Portuguese explorer Diogo Alvares suffered unpropitious predicaments whilst negotiating the cruel and trackless oven of the Kalahambara desert. Indeed, his behemothic series of misfortunes persisted when he and his beleaguered caravan momentarily escaped the endless furnace and chanced upon the perceived sanctuary of Wadi-Washm. This mountainside settlement (carved into the yielding rock until, over the centuries, it achieved the wondrous complexity and intricacy of a subterranean municipality on a par with any provincial conurbation in England) had once hosted a thriving community of Tuerian citizens. The Tuerians, by Salaam's account, were a singularly sophisticated and ingenious tribe who, in addition to their considerable excavatory abilities, also succeeded in harnessing the power of a most fearsome creature for their continued wealth and sustenance – namely the Kalahambara Wasp. Unhindered by climate, this particular insect had exceeded all previously-known laws of entomological proportions and had achieved dimensions

181

broadly commensurate with our elusive and lovable fellow, the common wren. However, its enormity was comp-lemented by a suitably capacious brain. Salaam recounts how this wasp would organise itself into regimented squadrons which descended on the multifarious enemies of the tribe in times of threat almost as if the settlement of Wadi-Washm was their own! In return for these charitable strategic campaigns against the advances of rapacious desert wolves and rodents, the wasp was rewarded with bowls of sweet goat's milk for the insects' continued sustenance. Tragically, this cool and ambrosial elixir gradually produced a calamitous transformation on the previously benevolent Kalahambara Wasp. Within weeks of ingesting copious quantities of this libation, the nubile insect experienced a hideous and apparently permanent metamorphosis from willing ally and defender of the fold to a vehement devil! Naturally, the response of the confused citizens of Wadi-Washm in encountering such a vicious and hitherto unrepresentative element of life's tribulations was to flee their mountain haven and unanimously rush into the unforgiving terrain of the mighty Kalahambara and, subsequently, into the welcoming arms of the Grim Reaper!

The unfortunate bones of the Tuerians lay a full fathom beneath the shifting desert waves by the time Diogo Alvares and the ragged remnants of his company chanced upon the ruins of Wadi-Washm. Feverish with excitement at a momentary respite from their usual tenure in precarious marquees with walls of ripped canvas (reinforced with the stinking pelts of expired horses), the men gathered their rags and climbed the stairways to the coolness of the dark, carved cottages up above. Deaf to the warnings of their captain regarding the twin-pronged stab of the fat-tailed desert scorpion (a most unsociable fellow who thrived in such murky domiciles), the men promptly succumbed to the narcotic spells of Morpheus.

Salaam-el-Duur recounts how Diogo was the first to be tripped from his weary slumbers by a reverberation which appeared to originate in the very core of the Earth itself. Alarmed to discover granules of sand dispersing around his hands as if they were dancing on the surface of a constantly beaten drum, the stout-hearted pilgrim jumped to his feet, unsheathed his sword and scanned the skies in full anticipation of meeting his doom at the claws of some previously un-encountered and fearsome desert ogre! But this fine warrior detected another sound within the Satanic rumbling – a sound so shrill and acute it forced him to drop his weapon and cover his ears for fear of being delivered to the very gates of delirium! It was then that Diogo Alvares witnessed a Stygian cloud of swirling smoke approaching him at the speed of a galloping Alentejo mare – mercilessly engulfing the ground like a d—able tornado! The mystery of the discordant cacophony was revealed to him as being the screams of his hapless men as they attempted, in vain, to outrun it! Diogo watched with despair as his crew were consumed in this nefarious vortex. Then, as he observed this vertiginous apparition advancing upon him – it became evident to him that this was no Earthly cyclone at all!

Regarding the origin of this malignant hurricane, I would beseech your indulgence for a few moments as I direct your attention to its source – namely the dank interiors of the lofty Wadi-Washm lodges. Here, long expurgated of the tragic human tenants, that Machiavellian fiend, the Kalahambara Wasp had colonised these hidden corners with characteristic assiduity – constructing vast nests which pulsated nightly with the energy of a Lancashire cotton mill. This impressive gnat had a most capacious intelligence and it possessed a vivid recollection of the somnific sweetness of the goat's milk which it had tasted in its infancy and (now that mankind had returned to the hitherto deserted upper echelons of the Wadi-Washm in the form of Diogo Alvares' desert-weary band), the Kalahambara Wasp had assumed that where there was Man there was also the likelihood of goat's milk. Aroused, therefore, into a frenzy by the anticipation of tasting once again this lacteal ambrosia, the winged devils had spilled from their barracks and instigated a nocturnal campaign against Diogo's exhausted party.

Diogo's surprising source of salvation from certain death was none other than the decayed corpse of a dromedary which lay nearby and whose muscle, crucial organs and bowels had been ripped out by ravenous packs of desert hounds. And thus it was that the rapidly debilitating figure of Diogo Alvares crawled along the ribbed and unforgiving trail of the Kalahambara desert within the protective shell of the increasingly pungent dromedary, propelled slowly – but effectively – by means of apertures he'd sliced in the bottom of the hide with his dagger. But the ireful cloud of hornets had persisted in following him from the Wadi-Washm and they besieged him – rapping the walls of his asylum like freshly-dispatched musket shells! But Salaam-el-Duur fancies how Fate must have been in good humour that day, for Diogo Paredus do Carmo Alvares was rescued and awoke within the walls of that last surviving secret wonder of the ancient world, Carthon!

On awakening from his involuntary period of dormancy, Diogo Alvares must have indicated to him that he had indeed slipped free of Earth's mortal bondage and entered the sublime pastures of Paradise! For were not the sheets which enveloped his enfeebled form woven of the finest silk? Were not the tables which surrounded his monumental bed overflowing with all manner of nuts, fruits and gelatinous confections? Salaam informs us that Diogo struggled to depart the wondrous haven of his berth, for this most commodious sanctum was as soft as a meadow in early summer! As if to further enhance this pastoral illusion, the chamber housed hundreds of tame songbirds whose fluttering wings and chirruping cantatas filled the room. When he eventually pulled back the silk sheets and approached the window, Diogo Alvares witnessed the full, irreproachable beauty of Carthon. He was enchanted by the voluptuous white domes of the temples, the jubilant cornucopia of mosaics which embellished the mighty city walls, the spear-like turrets of the shimmering minarets and the maze of alleys and thoroughfares which wove a magical tapestry around the bustling bazaars, piazzas and palaces. But his admiring gaze was suddenly disturbed by the sound of the doors to his quarters being thrown open.

Enthusiasts of the *Histories of Persia* often cite the startling appearance of King Ramak-el-Beyerty as one of the most arresting passages in the entire opus! Salaam-el-Duur's quill delineates a most splendid figure sporting a large barruk turban (woven from the gossamer silk of the Ragano worm). His corpulent form was cloaked in abundant blue robes whose lengthy train was suspended from the delicate hands of twenty beautiful young women – each plucked carefully from the most elevated regions of the King's fruitful harem. So ethereal were these mademoiselles that we are told they skipped across the floor without emitting a sound rather as if nature had somehow reprieved them of the more burdensome aspects of palpable physicality! Diogo perceived immediately that the King had the bejewelled scabbard of a barbarous kareka hanging from his belt and, fearing for his life, his initial instinct was to deliver an inarticulate plea for mercy but King Ramak-el-Beyerty sensed his unease and reassured him with a smile. He stepped into the middle of the room (allowing Diogo a tantalising glimpse of his emerald-coated talaria), unfurled a vellum scroll and began to declaim in imperfect – but commendable – Portuguese.

'Dear honoured guest, I, King Ramak-el-Beyerty – Ruler of all the Western Plains of the Kalahambara and Emperor of the Ridged Desert of Washm from the Rugut Oasis to the Palm Rings of Ammaraud – on behalf of all the proud burghers of Carthon do greet you and now extend to you our boundless hospitality. It is the proud custom and tradition of the city of Carthon to excel in the arts of hospitality. Our reputation for the provision of pleasure to our sadly infrequent guests is celebrated in verse by all the finest poets from the Jebel scrublands of the north down to the desolate southern slopes of Adrar.'

The King clapped his hands once more and the doors at the far end of the chamber opened to reveal a procession of servants holding aloft golden banqueting trays heavy with the ambrosial cargo of Carthon's masterly culinarians. Cuts of mutton garnished with fragrant sprigs of rosemary and mint! Thin strips of roasted fowl basted with apricots and olmehra leaves! Lamb kio-babs with peppers and fenugreek seeds on a steaming mound of fragrant rice! Sheep's milk sweetened with wild vanilla! Is it any wonder, dear reader, that Diogo fell victim to mild bouts of delirium as he observed how these plentiful trays were carefully laid, one by one, at his feet?

'Honoured guest, please accept these humble offerings as a measure of our meagre philanthropy. Feast, dear visitor, without abstemiousness, upon the unworthy products of our cooks – woven from the fruits of our beleaguered pastures –

and when your hunger is satiated I beg you to enjoy the fleshy temples of these, my finest concubines.'

The legendary hospitality of Carthon did not abate and over the following days and weeks Diogo Alvares was awoken with a feast worthy of Demeter herself! Once satiated, the empty salvers would be returned to the kitchens and twenty further jewels from the royal harem were ushered in, quickly lavishing upon Diogo the fruits of their specialised apprenticeship. This feast of various delights was visited upon Diogo thrice daily and such were the plentiful reserves and variety of Carthon's famous hospitality that not one dish, nor one maiden, was ever visited upon him a second time!

But Diogo Alvares was fired by peril and uncertainty – not lust or gluttony – and so this legendary city soon became a wearisome, cushioned prison of frippery and carnal indulgence! Witnessing his rapidly accumulating corpulence, he cursed the pertinacious attentions of Carthon's cooks! Indeed, his body had now bulged so dramatically that his ragged apparel, stretched to the limits of its durability like well-worn sails (swelled by the pitiless gales of Rio Madre Bay), had finally surrendered to the inevitable, and disintegrated! But still, as the months passed by with inexorable mercilessness, there was no discernable diminution of the daily luxuries served upon him by the industrious servants of King Ramak-el-Beyerty.

Finally, after twelve full months had elapsed (and with his bed long-since collapsed from the burden of his obesity) Diogo arose after yet another mountainous breakfast (and the diligent attentions of the latest selection of nubile treasures from the King's harem) and, using all that remained of his dissipated strength, he clambered like an unsteady giant towards the arched window of his chamber. He peered into the square of the bazaar down below and calculated that the distance between the ledge of his cell and the sanctuary of the ground was but roughly equivalent to the height of a mizzen-mast. Naturally, having negotiated similar heights many times previously during his adventures Diogo Alvares concluded that here was a most felicitous means of escape from his peculiar confinement! But whilst it was doubtlessly true that, ordinarily, Diogo Alvares would have succeeded in negotiating a leap of twenty feet with no critical impediment to his flight, the addled buccaneer had overlooked the painful particulars of his present condition. Alas Diogo – in his eagerness to abscond – had committed a calamitous miscalculation! For whereas in his imagination the Portuguese explorer persisted in envisaging himself as the agile and lean athlete who had swung so effortlessly from the masts of the *Santo Antonio*, in truth he was now a gargantuan figure and this disparity between the concrete and the fanciful formed the crucial basis for this mission's failure!

Cousin, it is never a pleasant task to chronicle the decline of eminent and worthy men – especially when, as in poor Diogo Alvares' instance – it is a tale of degeneracy supplemented by indignity and humiliation. But regardless of this fact, Salaam-el-Duur informs us how, for three long days and three equally interminable nights, fifty of King Ramak-el-Beyerty's finest warriors pulled hard on the ropes that had been tied around Diogo's inflated form in an effort to release him from his predicament of being trapped in the window of his chamber. In addition to these efforts, fifty burly cavalrymen of His Majesty's camel troop were subsequently instructed to augment this desperate action by occupying the interior of the chamber and pushing Diogo from the rear in the hope that it would dislodge his fleshy bulk. Despite these Herculean endeavours however, Diogo Alvares remained cemented in the window – his face transformed into a deep shade of heliotrope by the malevolent furnace of the sun. But King Ramak-el-Beyerty was a most resourceful and astute potentate and, realising that inordinate measures were called for if a terrible conclusion were to be avoided, he raised the ceremonial trimpitta to his lips and produced a shrill alarum.

Ah reader, what a most singular spectacle followed this call! The very ground shook and trembled as the combined forces of the King's elephant guards thundered forth on their magnificent steeds! Twelve immaculately-attired Carthonites sat astride each beast, each clinging on to a sturdy leash woven from the sinewy fronds of bohamash grass (a grass peculiar to the wild and wind-whipped plains of Korahestan and renowned for its durability under strain). Slipping down from their elevated positions with liquid grace, the riders looped thick ropes around the elephants' flailing trunks and – after striking their steeds' leathery hides with their ebony katrams – the obedient creatures responded by heaving with all their considerable might until the network of ropes tightened and sang, producing notes deeper than any that were possible on any conventional guitarra! King Ramak-el-Beyerty was overjoyed for, in a mere matter of minutes, he could see that Diogo's body was loosened from the painful grip of the window!

But, oh, how fickle the whims of fortune! How instantaneous the transformation from joy to despondency!

Reader, the breathtaking depth and capacious dimensions of the crater which was formed in the central square following Diogo Alvares' forced descent is said to have rivalled that of the infamous basin in the southernmost regions of the Kalahambara desert! After the mighty clouds of dust had finally dissipated, King Ramak-el-Beyerty and his assembled subjects tentatively gathered around the edge and peered into the abyss in astonished silence. The unhappy sight that greeted them was that of Diogo Alvares' lifeless body splayed out in all its naked indignity – lying upon four crushed elephants.

Weeping furiously, King Ramak-el-Beyerty dropped to his knees in despair and declared that Diogo Alvares – as a most treasured guest of Carthon – would immediately be accorded the rare privilege of a memorial tomb hewed from the soft, fibrous stone of the Washm plain. It was, declaimed His Majesty, to be designed and executed by the finest craftsmen, summoned from all corners of the Kalahambara territories.

The fifth volume of the *Histories of Persia* recounts how Diogo's monstrous corpse was transported across the Kalahambara desert by eight powerful elephants drawing a specially-constructed salrom. Then, by means of a labyrinthine mass of ropes and pulleys, he was finally laid to rest in the cool cradle of the Washm.

King Ramak-el-Beyerty's grief at his guest's undignified demise was most profound and it was peculiarly undiminished by the passage of time. Thirty years later – when this most sagacious monarch himself succumbed to the Reaper's callous scythe (after innocently upturning a stone and encountering the wrathful ire of a green-ribbed scorpion) – his advisors discovered that he had long-since expressed in his private papers the heartfelt desire to be interred after his death alongside Diogo Alvares in the self-same tomb on the Washm expanse. This was duly arranged and Salaam-el-Duur documents how the King's funeral was a most singular event! It is reported that four hundred loyal Carthonites followed the train of camels which transported his body through the city gates and out across the tundra but that only fifty of them succeeded in completing the journey back. The remainder lay strewn around the tomb, their faces frozen in expressions of abject terror. Their ravaged carcasses a seething mass of wasps.

The Moon and the Broomstick

Jo Mazelis

There had been three, perhaps four miscarriages already. Two had happened when Maria's pregnancy was already far advanced.

The midwife examined her hips, her teeth, the taut muscles of her stomach.

She was treated like a naughty girl. Ordered, now she was pregnant again, to give up all violent exercise. Maria's mother, the Russian acrobat and contortionist Tatiana Britt, had never abandoned her calling – practising her own skills behind the scenes when she became too unwieldy to perform for the public.

But she dearly wanted a child, and so at winter's end when she was five months pregnant she bid farewell to Stan (or the Great Bendini as he was known) when he left to begin the season with the travelling circus.

She felt lonely and bored, but spent hours at a time resting with her feet propped up so they were higher than her head. She wrote Stan long letters asking after all their friends, mentioning the small towns that she knew they would be going to, reminding him of things they had once done together, telling him she loved him. He replied twice. His letters were concise.

But Maria was grateful for all the benefits modern medicine had bestowed. It was a young century, the atlas still sported many splashes of pink to show that Britannia held on to her empire, and scientific progress had transformed the lives of many.

Children no longer worked in the mines or factories, fewer women died in childbirth, though there was still a very real risk. And babies and children, even once safely delivered, might yet die from any number of causes.

Guiltily then, she ignored her impatience and boredom, and submitted to examinations and thermometers and bed rest.

The sheets on her bed were starched white cotton, crisp and cool, the food was bland and lukewarm, and she had been disallowed not only brandy, which she liked to take a lick of now and then throughout the day, but also coffee, as it was thought to induce miscarriage by quickening the heart.

Tea was offered instead and she grew to like it well enough, but it was a pale substitute.

Her belly ballooned; so much so that she was cross-examined about her dates, about her monthlies and her marital relations with Stan. When she told the nurse that she and Stan were intimate frequently, once or twice a day, sometimes in the afternoon, and even, shockingly, during her menses, the nurse's face grew ashen and she looked as if she might faint. When the nurse had recovered, she said that this was *unnatural*, a woman's body was not designed for such overuse and he, Stan, must learn control and shouldn't make her suffer so.

'But it isn't suffering,' she'd protested, 'I like it.'

The nurse shook her head slowly in reproach.

'But my dear, you've lost four babies. Don't you see?'

Maria saw.

Next they accused her of overeating.

'Mother must eat for two, but she must not overindulge.'

Finally they began to suggest that she might be carrying twins, and searched her belly, pressing the stethoscope first here, then there to detect a second or third heartbeat.

By her seventh month she was instructed to prepare her nipples for breast-feeding, something that she could not understand but endured. She was given, as were all the newly expectant mothers, a small nail brush and a bar of disinfectant soap and instructed to scrub her nipples twice a day. It was painful but she did as she was told, marvelling at how women in more primitive countries, or in the past, or Eve herself, mother of Cain and Abel, had managed to procure a nailbrush and carbolic. How had the human race managed to survive and thrive without? Well, she considered, perhaps something was done with bunches of twigs and herbs?

Then she began to imagine her twins (which by the rough and tumble that went on in her belly she was convinced must be boys) tasting the carbolic soap on her nipples when she first offered suck, and pulling nasty faces before refusing her delicious milk. So secretly, a month before they were due, she stopped using the soap and after one week of grating the wet brush on her weary nipples, she abandoned that too.

Stan wrote saying that they should name the boys Romulus and Remus, and included a diagram of a she-wolf he'd had the idea of constructing. Concealed inside the animal's teats were two baby's bottles filled with cow's milk. He was always coming up with new and wild ideas for the circus and while she could see the appeal of this one, she didn't think it would work, not for her two boys anyway; and she wrote that perhaps it would be better performed by dwarves in diapers?

But the names were nice enough, and they could always give the boys a whole clutch of names so that they might decide later on which to use in their act, which for friends and family and which for the world beyond the circus. So, Romulus Samson Jacob John and Remus Nero Alexander Harold grew in her imagination, not weighted down by their freight of names, but strong, agile, handsome and clever boys who would become great men.

Two weeks before the babies were due, another woman was brought into the ward. Like Maria, this woman was expecting twins. Her belly was prodigious and vast, her insect legs and arms tiny in comparison, her small pale face fearful and timid like a mouse's.

She was a vicar's wife, as devout as a nun. She called out for God's help in a choked whisper between bouts of weeping. Her labour had begun thirty-six hours before in the vicarage, a long and rackety drive away from the hospital. The babies were stuck and despite all the manipulation and coaxing from the midwife they would not budge. In a few hours, if natural childbirth did not occur, the babies, dead or alive, would be removed by Caesarean section. If not, mother and babies would be lost.

They wheeled the woman off at close to midnight, her cries echoing down the tiled passage, 'Oh God, oh God, oh Jesus, Jesus.'

Perhaps the same thing would happen to her, for Maria surmised if God punished and tested even the virtuous vicar's wife, what might he do to her; an unvarnished sinner who had only jumped the broomstick with her Stan and not legally married in God's eyes.

She lay in bed terrified for what seemed like hours. Waves of spasmodic pain were passing through her body. It was two weeks too early, but it was now, and now was implacable, irresistible, she couldn't fight it. She struggled to sit upright, the twins seemed locked in a tight knot of stillness in a different, lower position in her body. Her eyes travelled up the ward to the desk where the night nurse usually sat in a quiet pool of yellow light, passing the dark hours by reading romantic novels or knitting Argyle sweaters for her sweetheart, but there was no one there.

Four other women slept in the other beds, all of them heaped on their sides, bulky as pigs under the covers.

She swung her legs over the side of the bed and struggled to stand. A contraction overtook her and she waited it out, rubbing her back to ease the pain and rocking her body like an Arabian dancer because that seemed to help, although it was probably forbidden.

Slowly, as every four or five minutes another contraction stopped her, she made her way towards the door that led out of the ward and closer to the delivery rooms. It was hot and airless, and despite the strong smells of disinfectant she could detect the coppery tang of blood in the air.

She heard voices up ahead, words spoken in urgent whispers, and these seemed to be coming from a lit room whose door was ajar, describing its edges with a sharp line of white light.

Another contraction overwhelmed her and she stopped near an open door. Resting one hand on the doorjamb to steady herself, she undulated heavily, sensing weakness in her once strong legs that must have come from under use. She wished that she could be with Stan; that instead of being here in this distempered place with its imprisoning walls, she could be in their little wooden caravan, breathing in the smells of the animals, the axle grease and the sweet, sweet air.

She gazed into the unlit room and noticed the silvery disk that hung beyond the window. It was a full, round moon with a hazy halo of light around it. She thought about Stan sitting on the caravan steps with his pipe, how he would look up and see this same moon. As soon as this idea came to her she felt she must get nearer to that moon, to stand by the window and press her hot cheek against the cool glass. If she thought hard enough and gazed intently enough at the moon, it would be as if Stan were with her and he would know that she was thinking of him.

She knew that it was forbidden to trespass into any room other than the bathroom, yet could not resist. She had gone forward only two steps when her stomach tightened again and a great wave of pain paralysed her. The rocking seemed to help, if only to focus her mind on something other than the burning cramped ache that coiled through her. There was no wall to support herself by, but her hand, groping in the gloom, found a metal rung, probably part of a bed, which she wrapped her trembling fist around.

When the contraction had passed (they were getting longer as well as more intense and closer together) she stepped forward still holding onto the metal rail. Now that she was closer to the window she stepped into the pool of its pale silver light, and she saw that what she had been holding was the foot of a metal crib, and inside it she saw two perfect babies' heads laying next to one another on the mattress. A single white sheet lay over the babies and their eyes were closed. She leaned closer, holding her belly as she did so. She did not think she had ever seen anything so perfect as these alabaster babies with blue-veined eyelids, and long black lashes and mouths so pale and perfectly formed. She immediately sensed that they were not breathing and thus not alive, but something about them convinced her that they weren't dead – or at least not dead in the way that something which has once been alive is dead. No, she had a barely formed impression that these were dolls.

Or not dolls as such, but something like. Perhaps they

were wax or bisque mannequins used for the purpose of training the doctors or other scientific research.

Another contraction and she gripped the sides of the crib and swayed. Again the pain passed away, retreating from body and mind momentarily and leaving behind the surprising nothingness of no pain.

She gazed at the baby mannequins again. It seemed both strange and frustrating to her that someone had lain them in this crib and covered them with a sheet just as if they were asleep. You'd think they'd be kept in a cupboard or under glass, not put to bed like a little girl's dolls.

Without thinking about it (as after all these were not real babies, they would not get cold and die) she drew back the sheet, and that was when she saw it, saw the strangeness of what had been done to the tiny naked mannequins. They were joined together. It was as if the wax or whatever they were made from had been allowed to melt and pool, fusing their lower torsos together into one unnatural trunk.

They were girls, and each had a clamped stump at her belly button and an elusive odour, sweet and sour at the same time. It was that which made her realise that they were real – not mannequins at all. She gasped and would have stepped back, but another contraction locked her in place, and she thought with terror of the violence inside her and she was suddenly more afraid than she had ever been. She who had soared through the air, somersaulting, balancing, with a leather strap in her teeth while her body spun beneath her, a cocoon of weight like a plumb bob.

She screamed. The sound was low, guttural and strangled, and the noise seemed to come from somewhere else entirely, as if it were the echo of another woman's voice, another woman's pain.

And then in answer to her cry, she felt a sudden hot gush

as her waters broke, and voices and people surrounded her. Hands were on her body pulling her away and out of the moonlit room, but the grip of her hands on the crib's rail was so strong that it jerked and rattled, shaking the wax babies so it seemed for a moment that they might wake. Alarmed, she let go and the crib clanked heavily and was still.

Her twins were also girls. Black-haired and button-eyed, with faces like fairy changelings, and perfect, perfect, perfect.

She made a promise to the moon the next night. She and Stan would marry. She'd been warned; she did not know what sin the vicar's wife, poor thing, was guilty of, but from now on Maria decided she must make amends.

Stan would understand. He invented the world as he went along; nothing was beyond him.

For years after, especially when the moon was full, she saw again the poor dead babies with their fused bodies and blue white skin and sometimes she thought she'd dreamt it all. Or worse, it occurred to her that the dead twins had been *her* babies, and these two bright girls, Charlotte-Kay and Georgina-May were the children of the vicar and his good wife, and somehow, by unnatural chance or charm, she'd stolen them.

And later still, when times were hard, and Stan told her of his latest plan, she saw the rightness of it straight away. She sensed that it had almost been the girls' fate to be Siamese twins, and now with tiny corsets stitched together at the hip and tiny beautifully made little double dresses, it became their destiny, and no one, not even their mother, thought it was a sin.

Yellow Archangel

Glenda Beagan

You can see time from here. You can see how it moves. I saw the colours come to the trees every year, of course I did, and I saw them blow away when it was time for them to go, leaving the trees' real shapes. I always liked their winter faces best. I was seeing what was happening on the surface of change. But the way I see time now is not a visual thing at all. So perhaps seeing is the wrong word.

Experience has taught me, and has taught many others too, those of us that are left, that we come and go so quickly, so easily and suddenly, we surely matter scarcely at all. To each other, yes. But in the great scheme of things? History would like to tell us otherwise but we're nothing really. Now I can see that time is one thing, and history another. One is a made thing, a construct that's never neutral. The other is. Simply is. All that remains is time and the land itself. And the land is its own story.

Now I'm old and slow and alone a great deal. Now I can see time.

To begin with we thought it a lot of fuss about nothing. Words like media, like hype, mean nothing now. Most people have no inkling of what they ever meant. It's scarcely recognisable.

Then there was no silence at all, unless you really looked for it. The opposite of now.

Admittedly, there'd been scares before. Each time there was an eager build-up. Then, when so few people actually died, it all became a kind of crying wolf and we got to take no notice. So when it really struck we were caught unawares. There was no time, no leeway, to isolate the latest mutated variant, develop a vaccine, distribute it. It was like the Virus was laughing at us.

In the first week to ten days people died in their hundreds of thousands. In less than three weeks they were dying in their millions. Soldiers were brought back from Afghanistan. Half of them had it to start with, then all of them. They had one task only: to dispose of the dead in mass graves.

As a child I saw the results of foot and mouth disease for real. I did not see this, not even on TV but I can imagine it. The powers that be (or rather the powers that were) deemed it best not to let those that were left see what was happening. But now there was only one television channel anyway. It played ambient music, the sounds of waves on a beach, and it broadcast a reassuring message on the hour. No one was reassured.

The devastation in the cities was almost total. Country people like us had greater immunity, maybe, closer to the earth and the animals, to dirt and dung. And ours weren't overcrowded like the urban areas. Mind you, plenty of us died too and we had to bury our own dead. Strangely, it was some of the younger, fitter ones went first. My husband, my brother and his wife. Here was I at Tŷ Chwarel with my daughter Kia, then five years old. My nephew, Nathan, now an orphan, aged four, came to live with us here. After doing its worst the Virus abated, reappearing from time to time when least expected. By now there was no central government, just cobbled-together committees of local people who couldn't do much but did their best.

I have lived longer than anyone I know in these parts but if I hadn't had the responsibility of looking after two young children I might have just given up. After Tom died I would have liked to have simply lain down beside him. That luxury wasn't available to me. I had to find strength from somewhere.

I missed him so much it was a physical pain. We'd met seven years earlier, on our first day in our first teaching posts. My subject was History, Tom's was Art and Design. His great love was ceramics. Not long before the Virus struck he'd had a kiln built here in the back. He'd such enthusiasm. What would he have thought of Nathan's idea of adapting the kiln for use as a communal oven for bread? Nathan was still only a boy when he thought that one up. It would never have entered my head. He was, and still is, full of wonderful ideas, not all of them practical, admittedly, though so many of them are. He often gets the original concept and then if he can't set it up himself he'll look for someone with the know-how and technical ability to make it happen. Mind you, there are few of those left.

The young generation never cease to amaze me with their adaptability and their resilience. We who know what it was like before, well, I don't think we ever recovered. The shock of seeing how quickly our world fell apart changed us forever. Nothing could be relied on any more. This nightmare was real. The young ones who came afterwards had no experience of how life used to be. Nothing to compare things with. So maybe it's easier in a way for them. Not physically of course. Scraping a living is plain hard work for everyone. But mentally, psychologically, they didn't have their noses rubbed painfully in the fact of their own vulnerability. We lost the people we loved. We lost the illusion of safety.

Here I'm conscious of the old long-ago me, sceptical, highly rational, and the new me, though she's scarcely new for heaven's sake, and these contrasting versions of myself are not in conflict any more. Time, and what time has done, constitute the difference. Now I'm a person the wind has blown right through for so long I'm completely hollowed out. I just can't describe myself any more, except as a survivor.

Imagine a small grey church in a green valley. The church is very old, the valley narrow and shallow, its well-wooded sides sloping gently like the sides of a soup bowl. A stream meanders here, its water so clear you can see the bottom at any point, sometimes glinty with pebbles and sticklebacks, sometimes smooth with tawny mud out of which watercress grows.

I have to imagine the church and the valley myself now. My antique legs won't take me that far, and I'm still a bit scared of horses. I'm too stiff to get up there, I joke. So here I stay, most of the time, looking out across the Clwydians, with the Berwyns beyond, more aware than ever of the colours in the landscape, how they change with the seasons, the weather and the light. Up there are the Iron Age forts, the familiar shape of Moel Famau.

Tom is buried near the grey stone wall at the back of the church, in the shade of a sycamore tree. Years ago, not very long after Kia's illness, when she was getting better and playing over at her friend Ingrid's house, across the heath from ours, I'd come here with Nathan to put flowers on Tom's grave. I found a plant growing nearby, a kind of dead nettle with yellow flowers. As a child I'd had a passion for botanising and this plant's name, yellow archangel, had struck me as magical. Here it was again. Insignificant? Yes, really, though it had acquired a sudden relevance. For a moment I had an insight into a kind of mindset very different from my own. I saw a whole sequence of links that really weren't there. But this is true. I understood how, and why, when people have been under great strain and have been living in fear of one kind or another, for so long, they need explanations that comfort them, that account for what's going on, that show them that things will, maybe, get better. It doesn't work for me. My education and a streak of innate bloody-mindedness put paid to that early on, but at least I can understand.

I'd recently very nearly lost my Kia, but not to the Virus. There was no organised health service of any kind by now. So many of the people we used to call health professionals died when the pandemic was at its height, though I know some people still had stocks of out-of-date drugs, dubiously acquired, no questions asked. It was five years after Tom's death, so Kia was ten years old, Nathan nine. I didn't think it was the Virus, but she'd been feverish for a couple of days and by now she was delirious. Desperate, I thought I'd risk driving down to the town to see if I could find a doctor or, failing that, one of the young trainees who learned on the job as best they could, often with doctors who'd come out of retirement to do what they could. I'd been given an address by Dewi Warner, whose wife had been so ill last year. Warily I set off, leaving Nathan with the shotgun, just in case, though there'd been no Ferals up here for a few months now.

A painfully young lad with freckles and red hair thought it might be meningitis but there was really nothing he could do, apart from advising me to carry on sponging Kia with cold compresses to try and reduce her temperature. He was brutally honest, warning me that even if she did survive, she might well be brain damaged. Well, survive she did, and without any lasting problems of that kind, thank God. But she was changed. She seemed so much older; quiet, melancholy. And there was another indefinable quality. Fey, maybe? She told us she was still alive because a yellow archangel had come for her and brought her back down the winter hill, carrying her in his arms and leaving her by the well. The archangel had a message for Kia. She had a task now, a special responsibility. She was here to help people and give them hope.

The first person to hear about the archangel was Kia's best friend, Ingrid. She told her mother, Ingrid's mother told her friends. In no time at all, it seemed to me, we had people turning up at our door, insisting on seeing Kia, quite convinced that she could cure them, predict the future for them, advise them on their relationships, solve all their problems. She'd come back from the dead, hadn't she? She had all this wisdom to share, didn't she? And this child was ten years old!

I would have liked to have brought them to their senses. Frankly I would have liked to tell them where to go. But Kia was adamant. This was why she'd been saved. I thought she was deluded but at the same time I saw how she grew into her role, relished it, thrived on it, becoming rather insufferable in the process sometimes, it must be said. There's no doubt she had a remarkable effect on people. I remember how I sometimes felt uneasy with her, and then guilty for doing so. It was as if a kind of crackly static was coming off her, a kind of energy. Once, I looked out of the window and saw her with a gaggle of friends. Ingrid, who in days of old would have made a remarkably successful publicist, was, as ever, prominent amongst them. They were all standing in a circle around Kia and they were holding their hands towards her, palms flat, fingers stretched out as if they were warming themselves by a fire.

Once upon a time Tom had his ceramics, his dreams of making a name for himself, of selling his planters and bowls at catch-your-breath prices, and making so much money he didn't need to teach any more, except for giving the occasional master class, maybe. It was his fantasy. Once upon a time I had my dreams too, of writing a book about the local folklore, legends and the like. There was a story about a ghostly dog and the spirit of a hanged highwayman who still haunted the crossroads where the roads met on the other side of the heath. There was a good deal of much older, more unusual pagan material too, hints of it in variants on the Green Man. Anyway when Tom died, and the Virus shattered everything, I no longer cared about folk tales or legends. What did they matter? They were trivial, frivolous. Nothing but a mockery now we were living in the midst of scarcity and chaos. How ironic then, that I lived to see my daughter become a classic legend in her own lifetime.

I use those cheap, smudgy words that used to belong to the forgotten concept of celebrity. Forgotten that is, except by old biddies like me. But I actually mean those words literally, in a much older, more respectful sense. Kia became an oracle. And then a kind of saint. Or maybe the word I want to use, but find myself hesitating over, though there were many that did not, is goddess. There, I've said it. Everyone was in awe of her. Everyone, that is, except Nathan and me. He was as cheeky and irreverent with her as he'd always been. This helped to keep her grounded to some extent.

Now, so long after she's gone from us, proving emphatically that she wasn't immortal after all, people still come here to the well to leave tokens for her hanging on the ash tree. Special wishes. Prayers for her to answer. I have lived long enough to see how a human being can become something more than human in the minds of needy people. And how their belief can strengthen them, can save them.

I was shocked when, in due course, Kia and Nathan

became a couple. They were first cousins and as they'd been brought up effectively as brother or sister, the whole thing felt incestuous. But I could see they loved each other. Always had, really. Wisely, as I've got older I've learned to let things be.

It was childbirth took her from us. This time it was Dewi Warner who rode down into town to look for someone who might be able to help. Ingrid and I delivered the baby after a protracted labour, Nathan now sitting beside Kia's bed, willing her to live even as her life bled away. Dewi appeared at the door eventually, alone, apprehensive. I'll never forget the look Nathan gave him, slowly, heavily shaking his head.

Nathan named his little daughter Kia and it was this little motherless scrap that saved him. It's uncanny how like my Kia she is. Come on now, I rebuke myself. It's not uncanny at all.

A few years later, nervously at first, thinking, maybe, that I'd be angry and resentful, Nathan brought Mai home to live with us at Tŷ Chwarel. Kia is thirteen now, and Mai has given Nathan two sons. That makes me some sort of odd combination of great aunt and grandmother. It's good to hear young voices in this old house. Nathan and Mai are very good to me and I suppose you could say I'm happier now than I've been since Tom died. Odd that, with my aches and pains and my sense of increasing distance from everyone and everything. Odd that I've become more accepting, calmer. Not before time, you might say.

No one round here ever talks about death any more. Not in so many words. We talk about the yellow archangel instead. My daughter's words have entered the language, and it can't be long before he comes for me.

The Pool at Wiene Street

Alan Bilton

The first thing I want to say is don't go to the swimming pool on Niblo Street. The showers are cold, the vending machine eats your money and the lockers don't lock. The second thing is: don't go thinking the baths at Mamoulian are any better. Not a bit of it! The pool stinks of chemicals and you'll notice a yellowish tinge to your skin for days afterwards. Trust me, such a tinge is not good for your health. So why go there? But the third thing I'd like to say is that the pool on Wiene Street is the worst of all.

I used to go there as a kid. As soon as our school bus would start to pull up, my insides would feel as though they were being wrung out like a towel. Just thinking about it brings it all back – my ears go fuzzy, my scalp starts to itch, I sweat all over. True, I've never been a confident swimmer. 'That boy could drown in a tea-spoon of water' (my dad). But at school, what could you do? I joined my schoolmates and helped form a disorderly line. The entrance stank of small boys' sweat. Dark stairs led down to the changing rooms. This is it! I thought as I descended into the depths. I fingered my wristband and squeezed hard on the locker key.

And then, many, many years later, I found myself standing there again. What are you doing here? I thought: seven years of misery not enough? But lately I'd felt myself growing slightly less trim. My waist had expanded, my limbs grown flabby. I'd had to let out my trousers to permit extra parking. There was no getting around the fact; I was no longer as svelte as I had been. Looking down, I could no longer tell if my shoelaces were tied. Climbing stairs, I sounded like a balloon losing air. This can't go on! I said, fixing myself another bowl of waffles. Most exercise however, was out. Strict moral and aesthetic strictures forbade me from the wearing of shorts or T-shirts. I had heard of gyms, but never actually seen one. The idea of running didn't do anything for me – what's more pleasurable to do standing up than sitting down, or better yet, lying prone? At least when swimming, the water does half the work. True, when fully immersed I tended to flounder like a man trying to attract a passing plane, but what did I have to lose? Maybe the water wouldn't give way this time.

And so, against my best instincts, I went back. As my grandmother said, 'A fool hits his thumb three times.' From the outside, the baths were just the same as I remembered them: a concrete lump that from the back could have been a prison block, a rendering plant or an abattoir. Black smoke was billowing from a chimney. In the car park there was broken glass everywhere.

But the worst thing was the smell. As soon as I pushed open the door I smelt it: a potent combination of sulphur, chlorine and dread. I mean, I suppose there were chairs, posters, a desk, but all I could think was: the smell! I was seven years old again, half a pound of nothing, skinny as the stroke of one.

Strangely though, the girl behind the desk looked at me as if I were a long-lost relative. She flashed me a dazzling smile and her big black eyes opened wide as a sunflower.

'Hiya old-timer,' she said, cradling her face in her hands. 'Couldn't stay away, huh?'

'That's right,' I said, keeping one eye on the door. The girl's head was propped up on the desk like a vase, her eyes as dark as tar.

'So how's the fitness regime going? Shedding those pounds?'

'Well, you know me,' I said. 'A slave to physical perfection.'

'Mm, so I see,' she laughed. Her big black eyes seemed to draw me in like a bee.

'It's true,' I said. 'The weight is falling off me. From the side I'm just a shadow.'

The gal eyed up my ample belly and smiled. 'Mm, from this angle I can barely see you.' Then she sighed, stretched and handed me a ticket. 'Well, there you go. Don't drown in the foot-wash.'

I smiled weakly and shuffled past. My face felt hot as a bowl of soup. I rushed down the dark stairs but tripped on the last three.

The changing room was the colour of a smoker's lung, and awash with dirty water and sweet wrappers. Some school class must just have finished 'cause a whole bunch of squawking kids were running around, flicking each other with towels and 'getting up to high-doh' (my mother). I waited until they'd gone before removing my clothes. Everything inside me, physical and spiritual, seemed to shrivel. Stepping in a puddle, I noticed a sticking plaster sticking to my foot. But what could one do? I stripped off, donned my voluminous trunks, and placed my clothes in the highest of a line of stained, rusty lockers. In my hand was a small, gold key.

But where, I ask you, is a man supposed to put such a key? In his beard? I possessed neither pin nor armband nor pocket. The changing-rooms seemed to be unmanned. I stared at the key and sighed: 'there's no point in asking a naked man for change' (my grandfather). So I carefully placed the key in the waistband of my trunks. The light was very poor. Without my glasses on all I could see were vague blobs and shapes.

The showers seemed to be full of naked old men chattering away, but luckily I couldn't see too much. They were skinny as a copse of ash-trees. As I tiptoed past them my feet seemed to flap and stick. Nobody looked up though and I made my way past the petrified figures as unobtrusively as possible.

Past the showers was another set of dark stairs and then there was the pool itself. Ach, what a sight! The pool seemed to be in some kind of draughty, badly lit bunker. Black waves lapped the surface but there was absolutely no one about, neither bathers nor spectators nor attendants. I edged my way to the side. The water looked cold and black. Best not go too far from the shallow end, I thought. Even my goose bumps had goose bumps (Bob Hope). A rusted metal ladder led down to the lower depths. I lowered myself in up to my ankle and – ah, me! – it was like dipping your toe in cold tea. Nevertheless, I allowed my extremities to edge south; when the icy waters made contact with my thighs I had to bite hard on my arm. And this, the shallow end? I tried splashing water on my arms and bobbing up and down, but nothing seemed to help. Well, that's enough for a first attempt, I thought, hauling myself back out. Strange shadows jumped on the walls and smeary blobs bobbed in the water. Best not over-do it before lunch. And so I retreated back up the stairs, my feet flapping and sticking as I went.

I was still breathing heavily from my exertions when I got back to the lockers. Ah me, I thought, dry land at last. But what about the key? I looked down in my trunks: nothing. Feigning nonchalance, I looked down at the floor instead:

nothing also. What was I supposed to do? I couldn't go back past the girl undressed. In this state I looked no great prize: my gut seemed to cover my trunks like an avalanche. Well, there was nothing to do but push open an access door and leave the back way, by the bins. This is what comes of such foolishness, I thought. Man is not a duck. I pushed open the doors and felt the cold wind buffet my belly. By the dual carriageway, it was even worse. Drivers blew their horns and pedestrians stopped and pointed. I shall not speak of what I had to plod through with my two bare feet. Tch, what a pitiful figure I must have cut! A round, bare man, hobbling along the side of the road. After a while it started to spit with rain and the sky made an angry face. My skin seemed to be powder blue. My teeth chattered like they were about to fall out. What a fool I'd been, what a goose! When I got back home and found a neighbour to let me in, I vowed never to set foot in a swimming pool again. What were these places anyway? Sink holes for the unwary. From now on I'd keep my feet on solid ground. And I'd have to go to the shops and buy a new set of clothes too.

Anyhow, months went by, and it's fair to say that I might have put on a few extra pounds. In bed at night, I felt as if there were an anvil on my chest. My knees and I were now on only a nodding acquaintance. Still, I thought, I have learned my lesson: physical activity and me do not mix. 'A beaten dog recognises the stick' (my Uncle Tibor). Nevertheless, a few days later I had to go on a business trip to a nearby town, and found that I'd been booked into a very swanky hotel indeed. Honestly, it was enough to make your eyes water: liveried flunkies, mints on your pillow, gold trolleys, the whole shebang. 'Ah yes,' I said, 'a man can get accustomed to such luxury.' Sitting there in my bathrobe, watching wide-screen TV, fluffy white slippers on my nippers, 'I was grander than

Solomon in all his splendour' (St Matthew). And it was just then, as I was flicking through the hotel's glossy brochure, that I noticed that the place also had a private pool. Just look at the size of that TV, I thought, how bad can the swimming pool be? And so saying, I plodded down from the top floor, room key in my pocket, and went to look for the spa and relaxation pool. Out in the corridor my slippers made funny little smacking noises on the woodwork.

And oh my friends, the reception was like a dream – soft lights, perfumed towels, pot-pouri by the bucket load. Yes, this was a different kind of establishment entirely. But then I suddenly clapped eyes on the girl behind the desk. Tch, I couldn't believe it! It was the gal from Wiene Street, only now in a white smock with her hair pulled back from her face. She didn't seem to recognise me though. Her eyes looked red from crying, and she handed me my trunks and towels without so much as a by your leave.

'Miss, miss?' I asked. 'Are you all right? What is it, what's wrong?'

Her expression was tragic, her button nose as red as a cherry on a bun.

'Oh, fella,' she said. 'What are you doing here? Why did you come back?'

'Me? But miss....'

Her face was crumpled as a tissue.

'Oh fella, don't you see? There's nothing left to do. It's finished now....'

My mouth opened and shut but nothing came out. Even the girl's ears looked red.

'Just take it, will you?' she said, handing over a gold locker key. 'We both know it's too late now. Why torment each other any longer?'

'But miss...'

'How did it happen?' she asked. 'How did we let it slip away?'

Ach, what could I do? I looked down at my wee bundle and then retreated down a dark stairway. As I turned back to see if I could still see her I stumbled and slipped down the last three steps.

Down below, I couldn't believe it. The changing room was the colour of dentures and absolutely packed with school kids. What were they doing here anyway? They climbed on all the benches, chucked bars of soap at each other, and tried to whack each other with towels. Aye, even here, I thought, as a missile went ricocheting off my head. I placed my clothes in a wee cubby hole and tried to ignore them. Nothing changes in this world, I thought. The school gates never close. I started pushing my way through to the steps but they kept grabbing at my bathrobe and trying to pull my trunks down. What a pack of monkeys! Just as I walked past them a sudden shove sent me stumbling into the naked old men in the showers. Close up, the old sticks were as shrivelled and wrinkly as papyrus.

'Scuze me,' I said, 'coming through,' and with that fled down the second dark stairwell, down to the pool itself.

The pool seemed to be in some kind of draughty, poorly lit cave. Black waves lapped the surface but there was absolutely no one about, neither bathers nor spectators nor attendants. I edged my way to the side. The water looked cold and black. It was like jumping into an inkwell. I tried extending one exploratory toe. Cold as a penguin's lunch. I placed my whole foot in. The pool was just unbelievably icy. There wasn't even a shallow end here, not even a ladder. Just a sudden drop, just me and the pool. Then I must have slipped, 'cause the next thing I knew my mouth was full of foul-smelling water and I was splashing about for my life.

Fortunately though, one foot found a slippery tile and after a while, so did its mate. Coughing and spluttering, I hauled myself out and flopped down on the side. Oh, the taste! Like the smell, only a hundred times worse. What was I thinking of, coming to this place? As my mother used to say, 'Never put anything on your plate that you wouldn't put in your mouth'. Shaking, I pushed myself back to the stairs. Clumps of hair lay all around me. When I pushed my hair back from my eyes, a whole kink came off in my hands. Feeling kind of wobbly, I didn't even bother to look for my locker key, but just ran back up to my room. When I got there I couldn't find my hotel key. My hair was coming out in tufts.

By the time the concierge let me in, I felt awful. I couldn't eat, couldn't sleep. My flesh seemed to sag like an over-stretched bag. By the time the trip was over, I'd lost nearly a stone. The weight kept sliding off and I was bald as a sausage. I could still smell the pool, though. Chlorine, sulphur, cleaning fluids. The devil's soup.

Ach, after a fortnight I had no choice. An ambulance took me to hospital. The doctors were baffled. I weighed no more than a shadow's suit. My hair refused to grow back. My skin was as wrinkled as a turtle's chin.

Strangely, all the doctors in the hospital seemed really short and really young. Indeed, several of them looked hardly old enough to be wearing long trousers. Instead of examining me, they seemed to just prod and poke, and kept telling me to take down my trousers. Finally, after being ferried between cardio-vascular, ears, nose & throat, and gastro-enterology, I was packed off to hydrotherapy. When I got there a little doctor winked and stuck out his tongue. A few minutes later a nurse came to get me ready. I was put in a hospital gown and given a small gold key.

'Don't lose that,' said the nurse, rather severely. She

reminded me of a teacher from my old school. Her breath smelt of Fisherman's Friends.

'Tell me, sister,' I whispered. 'What is it with this place? Why are all the doctors so little and so young?'

She glared at me through her glasses. 'Hm, well, and what about you? Why are you so old and so wrinkled?' And I have to admit, I didn't have an answer to that. Then, with a whole line of shrunken old fellas, I was led along a dimly lit corridor and into a side building, my feet flapping and smacking on the lino. As soon as they opened the door I smelt it. Well, what did you expect, I thought? *Après la dernière marche, la grande chute* (Voltaire).

The girl behind the desk looked at my file impassively. She didn't even seem to recognise me. Just one strand of golden hair escaped from under her nurse's cap.

'So how are we today?' she asked, flicking through my file. She looked younger than ever, whilst in the last few weeks I had shrivelled up like a punctured balloon.

'Oh missy, I haven't been so well,' I said, my tongue sticking to the top of my mouth. My ears felt fuzzy and my insides felt twisted like a dish towel. 'But oh, my dear, do you remember me at all? Do you remember how I once looked? Ah, miss, what happened to the two of us? How did it go by so fast?'

The girl looked at me strangely.

'Let me take your robe,' she said. 'That's it; off you go, down those dark stairs. Mm, just there, that's right. Take care not to slip on the last three.'

The pool seemed to occupy a kind of draughty, dim hole in the ground. Black waves lapped the surface but there was absolutely no one about, neither bathers nor spectators nor attendants. The waters were as black as night. Somewhere above I could hear the junior doctors laughing and playing.

But where was I supposed to go but down? With the other stick figures I entered the pool. The slope was surprisingly severe and pretty soon I was up to my neck. What could a naked man do? 'No one digs a hole from the ground to the sky' (my mother). The smell was pretty bad. After a few minutes I started to lose feeling in my arms and legs. This is it, I thought, the deep end at last. I was calmer than you'd expect, though. I felt numb rather than cold. When I looked down I couldn't even see myself. My belly, my trunks, the little gold key – all had gone. Darkness seemed to surround me. Yet, though my eyesight was fading fast, I could just about make out a sign on the wall next to me. No petting, no bombing, no splashing. Aye, that's right, I thought: no petting, no bombing, no nothing. And then the waters claimed me.

Three Cuts

Roshi Fernando

My mother shouts, 'He is come! He is come! Hurry!' and the scratch of mice feet, I can hear, as I lie still and quiet on the bed, and voices in the garden and the clean cut of a spade through dark earth. At the front of the house, my elder sister Javotte shouts for me, 'Hele! Hele!' and I hear birds singing, their twittering, their excitement, for he is come, and we are to know what will happen next.

I wonder whether they asked my younger sister to clean up after me? Which box did she put me in? I thought to search the house would be a good beginning. I went up to the dressing room and found the sofa was clean. She must have scrubbed it for hours, for I bled and bled. I looked on the mantelpiece, in the silver tinder box. Nothing. I looked in her workbasket, and found only pins in a velvet cushion, a needle case made from her home-made felt. I watched her dye the wool red with bark, then on the kitchen table rub it and rub it, rub it and rub it; soapy and matted, it became itself. And she cut it and sewed it and shaped it. Into a little book for needles, tied with ribbon.

It's playing up down there. Sometimes, it does. My legs too, sometimes they just won't move. Javotte shouts again 'Hele! Would you just come? He brings the shoe!' Yes, I heard he would bring the shoe, but I know who it will fit. It will be Javotte – she is the eldest. I am the second daughter, and I have found I'm good for nothing but diplomacy. Go between, and quiet reader, that is my lot, and if Javotte were to marry him, I would be happy, for her tongue would slap him and not me, with her demands and wily manipulations. I would not mind, and nor would our sister, who even now I hear in the room next door, shut in for pity's sake.

'Hele!' my mother calls, and I sit straight up on my bed, smooth the hair, feel the heavy lack between my legs. Pain and nothing there, where once there was – something.

When Javotte tries it on, it does not fit. My mother says, 'Hele must try too! But Javotte, I need to see you in the kitchen, my dear,' and she looks at me with eyes that tell me to stay where I am, stay with my foot suspended above the shoe. I look at the men. They are bored. I say out loud, 'Can you save me please?' and they both looked startled. 'Help me?' The older man coughs. He has blue eyes, but his face is brown. His moustache is flecked with grey and red and black hair like a squirrel's tail. His nose is splayed and the pores on it look like pock marks. I say, 'I can pay you. I have this,' and I show them both my necklace. Pearls and diamonds. They look, but they do not see the necklace, they see the flesh beneath.

When Javotte is in the carriage and firmly on her way, my mother calls my sister and me to the kitchen. My sister is behind me and holds my hand hard. Mother looks at the corner. It is a painting in its way. A three-legged wooden stool, lying on its side. The sun pooling on the grey floor, the knife lying there in the middle of it all. By the fire, the familiar carbon grey of our kitchen knife, the red mess sliming the handle and the blade. I see flecks of flesh there too, and I shrink away. Javotte's big toe, her scold's toe, the one my father said would make her husband unhappy, there, next to the knife, alone now, her sorority carried away by the stranger.

My sister moves forward and pulls me with her.

'We must,' she says. My sister is unclean. She is whole below her stays. She may sweep and wash but she may not touch food nor wine. If she should marry, the organ she carries down there would kill her husband. She would be an unreliable wife. Her labia would poison the milk. I know this. My mother told me. My sister picks up Javotte's toe as if it were a baby mouse, as if it were a friend of hers. She takes a wooden box from the mantelpiece, the one she carries to light the fires. She empties the tinder and, tearing a piece of plain muslin from her underskirts, wraps the toe within it. I am in pain again, and she sees me wince.

'Come, sit. Do you bleed again?' she asks. She dresses me: my hair in plaits and curls, my ears with cherry blossom, my skirts of silk and taffeta and my wounds. She washes them clean, bringing warm salt water and bandages. When she finishes, she rolls silk stockings up my legs, and pulls my skirts down again. I watch her from my window, taking the bloody water to the squashes in the furthest patch. How the pumpkins grow!

I was tricked. They said they had a surprise, for me, for my husband. Come to the dressing room, they said. I went directly, anticipatory, the door opening with a measuring tape click. I see Javotte's eyes now as she turned suddenly, the eyes of a woman. She smiled, and Mother smiled, and behind their rustle, a woman in black, and laid on her table a set of instruments. My younger sister sang in the kitchen, I remember. Undress! I was told. Quickly undress!

I had never undressed or dressed without my younger sister's help. Javotte came toward me and tugged and pulled at ribbons and strings. My hair came undone. The flowers fell from my breast. I stepped from the yellow skirts, and my mother said, 'Remove the petticoats. I had never removed the petticoats myself, so my mother came and untied them carefully with cold fingers. I stood in my pantaloons and my shift. The woman smiled, and pointed her chin at my legs. Remove the pantaloons, my mother said. I knew how to lower these, but had never taken them away from my private places in front of others before. My mother and Javotte moved toward me, and I stepped back.

'What sort of dressmaker is this?' I asked them all. The three walked toward me until my legs met the sofa. Javotte held my knees, looking out toward the orchard. My mother held my shoulders, leant down on my chest.

'You will be clean for the Prince. Beautiful for the Prince,' she cooed.

'No odours!' the tailor cackled.

'And beautiful soon,' Javotte entreated.

With a sharp blade, she took my finest feather, my sweetest pleasure, and the round, small wings sliced clean off. And then she sewed it all up, leaving a tiny hole. I screamed enough for my younger sister to leap two flights like a swallow.

'Hele! What is wrong?'

And Javotte met her at the door, saying, 'Your turn will come, Cinderella.'

Javotte is returned to us the next day. The bleeding will not stop, we are told. But it is not her toe they talk of. The prince has tried. The tailor was called who loosed the stays. The prince tried again, and tight and satisfying as it was, he realises now he made a mistake: Javotte is not beautiful like the girl who lost the slipper. Javotte will not twirl a ballroom again with a crippled foot.

He will return tomorrow, he tells my mother. He is certain when he followed the beauty home from the ball she came to our house. My mother says: 'Your turn tomorrow, Hele!'

Javotte is on all fours in the corner of the kitchen, searching, searching. When Mother leaves the room, my sister gives Javotte the tinder box, and Javotte takes the little package from it, unwraps the muslin and tenderly extracts her toe. She kisses it, puts it down to the scabbed foot. The bloody end is silver and green, iridescent like a bubble from soap. Or bacon gone bad.

I keep on looking for my precious pieces. I look in the music room. I look in the cellar, where the coal makes my skirts black dusty dead. I sit on the bottom stair in the hall and look at the road with its travellers going by. And when I hear the trumpets singing his arrival, I wait patiently for the next moment of bleeding.

It is not important what happens to me. She cut my foot, my heel. I have no real sympathy for a heel, no real nostalgia for a part of my foot that is so integral, the place that meets the earth, the round pocket that cushions my fall. In a shoe, a heel can be done without. And the cutting of the wounds, so new, so fresh – one mess after another. I have learnt to be quiet. I have learnt to understand that pain is what others guide you to. When his parts push into the hole, it is as if he would comfort me. As if he says – this part of me fills up that part of you missing. He hurts me, he fills me, he comes away. I take it, take it and flee my body back home to my sisters who sit by the fire and think of me. I sit with them, and we hold each other. And when his mess mixes with mine, he prods me off the bed, which is covered in my blood. He calls for water and help and they wrap me in a sheet and take me home. I bleed and bleed – my foot, my entrance, my eyes. From my eyes, the blood is transparent.

'Have you another daughter?' I hear the prince's steward ask from my place with my sisters next to the fire.

'She is unclean sir.'

'Bring her forth,' the steward cries. Javotte prods my sister forward. Javotte sees my sister's chance as her own. No honour lost, if Cinders wins! I cry out, 'No!' and pale they all are as they look at me seeping to death. My mother ushers the steward upstairs. No one to send for the tailor, she calls for the crone at the end of the garden. Some say she is a witch. The crone comes with a broken scythe blade.

'I will hold her down,' my mother says.

The crone nods politely. Her hair is white and scatters about her face. There is magic about her.

'Bring me beans from the garden,' she says to my mother. Mother goes and picks dark purple french beans. The crone places a bean in Javotte's lap, and another in my own. She mutters some words, and light springs from her fingers so that pudenda bud between our legs.

'Bring me doves from the dovecote,' she says. Mother brings two doves, and again, magic words are cast, and dove wings sprout from our pelvic bones. The doves grow new wings and fly away.

'Bring me a courgette and a beef tomato,' she says. And my sister runs to the garden and brings both. The courgette becomes Javotte's toe. The tomato my new red heel.

'And now for Cinders,' the crone says. She takes her rusty scythe from her basket and says, 'Who will hold her down?' Javotte stands up. Javotte takes the knife that chopped her and stabs our mother through the heart. I hear the trumpet scream.

'He is come,' I say. My mother's heart pumps onto the kitchen floor.

'And you?' the crone asks me. I take the scythe. He knocks on the door. The crone says, 'And you?' and I say, 'No, please no,' because of course, my mother is alive, I bleed still, Javotte sits near dead. And it is my sister's turn next.

Neptune's Palace

Christine Harrison

When the journey began, of a winter's morning, it was pitch dark. By the fourth stop you could see, more or less, what was out there. There was light by the seventh stop – journey's end for Colin.

The seven ten was two battered carriages strung together and pulled by a spent-looking engine. It waited, covered in frost or dew, for its usual little crowd and pulled out at ten past or thereabouts. Sometimes it pulled out earlier than it should – getting things over with. It was an effort every weekday morning for Colin to board it. It wasn't like travelling. It took you somewhere else, that's all – somewhere you didn't particularly want to go. In spite of all this he could not deny the mournful charm of the journey with its gradual emergence from darkness into light.

The view, when it appeared, was sullen scrubland, huddled sheep, and later, melancholy estuary and mudflats, cheered only by its bird life.

There were almost always the same people on the train who kept to their usual carriage, and if possible sat in their usual seat. They had the look of black and white woodcuts – that chunky, slightly dreary look. Not dreary exactly. More a sort of heavy dullness, as if they were not really living people, each was in his bit of space separate from the others. There was one man who always occupied a corner seat and kept his gaze on the passing countryside.

What with one thing and another the journey would have been almost unbearable but for one oasis of interest. Colin's heartbeat always quickened as the train approached it. The carriage would take on a different aspect and loving feelings well up in him. He regarded, for a short while, the other passengers with a glimmering of goodwill – though amazed and relieved that no one else seemed to notice, seemed hardly to spare a glance, for the thing which made his heart leap.

Neptune's Palace, it was called.

Just before it, the train rattled over a bridge, across mudflats. Then there it was, isolated, not in a village or near houses or near anything, just the mudflats and Neptune's Palace. The sight of it made his journey possible. His life's journey easier.

In the half-light, there it stood. It loomed with a brave jauntiness, an actorish bravado. Classical columns each side of the door, a painted lintel and antique lettering proclaimed

Entertainments

Music

Pictures of mermaids adorned it.

It spoke of life's promise.

And the train stopped here – the station just alongside the Palace – a station where no one ever got on or off. This station seemed to be just for any possible clients of Neptune's Palace. The shaft of joy was prolonged as the train went through a short tunnel throwing images of what he had seen, as in a cave painting.

But for this, the whole business of his life was killing him. He knew that slowly, with careful steps, he was being stalked. A shadowy figure watched from behind winter trees, from across wet pavements. Some ruffian footpad perhaps, poor and ragged, followed him, always at a little distance.

Only when he turned his mind to the mermaids combing their hair, so beautiful and self absorbed as they flicked their tails at the sea horses floating in their fixed way on the painted sea, only at such times was he reminded of life's glamorous promise, and cheered up.

So it was with peculiar excitement, after he had endured the journey to and from work for three years, that one morning in April the train, having made its bridal way through flowering banks of blackthorn, stopped briefly as usual, and Colin glimpsed a young girl coming through the painted door of Neptune's Palace. She slipped out of the door like a fish. Such a slip of a girl. Come into the world for the first time. Brown hair neither long nor short, an olive skin, bare legs.

Colin willed her towards the path that led to the station platform, white with blown blossom. He willed her onto the train and she slipped on with a second to spare. She sat opposite him.

'I'm a dancer,' she said, 'and a trapeze artiste.' He watched her falling through space. 'In the evening I dance on the tables.' Someone rattled his newspaper with a slitting sound.

The girl was wearing a tangerine-coloured summer dress and her blue cardigan had moth holes in the sleeves. She shivered.

'Are you cold?' Colin wanted to warm her, stop her shivering. He leant towards her as far as he dare. 'It's still only April,' he said. Perhaps she had come recently from a warm country. Italy probably. (She had some sort of accent.) Come without her coat. 'Never seen you before on this train.' Nor will again, she told him. 'We're off to somewhere else.'

'Where will you go?' He wanted to know with a desperate intensity.

'Just on the move – just out of this place.' She got up lightly on her dancer's feet. With alarm and deathly sorrow he realised she was going to get off at the next stop.

'Where will you go?' he said in a clear, stern voice.

'Maybe Bristol,' she said, giving a little shrug of her shoulders as if used to fending off unwanted questions.

She stepped off the train at another remote station in the rain. There were no houses in sight, only wet fields with lambs and further off a dismal stone quarry.

He had let her go.

After that he looked out for her every day even though she was possibly in Bristol. He even took to making the journey on Saturdays. There were no trains on Sunday. This went on for several weeks and the sight of Neptune's Palace became harder and harder to bear. Things went on in this slavish way, but nothing goes on for ever.

One summer morning the train stopped at the station alongside Neptune's Palace and broke down there. It was as if it had given up.

After a while everyone got off the train. At first they sat about on the little platform in a forlorn way, but later began to chat to one another, at first tentatively and then in a lively way until there was a buzz of conversation. Someone began organising a cup of tea in the little waiting room – the driver had set out on foot to the nearest signal box. 'We'll be here all day,' said someone happily.

Colin climbed over the stile next to the platform and went over to Neptune's Palace, his heart drumming in his ribcage.

As he came close he realised there was something

strangely insubstantial about it. It wasn't a real building as he had thought. It was a façade. He opened the door from which the girl had slipped out, but it opened onto the landscape behind. He walked through the door only to find himself looking at the mudflats and sky. It was a stage set of some kind. Behind the reinforced plywood façade there were several large packing cases lying around. The head of Neptune himself peered out of one of them, his stone curls and eyes that were not stone, blind but painted on, and flashing angrily to be boxed up like this away from the sea.

In the stillness of this spell-stopped place, Colin was held in a terrible grip. Around him strong shadows were thrown up like prison bars. When he looked up he saw a sheet of lead being drawn implacably across the sky. He looked down into one of the packing cases, wondering if he could climb in and perhaps eventually be transported to wherever Neptune's Palace was bound. At the bottom of the packing case was a stone foot broken off at the ankle. He thought it the most dreadful thing he had ever seen.

At last, trembling, his heart now battering against his breast, he went back to the platform, where everything was humming with pleasure and good humour. 'Do you take sugar?' someone asked. After an hour or so a leisurely engine appeared in its benign way to take the passengers on the rest of their journey.

But after this event the daily journey to work took on a different atmosphere altogether. The passengers greeted each other by name. They chatted about their families, contents of their newspapers and the weather. Colin could not bear it. The journey lost even its mournful silence, and then one day he saw that Neptune's Palace had gone. It simply wasn't there anymore. Perhaps only a ghostly reflection remained in the sky and against the mudflats. Colin wondered if he had imagined the whole thing, even the girl. The entire journey was now torture to him. He gave in his notice at work and moved to Bristol. A man can stand only so much. He found another job and spent his evenings searching the places of entertainment for the girl with the look of Italy about her.

After two more years of this, hope left him and he met and married a thin fair-haired women called Karen who worked in the shipping office; she was a quiet woman, sensible, stoical and kind. They had a little boy and called him Brian, and Karen gave up work to look after him. Colin still sometimes roamed the streets of Bristol: it was a habit he had got into. One wet evening he surprised the footpad on the Christmas steps – after some other quarry, no doubt. Soaked to the skin, his clothes hanging off him. Poor wretch.

Trains were no longer part of Colin's life. He went to work on a motorbike. Once a year though, the family took the train to Weymouth to stay for a week's holiday in a guesthouse. They had bed and breakfast. They always ate a big breakfast which lasted them all day until early evening when they got fish and chips. Karen always bought a souvenir of their holiday. At home she had all these arranged on the mantelpiece; I'll put you here for a change, she would say as she dusted and rearranged them.

It was on one of these holidays that Colin caught a glimpse of the Italian girl. A train was pulling slowly into the station which ran alongside the sea. She did not smile or wave and neither did he. He wasn't sure if she had recognised him but he looked much the same, being one of those men who scarcely alter with age. She looked the same to him for he saw her inward self. There was not two of her in the world. She was wearing a nice hat with red flowers of some sort.

His whole life was overturned by this encounter. All the rest of the week it was as if he were mad. Restlessly he combed the streets of Weymouth. He glimpsed her in cafes but it turned out to be someone else. He saw her running just as she had run in the rain that day – when he had not followed her, when he had not jumped off the accelerating train and followed her. He saw her half hidden behind curtains in Georgian houses and did not knock the brass knockers. He was in hell. What was the use of the rest of the world? He stopped eating. He could not eat his breakfast and Karen shared it out between herself and her little boy who especially liked fried bread with tomato sauce on it. Karen pocketed the leftover toast for later. She would try her best not to have the holiday spoiled. Her husband had turned into a complete stranger.

On the day before the holiday was over it was hot and inclined to thunder. It was as if Colin's life was running out like the sand in the egg-timer souvenir of Weymouth that Karen had bought. But that afternoon Colin happened to see, as in a vision, a poster which proclaimed:

Neptune's Palace will come alive
at the railway station at 7pm

The poster was like an illuminated scroll decorated with mermaids and beautiful scaly fish.

Trapeze Artistes
Jugglers
Fire Eaters
Mermaid's Cavern Extra

Weak from lack of food as he was, Colin nearly fainted. Without stopping to recover he went to the beach to look for Karen and Brian.

'That'll be nice,' said Karen, not commenting on his pallor. 'How much is it?' Kneeling in the sand she offered her husband a piece of bread and butter. 'Are you hungry?' she asked him, but he did not hear her. 'How much is it to get in?' she said slowly.

He frowned.

'We needn't go into the Mermaid's Cavern,' he said.

'What's a mermaid?' asked Brian looking up from his sandcastle. 'Can I go in the mermaid's cavern?'

'We'll see,' said his mother.

That evening at seven o'clock, Colin led his wife and little boy through the façade which said Neptune's Palace to the railway station behind.

'Why are they having it in a railway station?' whispered Karen.

'I don't know.' Colin sounded impatient. His eyes looked quite cruel and crazy. Perhaps it was the light off the sea.

'What is that lady doing up there?' shouted Brian. He pointed up to the girders of the station high above them.

'Be quiet,' said Colin.

'Where's the Mermaid's Cavern?'

'Ssh, it's extra,' said his mother.

The girl with the look of Italy swooped down time after time like a ravishing swallow. A drum rolled. Then silence. Then she swooped. There was no safety net.

Afterwards Colin led his family blindly from the place. Brian had picked up coloured shiny scales like confetti from the platform; he threw them over his father.

'What's a mermaid, Dad?' he shouted in his shrill voice.

'Is it a fish? Or is it a lady? Why has that man with the drum got his coat done up with safety pins, don't like him.'

Next day they spent the morning on the beach. There had been a thunderstorm in the night and everything looked different. Wilder and cleaner. Yapping dogs chased balls of seaweed rolled about by the wind, and Brian's castle was washed away. But there were fresh footprints in the smooth damp sand. Colin stared at them for a long time, then he said, 'It's time to get on the train.'

Karen and Brian fell asleep leaning against each other on the journey home.

Soon the train slid quietly into a tunnel. It was a long tunnel and Colin thought he would see the girl swooping in her bright spangles or looking out of the train in her hat with red flowers or running in the rain or even sitting shivering as she had years ago when he first saw her.

He summoned these pictures to the walls of his black cave but they did not come. Instead he too fell asleep and dreamed of a man in an old raincoat done up with a safety pin, feeding the birds.

'I am your quietus,' he told Colin. 'I have been following you for ages.' He spoke in a matter-of-fact voice. 'I've caught up with you. You hardly ever noticed me for I am a quiet person.'

When Colin woke they were in the next tunnel which was even longer. He saw only a deep darkness lit sometimes by flares, but leading into an even deeper darkness, the flares fainter and fainter as if they had shown him only so far. And so he slept on.

The train pulled into Bristol. The platform was busy but Colin straight away saw who was waiting for him. The sun had come out after rain, the platform shone and a stranger who was not a stranger was waiting calmly for him. There he was sitting on the bench, his hair neatly combed, dressed in an everyday ordinary suit, a little worn but respectable as if he had done his best for the occasion, the raincoat folded over his arm – no doubt to hide the safety pin. He was feeding the pigeons, legs stretched out in front of him. Seeing Colin, he raised his hand in greeting and recognition, a bright smile on his face. Colin had expected a rougher sort of fellow.

The Pit

Jon Gower

Workers at Wales' last remaining deep pit, Tower Colliery near Hirwaun, had to abandon work yesterday when human remains were found in a recently excavated drift. Two bones, believed to be a femur and part of the collarbone, were taken away by police and are being examined at the Forensics Department in Bridgend.

Broadcast on BBC's *Good Morning Wales,* 6.9.07

The tunnels are long and preternaturally dark. Down there naked eyes are useless. In such recesses, where there isn't so much as a glint or a hint of light, the ears are forced to compensate, so the sound of a scurrying rat seems swollen to twice its size, the rustle of hairs on its rancid pelt like brushfire. This is the darkest labyrinth, the passageways connected in ways that no one remembers nowadays, now that the mine entrances are padlocked. After what happened down there.

There's a myth among miners that a robin sighted underground is a portent of death. A shot lighter was reported to have seen no fewer than four robins in a shaft at Caled Number Four.

Known by some as 'the deadliest colliery in Christendom', Caled Number Four near the village of Maerdy was opened in 1873. It was one of the biggest employers in the industry as a whole. Three thousand and three men sweated and coughed there. Miners were like ants burrowing into Allt y Fedwen following an incline called the Trimsaran Sink. The secondhand winding gear above ground was arthritic: when the big wheel turned it made the sound of a badger being flayed.

First timers, twelve or thirteen year olds on their virgin shift, would double-take when they saw the shot lighter who was blind and had to be shown where to place his fuses and how to light them. The man also had the shakes. But despite the creakingness of the machinery and the oddity of some of the senior men, Caled Number Four had rich seams of luscious coal, producing masses of hard nuggets which were long-burning and sought after by the British Navy for their Ironsides. But there was always something curious about the workings. Lit by candles, in defiance of marsh gas, surveyors who measured the growing tunnels could never quite make their sums add up. There always seemed to be more space than accounted for by their instruments. Roofways seemed twenty feet higher than they actually were. There were caverns that might have belonged to a forgotten race, halls of lost kings, troglodyte rulers of the darkness under the land.

Davy Jones was a miner in Caled Number Four, though everyone called him Cross Eyes. When he was born they said that storm clouds had galloped down from the hills and lightning had struck the tree outside his mother's room. He was a lonely child because other children were merciless and the only friend he had was a gimpy girl who ran on sticks because of polio. She was called Catherine and kissed him once, full on the lips before apologising and saying she had the mumps. His parents were of that hard generation that never gave him love, so he grew up a stunted flower.

But he did get married, to a scrawny little thing called Anne he met after chapel on the Monkey Walk, who loved him like life itself. They had a child even though neither could work out how exactly that came about. They rented a tiny terraced cottage above the canal with money he borrowed at a high rate of interest from his dad and bought two fine chairs so they could sit of an evening and discuss the previous Sunday's sermon. Davy might have said he was happy then. His wife's porcelain skin in the flickering light. The metronome ticking and tocking of his grandmother's grandfather clock. New potatoes from the garden where he'd planted autumn's peelings and saw them return and take shape under the soil. But it was a brief happiness. The work at the mine dried up just before the General Strike and because he was proud and stubborn like his parents, Davy couldn't ask them for help when the money dwindled. He watched his wife turn skeletal and his baby run out of life. First the bawling of the baby stopped, then his whimpering, and finally Thomas stopped breathing. Anne faded like the last note on a pipe. So he had a bag of bones for a wife and a grey lump of flesh for a son.

His wife only lingered on this earth for some days. Davy had to live with the image of the two tiny coffins in the graveyard at Gerazim, borne so lightly. It was an afternoon of sleeting rain. Davy's parents died soon after, leaving him alone to contemplate the savagery of his personal God. *Duw Cariad Yw* is what the Bible said. God is Love.

When the local mines reopened after the Strike, some of the former workers were so rickety from lack of nutrition that their hips snapped underground. One man's elbows broke when he reached for a rope. Another broke a vertebra just looking up. And among the legion of the starved, the most pitifully lean was Davy, with his pipe-cleaner legs and flesh so thin you'd swear you could see his heart beating if he left his shirt collar open wide enough. Some days, as he chipped forward with bandaged hands to soak up the blood, he heard his son's crying as clearly as the church bell.

Davy might have worked out his days on earth in Number

Four were it not for a tragic day when a runaway spake smithereened a dozen pit props as it careened its way down one of the deepest tunnels, breaking men's bodies like snapping chicken bones. Hitting the bottom, the reverberations set off a rumbling reaction in the earth and almost all of Caled's labyrinth of tunnels collapsed amid whirlwinds of cloying dust.

He might have been concussed for a day or more. When Davy opened his eyes he could see nothing in the pitch dark but was aware of a burning pain in his right shoulder which had been severed from its arm by a falling mass of coal. The weight of it pressing down on him had staunched the flow of blood, had near cauterised it, while threatening to collapse his rib cage. The arm lay there in the dark, its fingers, despite the congealing of the blood, still making attractive suckling for a rat, the only other living animal in the tunnels. He coughed, and Davy could hear nothing other than the tiny claws of the animal scarpering, his blood on its whiskers.

He had no sense of time other than the rate at which his hunger gnawed inside. It grew in intensity so that his mind was filled with images of cauldrons of his mam's cawl, with luscious aromas. He had visitations of marmalade, bore witness to hallucinations featuring sides of hanging ham.

On the third day Davy casually picked up the limb and sucked his own forearm, knowing that meat lasted long underground, something about the air, or the depth away from the sun, or the near absence of microbial life. It was a white taste and without thinking about it he drove his incisors into the meat and started tearing chunks away from the tendons. He carried on until he was sated and at that point the rush of nutrition gave him sufficient strength to attempt to lift the fractured spar of wood that had him pinned to the floor. It lifted, slowly at first, but then with magical strength, he lifted it as though it were balsa. On his hand and knees he crawled along the floor, fingers splayed out before him, searching in the dust for a candle, which he lit with the flint box he always carried with him.

It was a garden of broken limbs, white tulip hands breaking through the dust stratum, faces of his friends now flattened or wrecked out of recognition, staring at him like dumb watermelons. He ate William Trefor's buttocks over a three-day period, savouring the vague hint of carbolic soap which adhered to his skin. Him being a miner, William's obsessive cleanliness had always provided a topic of conversation.

As he grew braver, Davy started on soft parts, spilled brain matter. The goodness hoovered up from Matthew Dunvant's stomach, along with a last supper of partly digested cheese and bread. Except for the sinewy footballers, he found some of the younger colliers quite succulent.

It was only on the fifteenth day that Davy managed to stand up straight in one of the chamber tunnels. By now his candles were long expired but he had found two places where the tiniest glimmers of light filtered through along with rainwater which pooled dangerously now that the pumps were no longer working. His nails felt strong as he started to scratch on a soft patch of coal and he found that soon he was making real progress, especially when he started to use his teeth as well, biting off gobbets of coal and spitting them out even as his nails made a high screeching noise.

He made it into the next colliery in the valley and decided to lie in wait, a lizard waiting for a fly. The father of three he snapped up was trailing his butties on the way back to the spake when Davy nabbed him, dispatching him with a spade. He dragged him into an air vent and started with the eyes, as if he were eating caramels.

And so he continued – always on the move – snacking as he went, or if he got a fat one staying awhile so that he grew plumper – reserves of energy he drew on as he moved across the coalfield. From feast to famine he went, investigating closed workings and thriving mines, able to gnaw through the earth like a rat through a ship's hawser. On and on, forever hungry and seldom sated. Blaenyrhaca. Pergwm. Abercwmnedd. Tyle One and Tyle Two. Along Ogmore and Rhumney, shadowing the rivers in their courses and unlocking floods of terror.

In 1963 there was a sighting. A hydrologist, checking out some pipe casings in the pit in Wyattstown heard a strange scuffling sound and then saw a deformed man run down a tunnel. By the time his description had been repeated around a frightened village the man had grown: his globular cross eyes were the size of dinner plates, like a gargantuan barn owl with a squint. The man's nails were those of a pantomime Mandarin and his deformed hump of a back thrashed around in the collective imagination like an eel arching on dry land. The teeth, man, they were as big as stalactites! I heard he chased this man and ran so fast he only got away by wriggling out of his coat! After that, teams armed with police truncheons were sent to check out every part of the mine, but to no avail. The monster was made of Scotch mist. He seeped away like a breath of methane.

It was Prime Minister Margaret Thatcher who did for Davy. As she took on the unions and closed down the mines throughout the United Kingdom, so too did she neutralise Davy's source of food. But there were side benefits to the Thatcher era for Davy, too. The police had less money to spend on trying to catch the monster that the popular imagination had cast like a Grendel inhabiting the land of fear. The National Coal Board was forced to up the danger money for anyone who worked underground. Police investigators over the decades remained dumbfounded that they hadn't so much as a single decent clue to go on.

And then the last pit in Wales closed and Davy could no longer smell so much as a molecule of new prey, for all his desperate, snuffling peregrinations along drift and through hard surfaces. So he had to leave the subterranean world. He had to go to the Overground, where meat was plentiful. He managed to make his home there, found a way to live. Snaring and surviving, stalking unwitting prey, along the empty aisles of late night supermarkets.

Recently there was another sighting, behind the loading bay of Tesco's in Llansamlet. But not enough of a sighting for the scared man to tell his mates, as he'd been drinking on shift.

He'd seen a man seemingly bent over on himself, dragging something heavy in the direction of the overspill car park.

Davy'd nabbed a fat man behind household goods, stunned him with a brick, then swiftly pulled him through some plastic flaps into the stockroom and through the back doors where some men were unloading pallets. Pulling the carcass swiftly now, as if it were on a sled, he got it out onto the ramp and pulled it with a dull thump to the ground, his actions urged on by hunger.

Safe in a clump of rhododendron, Davy scrutinised his victim: plenty there for a long feast. The miner got out a knife, a fork and a threadwire saw, ideal for cutting bone. He started carving, pulling back the delicate thin meat over the forehead with all the care in the world.

The White Mountain

Charlotte Greig

Môn Gwyn Studios, Tuesday 6th January 2009

I can't believe what's been happening here. I don't need this hassle. I've come up to Môn Gwyn to work, but the place is doing my head in. I can't think straight. I feel like I'm going nuts. It must be the mushroom tea Arianrhod's been giving me, or maybe the spliffs that Brân keeps rolling. Whatever it is, it's got to stop.

I'm sure if I write this all down, I can make sense of it. The trouble is, it's so weird up here. I feel as though I've stepped into another dimension. It's always so dark, so wet. The mist hangs in the air, the trees drip in the rain, the wind whines around the windows, and you start to feel worn down by it, as though you'll never have the energy to escape…

…or worse, that you don't want to escape, even if you could….

Right. Enough of that, Gwydion Griffiths. Get a grip on yourself. Write it all down now. Begin at the beginning. Then you'll know where you are.

Okay. Here goes, then. This is the story.

I came up here yesterday – God, was it only yesterday? – on the train from Cardiff. It's a weird train, it is. Small and packed, with an odd collection of passengers getting on and off. A hippie girl with a ferret in a basket, for instance. It kept poking its nose out and looking at me. I could tell she liked me, this girl, especially when she saw my guitar. She asked me where I was going, and I said I was off to a studio to record my first album. What label are you on, she asked, and when I told her, I could see she was impressed. She asked me my name, so she could look out for the album. I didn't ask hers. She wasn't my type. One of those Celtic goth girlies, all *Lord of the Rings* and tongue piercings.

Anyway, when I got off, Brân was there to meet me. He's the studio's resident engineer. Nice guy, bit older than me, around thirty maybe. We got into his car and he brought out a spliff, and we drove along all these tiny little roads in the rain, up hill and down dale, past all these waterfalls cascading down the mountainsides, and it was so atmospheric, I thought, this is going to be great.

When we got to Môn Gwyn, I almost burst out laughing. The house was like something out of a Hammer Horror. Big iron gates, and beyond them, at the end of a long drive, this crumbling gothic mansion, with turrets, pointy windows, stone lions, the lot. When you got near it, it didn't look quite so good: in fact it was all falling to pieces. But it was still amazing.

Inside, more of the same. A massive old wooden staircase leading up to the bedrooms. Brân took me up. I was staying in the best one, he said, which made me feel good. It was incredible, completely round, because it was in one of the turrets. It faced out over a huge front lawn with a big palm tree in the middle. Above us, Brân said, was Môn Gwyn itself, the white mountain, but you couldn't see it today because of the clouds. In fact, he said, you hardly ever saw it, because the weather was always so terrible up here.

Brân went off to the studio, which was in one of the outbuildings, and I said I'd be down in a minute. After he'd gone, I stood looking out of the window. As I did, the clouds parted for a moment and I caught sight of the mountain. It was sparkling white, covered in snow. I was excited, elated. Here I was, on my first visit to the studio, and already I'd seen it. I thought it must be a good omen. I tried to take a picture on my mobile, but just as I pressed the button, the clouds closed in again, so all I got was a load of drifting grey mist.

When I went over to the studio, Brân and I got straight down to work. I ran through the songs while he scuttled about placing microphones and getting levels. It was only me and an acoustic guitar, nothing complicated. But he took a lot of care over it. He's known for getting an incredible sound, whether it's a band or a solo act, which was why I'd wanted to work with him.

We decided to record all the songs live first, just vocals and guitar, and then think about what, if anything, to put on later. With me, it's the songs that matter, nothing else. If you put too much instrumentation on, it distracts from the song. That's my opinion, anyway, and at last I'd found an engineer who understood what I wanted. Which is pretty rare. They usually want to throw in the kitchen sink.

I was a bit worried about the number of spliffs Brân was smoking, but he seemed to be doing a great job. I was relieved, because I'd chosen the studio, and him, myself. The record company was paying for everything. This was my big chance, and I knew if I blew it, I wouldn't get another.

We worked all day without stopping, and then went over to the house for dinner. I was starving by then, I'd missed lunch on the way up. Brân said that Arianrhod, the woman who owned the studio, always made dinner for her guests, as she called us. She was a good cook, but she had a tendency to take hours over the meal and keep everyone waiting.

We went into the kitchen, a great, dark room with trees outside the window that grew too close to the house. Arianrhod was standing over the cooker with a fag in her mouth, stirring something. When she saw us, she turned around and gave us a big grin. I noticed she had a gap between her two front teeth. I guessed that she was in her early sixties. She'd obviously been very attractive at one time – her eyes, boldly outlined with khol, told me that – but now her face was lined and her hair was grey. She wore it long, as though she was still a young woman. Her gestures, too, were those of a young woman – flirtatious, tactile. When she laughed, which she did quite often, she threw her head back and tossed her hair, showing her wrinkled throat.

We sat down to dinner and she brought over the food. It was some kind of vegetable casserole with couscous. She and Brân were vegetarians, she told me, and I told her I was trying to be. The food was ace – spicy, warm, and sweet, like a Moroccan tagine. I complimented her on it. Thank you, Gwydion, that's very sweet of you to say so, she replied, and then she and Brân laughed. I wondered if there was anything going on between them.

We all drank quite a bit, red wine it was, and I was so tired and overexcited it went straight to my head. Arianrhod kept calling me 'darling' and leaning forward to fill my glass. Each time she did, I caught a glimpse of her cleavage. Fair play, it didn't look too bad, though it was a bit crinkled at the top. I didn't know whether she was flashing it at me on purpose or whether that was just her style. Brân had told me that she'd been a pop star in the sixties. Arianna Black, her name was. I'd never heard of her. But anyway, she carried on the way a woman like that would, giving Brân an eyeful as well as me, so I didn't take it personally. Not at that stage.

After dinner, Brân lit up another spliff and Arianrhod asked us if we'd like some of this mushroom tea she'd made. *Tisane*, she called it. I wasn't very keen at first. I wanted to make sure I kept a clear head for the next day, but she said it was pretty weak, that it would help me sleep, dream sweet dreams. So in the end I gave in.

The tisane tasted odd, woody and bitter, but I finished my cupful, just to be polite. Brân passed the spliff around, and then, when we were all pretty stoned, they started joking about the house being haunted. Apparently, the ghost of a thirteenth-century Welsh princess called Gwenllian, who'd been imprisoned in a castle nearby, came out at night and wandered about moaning. But she only appeared if the white mountain was visible, and because of the dreadful weather, that wasn't likely to happen any time soon.

When I went to bed that night I didn't worry too much about the ghost to be honest. The weed and the mushroom tea – *tisane*, I mean – knocked me out straight away, and immediately my head hit the pillow, I fell asleep. I slept like a log. And then, around four in the morning, I suddenly woke up.

The room was bathed in white light. For a moment, I didn't know what was going on. And then I looked over at the window, and I realised I'd left the curtains open. Outside was the white mountain, looming up at me, covered in snow. There was a full moon above it, and a dazzling array of stars all around it. Over the summit, there was a pale streak in the sky that must have been the Milky Way.

I caught my breath. I'd never seen anything so beautiful in my whole life. The snow on the mountain seemed to be luminous, pulsating. I began to wonder if the mushrooms were giving me hallucinations.

It was then that I heard a knocking at the door, and a soft moaning. I remembered about the ghost, Princess Gwenllian, and a shudder of fear ran through me. I pulled the duvet closer around me and turned my face to the wall, telling myself it was just the wind. The knocking stopped, and I tried to go to sleep, but I couldn't. Instead, I kept opening my eyes and staring at the wall. It had some hand-painted wallpaper on it in a pattern that made my head ache.

As the minutes ticked by, I began to feel more angry than frightened. Angry with Brân and Arianrhod. I'd come up to this place to make an album, not to piss about getting stoned and listening to a load of crap about ghosts that was going to keep me awake half the night. I'd made a mistake about this studio. I should have gone to a professional place in London. Instead, here I was, halfway up a mountainside with a pair of nutters.

The next thing that happened nearly gave me a heart attack. The door opened and a woman walked in. It was Arianrhod, as far as I could make out. She was wearing some kind of white gown. She walked straight past me and stood in front of the window. In the moonlight, with the mountain glowing behind her, she looked completely different. For a start, her hair had gone black, jet black. I sat up in bed, my heart thumping, and whispered her name.

'Arianrhod. Is that you?'

She didn't reply. Instead, she slowly took off her gown. I watched in horror, and – I must admit – curiosity. Underneath, she was stark naked. I could see the outline of her body, silhouetted against the white of the mountain. She had long, smooth limbs and a slender waist curving to narrow hips. It can't be Arianrhod, I thought, she looks so young. But when she leaned over and stretched out her arms to me, I recognised something in the way she moved, so I shut my eyes.

I can't remember exactly what happened after that. The mist came down, the room went dark, and the woman, whoever it was, came over to my bed. She got in beside me. I was terrified. I wasn't sure if she was Arianrhod or the ghost, but whichever it was, I didn't want her in bed with me. I started to shake with fear, but she leaned over and kissed me on the mouth, and then… well, one thing led to another, and I stopped being scared and got horny instead.

Thinking about it now, it doesn't seem real. And yet it does. So real. Hyper-real, in fact. Whether she was old or young, real or a ghost, I couldn't say. It was pitch black in the room, and I was a bit out of it on the mushrooms. All I know is, she was flesh and blood, no doubt about it, and she really turned me on. Blew me away. Maybe it was the fact that I didn't know who she was. Maybe it was what she did to me. I'm not going into details, mind, but she didn't seem to have any inhibitions at all. Maybe it was that she was so warm and soft and… Oh God, I don't want to think about it any more. I shouldn't have done it. Shouldn't have let her…

Anyway, we went at it pretty hard that night. She wore me out, to tell the truth. I was exhausted by the end of it. I couldn't go on, although she still seemed to want to. Just as it was getting light I thought, I've had enough of this, I've got work to do in the morning. So I turned over and fell asleep, and when I woke up again, she'd gone.

I got out of bed, walked over to the window, and looked up at the mountain. There was nothing to see up there. The clouds had closed over it again. A weak sun was filtering in through the mist, and it was raining – that constant, light drizzle. I looked out at the palm tree in the middle of the lawn. It didn't look as good as it had done the day before. Not as impressive. I noticed that some of the leaves were yellowing, and it was a bit battered at the edges. Probably all this wind and rain, I thought. The wrong type of climate for a palm tree.

As I stood there at the window, Arianrhod came out onto the lawn. She was wearing an old brown anorak and green wellies. Her hair was wet from the rain and hanging in grey strands like rats' tails around her face. In one hand, she carried a black bin bag full of rubbish, and in the other, a fag.

I put up my hand to close the curtains. But just as I did, she looked up and caught sight of me. Her face broke into a broad grin and she waved cheerily. She didn't seem in the least bit fazed by me standing there naked, so I waved back, my free hand covering my private parts. Then she blew me a kiss and went on her way.

I had a shower, got dressed, and went over to the studio. Brân made me tea and toast, and then we got down to work. I didn't say anything about the night before, but to be honest, I couldn't stop thinking about it. It didn't seem to affect my performance, though. We recorded two songs today, and we've got eight to go. If we keep on at this rate, we should have the album finished on schedule, no problem, and there'll be plenty of time for mixing.

After we'd finished working, we went over to the house for dinner again. This time, the food was on the table and Arianrhod was waiting for us, smoking and reading a book. I avoided her eyes as we sat down, and looked away when she leaned over to dole out the food. It was baked potatoes and some kind of quiche type thing. *Pissaladiere,* she called it. I felt uncomfortable when she asked me how much I wanted. Just a small slice, I said. I'm not very hungry.

While we were eating, I couldn't help glancing at her surreptitiously. She was wearing a baggy black jumper instead of the low-cut top, so I couldn't see much of her body, but I thought, there's no way this is the woman who was in my bed last night. No way. Her whole shape was wrong: kind of hunched and bunched and bulging at the waist. An old woman. Nothing like that young girl with the long narrow limbs that I'd seen standing at my window in the moonlight the night before.

Brân started talking about an album he was making himself. Apparently, he'd come up here to record it ten years ago, and ended up staying on as studio engineer. He loved the job, he said. Always working with new people. More bookings than he could handle. But the album still wasn't finished.

I wasn't really listening. My mind was on other things. When we finished eating, Arianrhod brought out the mushroom tisane, but I excused myself, saying I was tired, and came up here to my bedroom. I needed some peace and quiet, time to think.

So now here I am, lying on the bed, writing this by the light of the bedside lamp. The curtains are open. It's pitch black out there. You can't see the mountain, or anything else. I wonder whether I should close them.

I keep asking myself the same question. If it wasn't Arianrhod last night, then who was it? The ghost? There isn't anybody else in the house, I'm sure of that. So either I've been sleeping with a sixty-year-old former pop star or the ghost of a thirteenth-century Welsh princess. Whichever it is, I'm scared I'm losing my mind.

Maybe I'll keep the curtains open. Just for now. If the mist clears and the moon comes out over the mountain, I wouldn't want to miss it.

I've been thinking, I wonder if I should add some more instruments to the album. I could have been wrong about that. It'd take more time, though. Weeks, months even. The record company wouldn't pay. I'd have to finance it myself. Unless of course I offered to help Brân in the studio, in exchange for more recording time…

I really should close those curtains, I suppose. Then again...

Oh shit, this isn't helping, writing it all down. I can't concentrate. My nerves are a jangle. I need to relax. Calm down.

I don't know. Maybe I was wrong about that tisane, too. Maybe I should go downstairs and have a cup after all.

It'll help me get a good night's sleep, won't it. Dream sweet dreams, like Arianrhod said.

Afterword

A Lovely Length of Slippery Ribbon

Gwen Davies

The underworld is imagined in the classics as fringed with willow and black poplar, ringed and riddled with deadly rivers, and guarded by a many-headed fearful dog. A place impossible to reach alive or return from without bribing gods and ferrymen, unless you are Orpheus about to lose your love for a second time, or Persephone off on a summer break sorted by your mother. It is a world where magic, the supernatural and the unexpected are expected, where the present and older, buried worlds overlap, and the dead are only a handshake away. The contemporary stories in *Sing Sorrow Sorrow* grow out of European, Arabian and Russian folk, fable, fairy tale, legend and myth – all porous categories – but they are dark tales which belong specifically to the domain of the underworld. Most have a black and, where necessary, violent twist – perfect for reading at Halloween, or rather the eve of its pagan Celtic predecessor, Samhain. These stories are chilling reading in their own right, but also fascinate in the overshading they make with other dark genres of horror, the ghost story and crime thriller.

Academics of myths assign their function to an explanation of origin and extinction, and as an account for customs and existing social systems. Such scholars have attempted to attach to myths (for example those involving ironworking or the use of horses) particular beliefs and precise historical periods. Revisionist theories, however, place more significance on abiding human nature and imagination. In these readings, ancient story sources play out universal anxieties about deformed babies; slow children and sexualised adolescents; infidelity; infertility; ageing; child abuse; cruel parents; male fear of women and vice versa; addiction; disillusion and the two-way traffic of child-parent murder fantasy. Fear of death and the unfamiliar, of pain and the possibility of afterlife may give rise to narratives with forest settings; bestial and supernatural subjects. Such fears endure and re-emerge even though contemporary writers may update situations and superficialities. Stories of rags to riches such as Cinderella and The Lady of Llyn y Fan tell of the unpredictability of love and money. Meanwhile, our persistent attempts to link endeavour with reward are represented by quest stories such as the labours of Hercules or the affiliated Mabinogion story of Culhwch's quest in *Culhwch ac Olwen*.

Many such concerns feature in this collection alongside themes, images and motifs which echo between stories, telling us about our current preoccupations. Most authors have chosen the direct intimacy of the first person narrative, and a slim majority are also stories told by or of men and boys. Broken limbs and members predominate. You will hear a strange buzzing from carcass-circling insects and murder weapons. Trumpets, conch-horns and whistles sound the alarm. Birds sing of truth and revenge; creatures shrivel and balloon like Alice; some strange animal scampers across your bed at night, and dogs are everywhere. Objects here have the peculiar power of fairy tale. There are mementoes such as a woman's samovar sold by her husband on their departure to her exile; ghastly trophies like a 'lovely length of slippery ribbon' and a slice of scalp, or just practical wooden boxes in which to secrete body bits, babies and the evils of the world. Puck appears in various guises, from old-school hobgoblin, through clubbable gent, to a translator who can interpret any symbol you care to name except his girlfriend's true nature.

Potions, as you'd expect, are powerful and mostly hallucinogenic, but count in their number innocent milk. Apart from one magnificent oasis feast, a tagine or two cooked up by a hippie, and vegetables which grow back missing bits of yourself, food is surprisingly scarce. Corpses are shelled out as hiding places; there is mutilation, blood, pain, gnawed sinews, extracted fingernails and sucked-out eyeballs. Witches, female ghosts and murderesses give the impression of women as feisty and amoral. While other women are hard hit, few are victims without the resources to recover. Men, in the meantime, are rather naïve, especially when in thrall to sexual desire. Blame winks at guilt reflecting back a knack for blanking blame in this hall of mirrors misted with the vapour of violence, murder and death. Addiction is toxic in the air, as are possession and obsession. Sibling rivalry poisons many characters; others are damaged by kidnapping and abuse. Childbirth is a breath away from death, and the complications, guilt and dangers associated with fertility are treated as the serious issues that they are.

The settings of *Sing Sorrow Sorrow* include abandoned villages in Almeria and a Middle-Eastern desert; Wales, Sri Lanka and Tokyo; the circus; a psychiatric consulting room, and a tailor-made shanty town. That folk-tale false utopia, the palace, appears in several guises but is inevitably the place where food must not be taken, women always want you and dreams (a studio session; that clinch with the girl you fancy, reprieve from persecution) may come true. But it is the threshold between worlds that exercises the writers here most.

In two stories this is portrayed as 'a crack' in a doorway which must be left open to release pressure on both sides. In others the underworld gateway appears as a scruffy well, circled with barbed wire; a cellar, lift- or mine-shaft. It is the graveyard wall which a dog, a latter-day Cerberus, vaults to trash the daffodils; the shoreline; a sharp descent in an ice-cream van. You will find it at the hospital or power point, and during grave illness. It is beyond a theatre façade set among mudflats, approached on one side by a railway tunnel and on the other, a bridal arch of blackthorn blossom.

Some see the job of myth as being to bolster national or tribal identity. The underworld locations of the Welsh myths of the Mabinogi and heroic folk stories are not as visually detailed as those in the Greek myths, although their geographical positions are just as precise. In *Sing Sorrow Sorrow* though, the writers of Wales flesh out and reinvent Welsh mythical and folk settings. Our ancestors would not be entirely conversant with the locations of the Welsh-set stories such as the camper van of a dysfunctional New Age family or Tesco's overspill carpark, although Moel Famau mountain and the post-pandemic Denbighshire countryside in Glenda Beagan's story would look unchanged. Jon Gower's valleys' coalfield-inspired labyrinth in 'The Pit' takes in the legacy of strikes, lock-ins, and Thatcher's decimation of the industry. Rhiannon, the teenage protagonist in Imogen Rhia Herrad's 'Rhiannon's Bird' is, like her namesake, determined and wily in the face of sexual threat. The eponymous summit of Charlotte Greig's 'The White Mountain' can only be seen in certain conditions, just like those islands that crop up in Welsh folk tale and mythology. Her characters borrow names – Arianrhod (a variant of Aranrhod), Gwydion and Brân – from the Mabinogi, and she keeps ancient motifs such as the Milky Way, known in Welsh as Caer Aranrhod. The author twists the conventional image of Aranrhod as a heartless bitch who refuses to acknowledge her son despite her brother Gwydion's elaborate ruses. Greig takes away Gwydion's magic and makes him an impressionable twenty-something whose life experience takes in guitar but not the music industry and certainly not the sex life of older women. Here Arian/Aranrhod is part ghost, part hag, part shape-shifting goddess, and all manipulation.

Folk tale and myth began in an ancient oral tradition. Since then they have inevitably been reinvented and repackaged, initially when they were first recorded, into another product with messages for their current readership. For example, the Mabinogi speaks to twelfth-century Christian Wales using themes and characters that reach back many centuries to the pre-Christian era. In the case of fairy story, Perrault reinterpreted and cleaned up folk tales, turning them into suitable seventeenth-century family reading. In the late eighteenth century the Grimm brothers' accounts were of stories gleaned from nursemaids and servants via ladies' parlours, and reflected a Romantic taste for melodrama and violence; these gorier aspects were in their turn tamed in later children's collections and of course in Disney films. The first English translation of the Mabinogion collection was published, in the mid-nineteenth century (1838-49), by scholar Charlotte Guest, who dedicated her masterpiece to her children. But it was not until late in that century that the marketing of Welsh myth and folk tale for a young readership got underway, when a small number of folk tales appeared in Welsh between the covers of O. M. Edwards' magazine, *Cymru'r Plant*. Juvenile English readers early in the following century had access to collections such as W. Jenkyn Thomas' *The Welsh Fairy Book* (T. Fisher Unwin, 1907) By 1955, Gwyn Jones' *Welsh Legends and Folk Tales* (OUP) had come out; this included extracts from his translation with Thomas Jones of *The Mabinogion* published six years earlier by Everyman's Library. By the 1970s, such titles for children had increased in number, with cheap editions and even colouring booklets of the Mabinogi stories available from publishers Y Lolfa. More recently, Gomer Press brought out a particularly outstanding collection: T. Llew Jones' *Lleuad yn Olau*, (1989; available two years later in English, from the same press, as *One Moonlit Night* in a translation by Gillian Clarke).

One motivation for translation and adaptation from other languages is the opportunity it offers the 'host' culture to create or promote a vogue for the 'exotic other'. One such instance is Arthur Ransome's *Old Peter's Russian Tales* of 1916, which would have made use of Aleksandr Afanasyev's eight-volume pioneering *Russian Fairy Tales* published in Russian between 1855 and 1863. Maria Donovan's superbly subtle and touching Russian Pwca tale 'The House Demon' tugs a long thread woven into the tapestries of both Ransome and Afanasyev. Set over a lifetime spanning our own and the previous century, the story takes as its main theme the tensions between the old superstitions at the source of oral tradition, and the pressure to conform to formal religion (*'I* am not afraid of demons,' [said the Minister, sniffily] 'I only fear for your immortal soul.') Siding with the characters who wish to protect the hobgoblin, Donovan returns the fairy tale to its taproot before superstition had been fully assimilated into Christianity. Formal translation is a publishing phenomenon which imports literature across territories. Its precursor was the easy slipping, with people as they crossed borders, of stories into new cultures. It is tempting to regard the appearance of a hobgoblin motif and its name – Pwca in the Celtic regions and Buka in Russia – as a marker of a hearthside story that travelled, although such international recurrences are more likely explained by a shared etymological source in the Indo-European language family.

Other additions to this genre of adaptation include the 'radical reappropriation' of Perrault for gender-aware Seventies readers by Angela Carter in *The Fairy Tales of Charles Perrault*, 1977 (Jack Zipes, Introduction, Penguin, 2008), and her Marquis de Sade-informed feminist stories, *The Bloody Chamber* (1979). Most recent is Canongate's ongoing series of short novels based on world myths and Seren's series, New Stories from the Mabinogion, launched in 2009 and based on the Mabinogi, with authors so far including Russell Celyn Jones, Gwyneth Lewis, Owen Sheers, and this anthology's own Niall Griffiths.

Classical mythology underpins many of our stories here. Persephone was abducted by Hades, god of the underworld: her story linked to winter's desolation. It is reworked twice here with different but brilliant results: Tristan Hughes' 'Just Like Honey' and Dai Vaughan's 'Persephone'. Vaughan's version is narrated by Persephone's mother, earth goddess Demeter, and is a sceptic's psychoanalytical dissection of the story's associations. Filling his narrative with pomegranates as well as corned beef and cherry pies, Vaughan's are intentionally leaden symbols of earth's fruits, just as his Disney dog Pluto sends the reader on a false trail. The main character of Gee Williams' 'The Crack', meanwhile, is Saul, a translator of Virgil's account of Aristaeus the beekeeper. This Greek god is often regarded as a localised version of Pan, who is in turn connected to the meddlesome Puck. Saul, an academic in the humanities, seeks the source of his new partner Julia's nightmares. The story suggests that because as a scientist Julia lacks the knack of story, she may not be able to articulate guilt or even express ethical doubt about the darker aspects of her work. Those of Williams' subjects which come directly from Virgil's story are neglect; animal cruelty; loss; guilt and payback or sacrifice. Gower's Minotaur, in the meantime, retains the original beast's culinary preferences. Deborah Kay Davies' 'Box' refers the reader to Pandora, the first woman created by the Greek pantheon as a divine punishment of Prometheus for having stolen the gods' fire. Made beautiful, like Blodeuwedd, to hide her deceitful nature, she inflicted on the world its woes as well as adding opportunities for misogyny to its literature. Told in attention-grabbing first person staccato, Davies' Pandora is a tour de force of evil. Jo Mazelis' 'The Moon and the Broomstick' is filtered through the burlesque fairytale vision of an Angela Carter circa *Nights at the Circus*. Playing on prejudices about circus freaks, Mazelis takes the changeling story back to its biological beginnings, tapping into mothers' fear for the outcome of their pregnancy. However, her conjuring of the worst-case scenario goes back to the classics – Poseidon's twin sons the Molionides were sometimes described as having a single body with two heads, four arms and four legs. Mazelis also evokes Hecate, the moon goddess said to be tainted by her association with another woman's childbirth.

Two of our stories involve a magical slipping between worlds, and focus on the idea of mythology. Lloyd Jones' dystopia of 'The City' is all grand-scale steel, and is patrolled by a rodent version of Cerberus. Jones has one of his trademark warm and witty oddball characters, ice-cream man F2, carry ideas about common and individual mythology, attempts to eradicate difference, and the value of memory. This book's second futuristic piece is Beagan's 'Yellow Archangel'. Millennial in its outlook on a stripped-down world, it is optimistic about how the next generation will adapt to drastic change; in fact it includes this collection's only utopia that doesn't crumble to ash. Beagan looks at 'old' (contemporary) concepts of celebrity and hype in connection with a healing goddess figure, Kia, and how these relate to myth. As with Donovan's story, 'Yellow Archangel' suggests that a valid role may come again for superstition: 'I understood how, and why, when people have been under great strain and have been living in fear of one kind or another for so long, they need explanations that comfort them, that account for what's going on, that show them that things will, maybe, get better... I no longer cared about folk tales or legends. What did they matter? They were... nothing but a mockery now we were living in the midst of scarcity and chaos. How ironic, then, that I lived to see... [Kia] become a classic legend in her own lifetime.'

Folk stories have long been bundled into the wider definition of 'folklore'. For this reason they have suffered a problem of status which Angela Carter condemned: 'She was scathing about the contempt the "educated" can show, when two-thirds of the literature of the world... has been created by the illiterate' (Marina Warner, Afterword to Carter's two Virago collections of 1990 and 1992). Words such as 'folksiness' have been used to denigrate and domesticate a culture belonging to the oral practice of unlettered people. This devaluation is part and parcel of folk story's re-presentation as fairy tale primarily for children. Compare the relatively recent queenly status of classical literature in academia and literature! The Mabinogi stories, while easily categorised as myth because of their foundation in belief, are often disregarded as folk narrative. However, an interesting example of revisionism which upgrades 'folk fiction' to 'national history' can be seen in the eligibility categorisation of the Welsh Books Council's children's literature prize Tir na n-Og, for which the Mabinogi stories are regarded as non-fiction! One way to raise the status of the Welsh myths may be to avoid a preoccupation with their historical, national or geographical connections, grounded in reality as these narratives may be. Rather, readers may revel in their persisting truths, while authors delight in the warped mirror they offer up to contemporary faces.

Parents' fear of their own children's sexuality, a terror so prominent in the old tales, is not expressed by the characters here. Perhaps in our society the incest taboo has been transplanted by paternalistic anxiety about child abduction by strangers. In *Sing Sorrow Sorrow*, the lost or stolen child appears as an innocent, blameless figure, another popular motif from the traditional stories. Richard Gwyn reimagines the miller's daughter of Grimm's story 'The Handless Maiden' whose title he keeps. She is the product of her father's persistent failure to put her first: an untouchable, slippery street child. The parents of Hughes' Persephone are deemed complicit by the narrator for having over-protected her – 'trying to hide the ugliness in our lives as if all that was needed was a sugar-coating of words'; the goddess of the underworld is a drug addict who has long lost interest in picking narcissus come spring. Niall Griffiths' 'Puck's Tale' shares a different theme with 'The Handless Maiden': the dynamics of group culpability and guilt.

Mary-Ann Constantine's theme in 'Absolution' is evergreen: romantic obsession. But hers is a softer take on a type of addiction than the tales above, making the story – which has affinities both with fable and ghost story – a marvellously-understated portrait of grief and vulnerability. The fabulous elements are in Constantine's conflation of a stormy blast of wind with an unidentified beast, a possible intruder and the narrator's own migraine. Desire is treated obliquely too, in Matthew Francis' 'The Lovers' where Walfisch and his equally-solipsistic public schoolmates cannot believe the death of their peer Nisbet could be down to anything other than his coveting their own current infatuations. Walfisch's image of women and girls is primitive enough, though: she is a hag or succubus, riding a chap at night and sucking out his life juices! Meanwhile Christine Harrison's love interest, the 'Italian' girl in 'Neptune's Palace', is a siren luring Colin to his fate. This story advertises classical connections but its mood is closer to Carteresque fairy tale.

The fairy story symbol of the bird as an ally of the weak is used by several of our authors. Animal attributes are attached by Gower and Griffiths to their main characters, linking the beast with a vengeful, grief-stricken or greedy man running riot, especially underground! The fairy tale and classical preoccupation with siblings is strongly present. In certain stories, the relationship is depicted as protective in the mode of 'Hansel and Gretel' and 'The Snow Queen'. But in the majority the dynamic is seen as negative, for example by Hughes, where the heartbreaking co-dependence of his brother and sister goes far beyond classical character sketch. Cynan Jones in 'The Epilept' keeps the conventional struggling widower but seems to turn the old-timey step-sibling into a foster-brother, an 'accident waiting to happen', whose relations with his 'fostered' sister may be as riven with guilt and betrayal as in any Grimm tale.

Despite the low status of the old narratives other than classical, they have persisted. Aside from the importance of their circling themes, this may be because they encapsulate some of the world's few basic plotlines. For these reasons, plus their taste for violence, wrongdoing and the supernatural, they have been appropriated into mass publishing and film genres such as crime thriller, ghost and horror story. This may not have helped their critical credence. However, several factors are currently ensuring that these old stories are spread in the broadsheets as well as the tabloids. These are the recent expansion of the family fantasy film; the new reach of horror (especially vampire sip-flicks) into the arthouse as well as the box office, and the rise in the past five years of TV's high concept drama serial.

The perennial genre of horror is undergoing a particular renaissance. The mainstreamed vampires of US Home Box Office (HBO)'s superior high-concept, bayou-set serialised drama *True Blood* broadcast in the UK in 2009 brought out the bloodthirst and prejudice in normal folk while straw-sipping artificial blood as though it were an alcopop. Meanwhile, author Stephanie Meyer's teenage fangsters gave a whole new meaning to 'heart throb' when her romance blockbusters stormed cinemas with the *Twilight* formula from 2008 onward. Unless you count Zillah Bethell's and Greig's ageing lady predators or Francis' soul-sucking secretary fantasised by schoolboys, I can detect no vampires in this collection. But we do have the full gamut of horror's freakish hallmarks. A human wake of nails scratched on wood; gore; dismemberment and flayed skin; omens and *dei ex machina*; fits, trances, deformity and obsession. Davies' mass-murderess possesses a filmic eye and no mercy: 'a tiny, scarlet mouth in a frothy white pram, a scream in the street, a fall, a silent, frozen crowd'. Anne Lauppe-Dunbar's equivalent in the title story is a Covent Garden tequila waitress in a story which recalls skin-obsessed *The Silence of the Lambs* but is a direct tribute to the casual horror of the Grimms' 'Jorinda and Joringel'. Both killers are in thrall to their knives and tools. Another of the Grimms' sicker stories, 'The Juniper Tree', involves infanticide, cannibalism, birthpangs, berries, bones picked clean, and a bird who aids the rebirth of a brother. It has many parallels with Herrad's contribution, where a winged phantasmagorical predator is pictured in technicolour:

'its skin is like glass, like a jelly fish... red snaking veins full of blood and... coiling purple intestines, its pulsing red heart and lungs spread like butterfly wings...' Roshi Fernando's reimagining of the grimmer Grimm version of Cinderella, 'Three Cuts', has an arranged marriage that ends badly. A blood bath with scattered body parts, this story is a fantastically paced, moving, gruesome feminist subversion. In contrast, Gower plays for laughs as well as gasps in his flesh-feast recalling zombie-pastiche film *Shaun of the Dead*. Gower's grand-guignolesque tastes put 'The Pit' firmly in the horror genre.

By today, story origins and their reflections in literature, film, genre writing and children's fiction, have formed a migraine-inducing disco ball where the source of light is often forgotten. Certain of the supernatural stories here mirror folk tale, or the gothic ghost story in the mode of Henry James' *The Turn of the Screw* (1898), or the chiller category of horror: the point of inspiration is lost. Among these is Cynan Jones' 'The Epilept'. This investigation into possession of the adolescent body has parallels with films such as *Village of the Damned* and *Poltergeist*. The tale appears to pay tribute to the changeling motif in its question: which of these two children seems most culpable? Jones' troubled adolescent boy is persuasive, and this, together with the story's grimly tantalising denouement, has you wondering what you should at the end of every ghost story: who really existed? Charlotte Greig's 'spirit' is a seductive one straight out of folk song and reminiscent of 'She Moves through the Fair', a ballad popularised by Fairport Convention. Griffiths' contribution is an exemplary fireside creepfest set in a timeless 'Victorian' gentleman's club, complete with cigar-smoke skulls; disappearing children who could have been snapped up from the foggy London streets by Philip Pullman's Gobblers; a ghost house, and the rumour of a spirit who may be just an alibi. Its concerns with paedophilia and class are handled in a similar way to McEwan in *Atonement*, but its sensitive exposition of sexual grooming and media hype around this subject is second to none. Griffiths recasts Puck not as a prankster so much as a complicated victim of the 'reappearance' of general human weakness and 'urges' that fill him with 'dread'.

Much of the fiction here involves murder, violence, cruelty and a preoccupation with the ethics of hurt and guilt: all elements of crime thriller. We have in *Sing Sorrow Sorrow* ex-cons and unsolved cases; jail-dodgers ('ducking and diving, darting and dodging') and lawbreakers who either couldn't tell a policeman from a traffic cone or could charm the pants off him. Some characters may be judged as both perpetrator and victim; others go down for a crime they may not have committed. Rough justice is meted out now and then but withheld in the most barbaric of examples. Akin with the old narratives but in contrast to police procedurals, our new stories tend to assume abuse is domestic: it will go unreported and must remain a mystery.

Ordinary people once observed, dreamt and began the whispering chain that is story. The themes, images and motifs of myth, folk and fairy tale remain common knowledge today because of popular film, children's books and genre fiction. But although they also supply the major themes and plots of great literature, these stories – especially in their more basic forms of myth or folk narrative – are not to every reader's taste today. Sketchy characterisation may be one reason. Carter notes (without criticism) in her collection of his tales, how Perrault's 'princes and princesses rarely have names; the technique of the folk tale demands they exist, in some degree, as abstractions... [it] tends to define identity by role.' (Carter,

The Fairy Tales of Charles Perrault, see above). Add to this the blurred settings of traditional tales, and baggy or formulaic narration, particularly in myths. Explanation is avoided (especially in myths, even more so in the Welsh ones). Chronology may be convoluted, making suspense flabby despite an eventful plot. Humour, except in surreal and absurd events, and in the dry irony of a reteller like Perrault, is scarce.

Yet for the contemporary author, these quirks offer huge potential for fun, either with filling in these gaps or by enjoying the spaces for what they are. Yes, you can do motivation and character, location, a plot which makes sense, a message and suspense. Or you can pour neat what's in the original bottle: ageless themes, a fundamental plot, refreshing narrative jumps and hallucinatory imagery.

As with a paucity of humour, dodgy gender stereotyping goes with the territory of the original narratives. If you are a woman who has managed to miss Angela Carter, you may find this wearisome. But for today's writers, especially those inclined towards subversion and pastiche like Zillah Bethell, here is yet another chance to poke that sourdough mixture and raise from it a whole gated mews of gingerbread houses. Bethell's 'Herself' is a hilarious send-up of romance, vanity and sexual fantasy. Its feet are planted in an early version of Beauty and the Beast in which a woman whose sexual advances have been spurned curses the younger man. Bethell's Amber Imogen is a cross between Barbara Cartland and Baba Yaga from whom hero Orlando/Giles escapes into Little Red Riding Hood where his grandmother behaves almost as badly as his ill-suited suitor. Best of all, Granny reassures us her juices haven't yet dried up!

Euron Griffith adds fun to the fable form in 'Being a Digression...', an excerpt from his forthcoming novel. In it,

Griffith satirises the high-falutin' tone of the Victorian explorer journal. But his Middle-Eastern settings are from Arabian fairy tale, as is his structure of story within story. The moral to this one is: avoid goat's milk and wren-sized wasps!

Alan Bilton also brings his unmistakable voice and humour to the fairy tale. His vision is filmic, his humour slapstick. All the key events in Bilton's nightmare at the swimming baths, 'The Pool at Wiene Street', occur three times: three gold keys, all lost; three sets of disrespectful kids; three sets of 'shrunken old fellas'; three marches into the unknown. But he has a lot more than three jokes, and the dilemmas are micro-scale – where do you put your locker key when the safety pin's gone walkabout? The laughter is controlled on just the right side of hysteria: 'maybe the water wouldn't give way this time'.

There is a Woody Allen joke about a nervous man at a funeral who is so scared of public speaking he'd rather be in the coffin than delivering the eulogy. Bilton's story is a peepshow into one man's embarrassing anxiety dream, and since fear of fear is said to be worse than the fear itself, this story is arguably the darkest of *Sing Sorrow Sorrow*'s lot. Alan Bilton's turnstile to oblivion is located in the swimming baths' changing rooms, packed with towel-flicking schoolkids: just beyond the chlorine footbath. For the reluctant swimmers among you, it doesn't get much scarier than this.

About the Authors

Glenda Beagan lives in Rhuddlan, Denbighshire. She was educated at the University of Wales, Aberystwyth, and at the University of Lancaster. She has published three short story collections: *The Medlar Tree* (Seren, 1992), *Changes and Dreams* (Seren, 1996), and *The Great Master of Ecstasy* (Seren, 2009) and a collection of poetry *Vixen* (Honno, 1996). Her short story 'The Great Master of Ecstasy' was a prize-winner in the Rhys Davies Short Story Competition, 1999.

Zillah Bethell was born in Papua New Guinea. She graduated in English from Oxford University. Her first novel, *Seahorses are Real*, was published by Seren in 2009 and her second, *Le Temps Des Cerises*, in October 2010. Her short stories have been published in magazines including *New Welsh Review*. She lives in South Wales.

Alan Bilton was born in York in 1969 and teaches literature and film at Swansea University. His first novel, *The Sleepwalkers' Ball*, published by Alcemi in 2009, is a comic love story inspired by (amongst other things) silent film: part slapstick comedy, part anxiety dream and part surreal city-tour. He is also the author of *An Introduction to Contemporary American Fiction* (2002) and co-editor of *America in the 1920s* (2004). He is currently completing a book on silent film comedy and working on his second novel.

Mary-Ann Constantine works on Romantic-period Welsh literature at the University of Wales Centre for Advanced Welsh and Celtic Studies in Aberystwyth. She has published one collection of short stories: *The Breathing* (Planet, 2008). She would like to thank Academi for a Writers' Bursary which assisted the completion of her story.

Deborah Kay Davies won the Wales Book of the Year Award 2009 for her first collection of stories, *Grace, Tamar and Laszlo the Beautiful*, published by Parthian. Deborah started writing and publishing poems and stories while she was a mature student at university. Parthian also issued her first collection of poems, *Things You Think I Don't Know*. Her first novel, *True Things About Me*, is published by Canongate in 2010.

Maria Donovan was born in Dorset and has lived in Wales since 1997. Her first collection of short stories, *Pumping Up Napoleon*, is published by Seren. An interest in Russian house demons was kindled by reading Gorky's autobiography, *My Childhood*, and by a history lesson. Website: www.mariadonovan.co.uk.

Roshi Fernando was born in London in 1966. She was educated at the University of Warwick and is in the final year of a PhD in Creative Writing at the University of Swansea. She has won the 2009 Impress Prize for New Writers for her composite novel, *Homesick*, which comprises a series of interlinked short stories about a community of Sri Lankan immigrants in London. *Homesick* is published in autumn 2010 by Impress. She has also been given a special commendation by the judges of the Manchester Fiction Prize, and has been longlisted for the Bridport Prize 2009.

Matthew Francis is the author of four poetry collections, most recently *Mandeville* (Faber 2008). His poetry has been shortlisted for the Forward Prize (twice) and for the Wales Book of the Year Award, and he was named in 2004 as one of the Next Generation Poets. His novel, *WHOM*, was published by Bloomsbury in 1989, and his current projects include a collection of short stories and a second novel. He is Reader in Creative Writing at Aberystwyth University, and lives near Aberystwyth with his wife, Creina.

Jon Gower grew up in Llanelli, graduated in English from Cambridge University, and now lives in Cardiff. A former BBC Wales arts and media correspondent, he has published ten books, including *An Island Called Smith*, winner of the John Morgan Travel Award. His latest novel, *Uncharted* (Gomer 2010), is the author's own adaptation of his acclaimed Welsh-language novel *Dala'r Llanw* (Gomer, 2009).

Charlotte Greig is a writer and musician. Her debut novel, *A Girl's Guide to Modern European Philosophy*, was published in 2007. She has made five albums of folk music, both traditional and original, the first entitled *Night Visiting Songs*, the last *Quite Silent*. More recently, she has been writing plays for stage and radio, including *The Confessions* which was broadcast on Radio Four. She is currently working on her second novel. She lives in Cardiff with her family.

Euron Griffith lives in Cardiff. His work has appeared in various publications including *Ambit, New Welsh Review, Poetry Wales* and the US anthology *In My Life: Encounters With the Beatles*. In addition he has written a comedy drama series for BBC Radio Wales entitled *The Rocky Investigations* and several episodes of the children's TV series *The Baaas*. In 2009 he received a Writers' Bursary from Academi and is currently in the process of completing a novel, *How I Became the Tower of Ectha, The Strange Confession of Hilary Durward Esq*, from which his story for this collection is an extract. He also plays guitar for Cardiff band The Soda Men.

Niall Griffiths was born in Liverpool in 1966, studied English, and now lives and works in Aberystwyth. His novels include *Grits* (2000), *Sheepshagger* (2001), *Kelly & Victor* (2002), *Stump* (2003), which won Wales Book of the Year, and *Runt* (2006). *Kelly & Victor* and *Stump* are being made into films. Niall Griffiths has also written travel pieces, restaurant and book reviews, and radio plays. His novella *The Dreams of Ronnie and Max*, is published as part of the New Stories from the Mabinogion series in autumn 2010 (Seren). His non-fiction includes *Real Aberystwyth* and *Real Liverpool* (Seren).

Richard Gwyn grew up in Crickhowell, South Wales. He studied social anthropology at the LSE and worked in factories and as a milkman before leaving London to spend ten years in aimless travel, settling for periods in Greece or Spain. He returned to the UK and took a PhD in Linguistics at Cardiff University where he now directs the MA in Creative Writing. He is the author of five collections of poetry and two novels, *The Colour of a Dog Running Away* and *Deep Hanging Out*. He has written many articles and essays and he reviews new fiction for *The Independent*. He has translated poetry from Spanish and Catalan, and his own poetry and fiction have appeared in several languages. His website can be found at www.richardgwyn.com.

Christine Harrison was born in 1933 and brought up on the Isle of Wight; she has lived in Wales for more than thirty years. She was drawn to the short-story form early in her writing career and has had many stories published and/or broadcast, some winning national prizes such as the *Cosmopolitan* short-story prize: a story collected in an anthology from Serpent's Tale. Recently she has turned to the historical novel.

Imogen Rhia Herrad is a freelance writer and journalist based in Cardiff and Cologne. Born in 1967 in Germany, she has also lived in England and Argentina. Imogen's collection of short stories *The Woman who Loved an Octopus and Other Saints' Tales* was published by Seren in 2007. She is currently working on a book about her Patagonian travels, and a novel set in first-century Wales and Rome, for which she received a Writers' Bursary from Academi. She also writes document-aries about travel, politics and social and cultural history for German public radio. 'Rhiannon's Bird' was inspired by the artwork 'Prophetic' by Rebecca Hale.

Tristan Hughes was born in Atikokan, Canada and brought up around Llangoed, Ynys Môn, where he currently lives. He completed a PhD thesis on Pacific and American literature from King's College, Cambridge, and won the Rhys Davies Short Story Competition in 2001. His books include *The Tower* (Parthian, 2003) *Send my Cold Bones Home* (Parthian, 2006), and *Revenant* (Picador, 2008).

Cynan Jones was born in Wales in 1975 and lives in Aberaeron. His first novel, *The Long Dry*, was published in 2006 and went on to win a Betty Trask Award from the Society of Authors. The book has since been translated into Italian, Arabic and French. Italian translations of a further two novellas are to follow. Other short work has been variously published, and the author was selected as the Hay Festival nominee for the 2008 Scritture Giovani project.

Lloyd Jones, born 1951, is a former farm worker, nurse and newspaper editor who lives on the North Wales coast. He has published two novels in English, *Mr Vogel* (Seren, 2004), which won the McKitterick Prize 2005 and was shortlisted for the Bollinger Everyman Wodehouse Prize for Comic Fiction, *Mr Cassini* (Seren, 2006), which won Wales Book of the Year 2007, and a novel in Welsh, *Y Dŵr* (Y Lolfa, 2009). He has also published a short story collection, *My First Colouring Book* (Seren, 2008).

Anne Lauppe-Dunbar is a writer and PhD student currently working on her novel *Dark Mermaids*. This uncovers secrets including the former GDR doping scam, Theme 14.25. Anne lives in the South West.

Jo Mazelis' first book, *Diving Girls* (Parthian, 2003), was shortlisted for Wales Book of the Year and Commonwealth Best First Book. Her second collection *Circle Games* (Parthian, 2005) was longlisted for Wales Book of the Year. She has been a prize-winner in the Rhys Davies Short Story Competition five times. Her stories and poetry have appeared in *Urban Welsh* (Parthian), *New Welsh Review*, *Poetry Wales*, *Big Issue*, *Citizen 32*, and *nth position*, as well as being broadcast on Radio Four. She is also a painter and print-maker.

Gee Williams was born and brought up in Flintshire and now lives on the Welsh border with her husband. A poet and a dramatist as well as writer of fiction, she has won and been shortlisted for various awards. Most recently her novel *Salvage* was shortlisted for the James Tait Black Memorial Prize for Fiction and won the Pure Gold Fiction Award, and her short story collection *Blood etc* was shortlisted for Wales Book of the Year 2009. 'My writing grew out of where I was born and the people I grew up with. Wherever it travels, its kernel is a sliver of Flint.'

Dai Vaughan is a former documentary film editor whose articles and stories have appeared in many journals. His most recent fiction publications are *Totes Meer* (Seren, 2003), *Germs* (Y Lolfa, 2004), *Non-Return* (Seren, 2005) and *The Treason of the Sparrows* (Terra Incognita, 2009).

About the Editor

Gwen Davies was obsessed with fairy stories as a child, especially any connected with snow. She is a translator from Welsh to English, and a creative editor. Her adaptation of Caryl Lewis' prize-winning novel, published in English as *Martha, Jack and Shanco*, came out in 2007 with Parthian and she is currently working on another of Caryl's novels, to be published as *The Jeweller*. Her critical writing has appeared in anthologies such as *The Babel Guide to Welsh Literature*, online, and in journals such as *Planet*. As translator, she is a contributor to Dalkey Archive Press' international Best European Fiction anthology, 2011. Her translations have been commissioned by the Book Trust and the Welsh Literature Exchange, and have gained the support of the Welsh Books Council and Translators' House Wales. She grew up in a Welsh-speaking family in west Yorkshire, attended Aberystwyth University and pretty much stayed in the town since then. Gwen lives with her husband, Simon, and their teenage daughter and son.

Acknowledgements

Thanks to the authors, especially to Mary-Ann Constantine; and to Penny Thomas at Seren.